THE
UNDERSTORY

≈ A Novel ≈

Elizabeth Leiknes

**bancroft
press**

Published by Bancroft Press ("Books that enlighten")
P.O. Box 65360, Baltimore, MD 21209
800-637-7377
410-764-1967 (fax)
www.bancroftpress.com

Cover Design by Peggy Fussell
Interior Design by Tracy Copes
Author Photo by

Library of Congress Control Number: 2012931382
ISBN 978-1-61088-049-7 (cloth)
ISBN 978-1-61088-050-3 (ebook)
First Edition
Printed in the United States of America

For Hardy and Hatcher

"When you come to a fork in the road, take it."

—Yogi Berra

"Someday you will be old enough to start reading fairy tales again."

—C. S. Lewis

ONE

There once was a woman named Story Easton who couldn't decide if she should kill herself or eat a double cheeseburger. As Story stared at her refrigerator, she decided it all depended on the cheese. Mozzarella—that would be fine. Cheddar—even better. But Swiss—if that was all she had, things were going to get dicey. Luckily, she found one last slice of pepper-jack, and thus decided to continue her unremarkable life.

Deep down, Story Easton knew what would happen if she attempted to off herself—she would fail. It was a matter of probability. This was not a new thing—failure. She was, and had always been, a failure of fairy-tale proportions. Quitting wasn't Story's problem. She had tried, really tried, lots of things during different stages of her life—Girl Scouts, the viola, gardening, Tommy Andrews from senior year American Lit—but zero cookie sales, four broken strings, two withered azalea bushes, and one uniquely humiliating breakup later, Story still had not tasted success, and with a shriveled-up writing career as her latest disappointment, she realized no magic slippers or fairy dust was going to rescue her from her Anti-Midas Touch. No Happily Ever After was coming.

So she had learned to find a certain comfort in failure. In addition to her own screw-ups, others' mistakes became cozy blankets to cuddle, and she snuggled up to famous failures like most people embrace triumph.

The Battle of Little Bighorn—a thing of beauty.

The Bay of Pigs—delicious debacle.

The Y2K Bug—gorgeously disappointing fuck-up.

Geraldo's anti-climactic Al Capone exhumation—*oops*!

Jaws III—heaven on film.

Tattooed eyeliner—eyelids everywhere, revolting. *Really* revolting.

Fat-free potato chips—good Lord, makes anyone feel successful.

Being a member of the Failure Club felt good. Mostly. At least she could close her eyes and pretend it did. So Story Easton lived in a not-so-far-away land, living a not-so triumphant life of failure without tears.

And one Sunday evening in October, the woman who came into this world too stubborn, too proud to cry, was fake-crying again.

She'd done it before. Once, when she was stopped for speeding, she'd broken into a whimpering sob just to see how it felt, for just a moment, to be someone who cried. At first the vulnerability was uncomfortable and foreign, but as she wallowed in it for a few seconds, pretending the weight of the world and the weight of the day had caught up with her, she pulled off an authentic performance.

But there were no tears. There were never any tears. Some things can't be faked.

So in the humble kitchen of her rented house she stood—a bona fide realist who hadn't truly cried since her father died when she was five, and even *that* she did in a closet where nobody could see. Something about lonely, quiet Sunday evenings always made her hungry, so she fried up a homemade cheeseburger, complete with extra onions—after all, who would she need to keep her breath fresh for? With paring knife in hand, she pierced the onion's outer skin, cutting it into two perfect halves. The aroma began to burn her eyes, and when they welled up, she pretended, for a split second, to weep.

But a slight laugh replaced her pseudo-snivel when she saw how the onions had strangely assembled on the cutting board—five rings had formed a sloppy, but recognizable, Olympics logo. Story marveled at the sight of them. They weren't interlocking—the rings themselves were intact—but still they gave the illusion of unity, which made Story feel even more alone.

A long time ago, back when she still believed in magic and saw tiny, shimmering mysteries in the flickering stars of the Phoenix skyline, even way back then, Story Easton wanted to be someone else. For as far back as her mind could remember, she imagined what it would be like to walk in other people's shoes—and not in a figurative way, either. She wanted, literally, to pull on boots, slip into heels, lace up sneakers, whatever it took to get a glimpse of how it felt to have purpose.

Instead, she drifted through life with the constitution of a wispy, misguided breeze. Her subconscious desire to explore other people's skins manifested in her clothing choices, and each day she wore different vintage thrift-store ensembles, hand-me-downs made from the fabrics of other people's lives, other people's stories woven into each second-hand thread. She hid behind these garments, disguising her real exterior, which was attractive, although she never bothered looking in the mirror. In general, her beauty was contradictory—her rich, auburn hair shined more than her attitude, and her soft, full lips, beautiful by any artist's standard, spewed out hard, caustic words. Like many things in nature, Story was simultaneously beautiful and dangerous.

So Story Easton pushed up the flouncy sleeves on her recycled peasant shirt embroidered with tiny flowers, and ate her cheeseburger. She then finished a game of solitaire. With her emerald-green eyes, she glanced at the confident Queen of Hearts that lay in front of her. *Ah, it must be good to be queen*, she thought. *With a fabulously sexy and witty king to sit by, throne-side, while servants danced about, delivering the day's exciting agenda with trays heaping with mini-cheeseburgers.*

But there was no king. And no exciting agenda, either. Earlier in the day, when Story had gone to the local grocery store to buy a bigger wine glass (that way she could tell herself she only drank two glasses on rough evenings, even though it was a whole bottle), the clerk made the mistake of getting personal.

"Just one?" the perky clerk had asked while scanning the bar code stuck to the bottom of the wine glass stem.

Story nodded, trying to avoid eye contact.

And then the clerk asked another question, unaware how Story Easton hated inquiries. "Doin' anything fun today?" she said, an annoying smile engulfing her face.

Hmmm, which should I do first today? Story had thought. *Romantic picnic or finish the novel my high-profile literary agent is dying to read?* Story decided to reply with something that would shut Chatty Cathy up, so she stared straight into the clerk's bright eyes. "I'm going to do something inappropriate with my cat."

But the clerk just giggled and wrapped the glass in brown packing paper. "Something inappropriate to your poor sweet cat? Why?"

Story rolled her eyes. "Not *to* my cat, *with* my cat. Isn't that wicked sick?"

"You're funny!" the clerk said with a wink.

Story slumped out of the store, realizing she failed even at humiliating herself. She wasn't, of course, going to do inappropriate things with her cat. She didn't have a cat. Pets were another of her failures.

But that had been her morning; she was hoping her evening would be better. With her belly full, and her games of solitaire complete, she picked up a small, worn slip of paper she'd found in a fortune cookie eleven months ago, a piece of paper that she'd saved and had been using as a bookmark in her copy of Kafka's *The Metamorphosis*. As with all of her books, she could recite from memory this story's first line—*As Gregor Samsa awoke one morning from uneasy dreams, he found himself transformed into a gigantic insect*—but she could not recite its last.

Story had always thought that reading a great first line was a lot like falling in love—surprising, but at the same time, comfortable. And she preferred beginnings to endings, probably because she harbored a subconscious aversion to accomplishment, but as of late, she'd become so disgusted with her own lack of ambition that she'd given up on expectations. In fact, she was so bored with herself that she'd resorted to reciting her favorite novels' first lines to replace her own worn-out words and ideas.

Thinking of it as a beginning she hadn't yet attempted, she opened up the small, folded-up fortune and read the familiar words—*Everyone gets one chance to do something great. Yours is coming soon*—but when the bitterness of the word "soon" settled in with an unpalatable aftertaste, she tucked it back into the book and, once again, reminded herself that things boasting of magic were usually caked in horse crap. And once again, she managed to find the shit-brown, shadowy side of things. From kindergarten through high school, Story's failings hadn't disappointed her. Sometimes she missed her apathy like she missed things in her less complicated past: Madonna with twenty extra pounds, *Fantasy Island* reruns, cherry Pop-Tarts with sprinkles.

One month ago, to recapture the feeling of being alive, of *feeling* alive, Story painted every room in her house a different shade of green, the color of life. The kitchen: pea pod green. The bedroom: hunter green. The bathroom: sage green. The living room: grassy green. But it hadn't helped her feel any more alive, or any more at home, so now, today, after she put her book away, she left her own disappointing house in search of another.

It was clearly nighttime—the time when Story Easton quenched her parched spirit by breaking the law—and so it was on that Sunday night that Story invited herself into a stranger's house for the fourth time that week.

Technically, she wasn't on the guest list.

Technically, she was a criminal.

If she'd given her nighttime actions much thought, she'd have pointed out that what she did hurt no one, but she didn't think about it—she *felt* it. It was a compulsion. One she'd had for three months now.

It had all started on a sultry evening back in July when the motionless Phoenix air too closely resembled her sad and stagnant life, and she'd started seeing the words *restless*, *irritable*, and *discontent* everywhere she looked. They swirled in her triple-shot latte, they sat perched on perky tree branches, and worst of all, they engaged in combat with more palatable adjectives as they passed by on the street with their very *satisfied*, *blissful*, and *whole* owners.

So there she was, three months later, starting the Sunday evening festivities without fanfare, going through rote motions with the fervor of someone about to brush her teeth. She drove around in her hand-me-down Volvo, keeping in mind practical things like parking, lighting, and the fact that she'd never visited this street before. And as she passed house after house, she tried not to let one of Zora Neale Hurston's first lines ruin her fun. *Ships at a distance have every man's wish on board.*

And then, like the unexpected beauty of a shooting star, she saw a house that intrigued her, a *life* that intrigued her. Boredom and discontent were replaced by exhilaration and possibility.

"Hmmm," she said to herself as she drove by the split-level she wanted to know more about. On the front stoop, a porch light revealed what the distracted homeowner must have forgotten and left behind in a rush—a brown paper bag full of groceries, with a bunch of bananas sticking out the top. Several other lights were on—twice as many as the other houses—exposing the goings-on inside, and Story was once again amazed at how much you can see into someone's life when it's illuminated. When she slowed the car, she saw a man sitting alone on his couch, pouring from what looked like a whiskey bottle. He displayed a Me-Against-the-World gaze as he stared out his front picture window at nothing at all. Or perhaps he was staring at everything—the overwhelming, all-encompassing *everything* of things he didn't have but wanted. Story could relate. And as selfish as it was, the idea of surrounding herself with people more screwed-up than her always made her feel better, or at least less screwed-up.

She drove two blocks and parked—this was standard procedure because it cut down on suspicion—and then, for stealth, she put on her light jacket over her dark navy flannel pajamas. Back in July, when she first starting doing this, she'd worn her street clothes, and it made for quite an uncomfortable night. And then there were a few nights when she'd brought her pajamas with her in a small overnight bag, but she found that traveling light enhanced the experience. Besides, changing clothes can get noisy.

As she walked closer to her destination, she realized the house could be a stand-in for Carol and Mike Brady's, complete with '70s exterior flair and a slightly more sophisticated station wagon in the driveway. Story considered possible entry points and decided, as usual, the back entrance was best, but first she grabbed the forgotten groceries on the front porch.

"Shit," she mumbled when she rolled her ankle on a rock in the backyard and dropped the bananas. When the motion light sputtered, she hugged the house to stay in the shadows, and instead of feeling cold, it felt warm and welcoming. When blackness returned, she made her way to a small patio and quietly checked the sliding glass doors she knew would be open.

"God, I could be a serial killer," she whispered while she slowly opened the heavy door and wondered why people didn't lock their doors anymore. Of the scores of homes she'd *visited*, she'd only had to pry open three locked doors. She'd become quite handy with her makeshift tools—the Leatherman worked well, but the best was an old, metal fingernail file she'd retrofitted for breaking and entering. Way more fun than a manicure.

After taking her slippers off so as not to track in dirt, she put down the groceries and scouted out the lower level of the house. There was one bathroom, a small living space, a kitchenette and, bingo—when she walked to the other side of the stairway, she discovered a bedroom. Its inhabitant was not home, and had been gone awhile, as evident from the layer of dust and overall sense of emptiness.

As Story entered the vacant bedroom, a colorful room with bright pink sheets, a yellow and orange bedspread, and a floor-to-ceiling rainforest mural painted in whimsical, swirling colors, she heard the television upstairs come on for a minute, bellowing a preachy commercial in which an airy, godlike voice asked a series of questions over a soundtrack of inspirational music. "Do you feel lost? Is your life empty and meaningless? Do you ever wonder about those unexplainable coincidences in life? It is all connected. *We* are all connected." She heard the man from the couch mumble something and then let out an audible, angry sigh. The commercial ended with a sped-up, "Paid for by the Church of Jesus Christ of Latter-day Saints." When the television went silent, Story heard the man pour another drink, and shortly after that, creaking bedsprings indicated he'd gone to bed.

Story examined her temporary bed. Above it hung a cartoon picture of a smiling sun—bright, golden, and peaceful. Propped up on two pillows was a pigtailed doll wearing khaki pants, a safari vest, and a little button that said, "Girl Explorers Rock!" And that rainforest mural had each of the forest's four layers labeled with black, hand-drawn words. *The Forest Floor*, it said at the bottom of the wall, near the carpet, amongst tree roots, leaves, and tiny saplings. The second layer, an area in the trees labeled *The Understory*, teemed with excitement, appearing as one interconnected world of action and secrets: brightly-colored birds flying about, tree kangaroos clinging incognito, howler monkeys leaping from branch to branch so fast there was an actual blurred brush stroke to illustrate it. The third layer, *The Canopy*, a roof of treetops, looked like a giant, carpet-like blanket draped over the whole forest. And the highest layer, *The Emergent Layer*, featured the few stray trees tall and hardy enough to break out of the canopy and stretch toward the sun.

And somewhere between the forest floor and the understory, a big white flower bud jutted out from a gray tree trunk. Having never seen a flower quite like it, Story walked closer. The vines held clusters of waxy, crimson leaves, and the flower itself was closed tightly, each petal hugging the next in layer after layer of silky white.

Story walked to the bedside table and saw a book, *Once Upon A Moonflower*, featuring a young blonde girl on the cover, alongside the same beautiful white flower from the wall. On the back cover was a picture of a man with salt-and-pepper hair—the same man she'd seen through the window—and underneath the picture was a short biography.

Martin Baxter, scholar and author, earned a Ph.D. in Botanical Sciences from Cornell University after enduring a lifelong obsession with plants. After discovering that plants were much more interesting than people (and much quieter), he focused his doctoral research on a phytochemical and pharmalogical investigation of Amazonian ethnomedical plants. Once Upon A Moonflower *is Martin's first non-academic book, and he hopes children everywhere discover the same magic and interconnectedness he's seen firsthand in the Amazon rainforest (or at least put off bedtime for a half hour). Martin teaches and lives in Portland, Oregon with his lovely and vibrant wife Katherine, who happens to hate plants, and his precocious but silly daughter Hope, who happens to be the greatest kid on the planet.*

It was written in third-person, but somehow, Story heard Martin Baxter, the stranger upstairs, in the words, as if he was hiding between the distant tone and the quirky sense of humor. The smile he wore in the book jacket picture was infectious, and with the smart-but-rugged thing he had going, he evinced a surprising sex appeal. But the interesting and vivacious man from the book jacket looked very different from the man she'd seen in the window. Something had changed since he'd written the book.

Something horrible had happened to Martin Baxter.

Story then walked over to an open closet and saw a poster of a city skyline, titled *Portland at Dusk*, propped up against the closet wall, its tone grayed-out and bleak. On the floor sat a large cardboard box holding neat little rows of carefully packed items, each wrapped in a dishtowel for protection. She unwrapped one on top. A stained coffee cup with a picture of a family on the front, it showed a woman with bright blue eyes standing close to Martin Baxter, and on his shoulders, a young blonde-haired girl, smiling and waving. Story wrapped the cup back up the way she found it and looked in the next dishtowel to find a woman's worn yellow slippers.

She then found another picture of the young blonde girl, sitting on a bed beneath the same golden, cartoonish sun picture, and in the background was the rainforest mural, but it was slightly different. On the back of the frame it said *Portland*, and it was dated two years ago. *Two almost-identical rooms*, Story thought. Somebody liked the décor enough to reproduce it. Somebody was hanging on.

After laying the picture aside, Story uncovered one more item. It was a framed piece of paper with a picture of the woman and young girl from the coffee cup, and these words underneath: *In Loving Memory of Katherine Anne Baxter and Hope Amelia Baxter.*

Story swallowed the lump in her throat, but she remained silent, avoiding the urge to look through the rest of the box and risk waking up the man who mourned upstairs, and who, as evident from the many discarded high-ball glasses on the bureau, occasionally mourned in the very room Story temporarily called her own. It seemed that Martin Baxter had fled from Portland to Phoenix, looking for sun, only to find himself still lost in shadows.

No wonder he'd forgotten the groceries. Remembering the milk, Story tip-toed her way into the kitchenette, put the canned goods and bananas on the counter and, like a good intruder, placed the milk in the mini-fridge. She watched the refrigerator light flicker, which meant a rolling blackout. Though blackouts were most common for Phoenix during summer's peak heat, during the last week, sporadic fall thunderstorms had prompted electrical interferences, and it looked like another one was probably on its way. She returned to her room before complete blackness came.

But then, just as Story was settling in for a good night's sleep in a total stranger's house, Martin Baxter stirred upstairs. Soon, he stumbled down to lock the very door that Story had entered through. Story caught a glimpse of him through the cracked bedroom door as he walked past, and thanks to the moonlight flooding through the hallway window, she noticed Martin's face as he glanced in her direction. He stopped and stared at the spare bedroom as if it were an old friend—one he knew he should let go of, but could not.

Story didn't know it yet, but she and Martin wanted similar things. Martin wanted to become the man he used to be, and Story wanted to become the woman she didn't know she could be.

Once Martin had returned upstairs, Story went to the closet and grabbed the final element in her quest to be someone else—the slippers. And as she snuggled into someone else's bed in someone else's house, wearing someone else's slippers, she began to fall asleep. But this time, in this house, the comfort didn't come so easily. She felt a little guilty. This was new.

Maybe it was something I ate, she thought.

Maybe I should unsubscribe to the Lifetime Channel.

Maybe I should grow a pair.

Maybe I shouldn't have seen the obituary for "the greatest kid on the planet."

Or maybe, just this once, for solidarity's sake, I should try not to dream.

TWO

Across town from where Story Easton secretly settled into Martin Baxter's home, Cooper Payne sat on the edge of his bed, dangling his eight-year-old legs in anticipation of his personal oasis—the one that always came at night. In Phoenix, even the most faithless Phoenicians could rely on at least one thing: sun. But with three hundred days of sun each year came thirst-causing heat, a constant reminder of the city's namesake, a fabled bird burning to death on its very own funeral pyre. Yet with death came the possibility of rebirth, and in Phoenix, any hope of renewal came at night, when body and soul dreamt of a fertile oasis amidst an arid wasteland.

So on this Sunday night, moonlight pierced through layers of clouds, some dense and stubborn, some sparse and carefree, all providing a soft filter for a night sky teeming with stars so brilliant, they flickered long after you closed your eyes.

But Cooper's eyes were wide open.

"Mom." That's all he had to say, because she knew what he wanted. It was what he always wanted. Instead of clinging to a soft security blanket, as he used to when he was younger, Cooper firmly gripped a green, wood-handled umbrella.

"Oh, Coop," Claire whispered as she sat down on his rumpled twin bed and caressed his warm bed-head. "I was thinking we could read the *new* book I bought you, the one about knights." She added, "It's got swords—and dragons!"

With resolve, Cooper rested the umbrella on his shoulder, folding his small hands together as if he'd wait forever. Too old to wear his little boy Spider-Man jammies, and too young to wear the shirt-and-pants pajamas he'd seen dads wear in movies, he wore oversized nylon basketball shorts, which exposed his legs, olive-skinned and bony. On top, he wore a *Star Wars* T-shirt with *Come to the Dark Side: We Have Cookies* centered on the front.

After a heavy sigh, Claire conceded by opening the drawer of Cooper's bedside table and taking out a worn, much-loved book. She put it in her lap, resting one hand on the front cover, and then tucked her other hand underneath the back cover, touching the dark underbelly of the thing that held a relentless spell over her only son.

They assumed their usual positions, backs against the walnut headboard, with two navy blue pillows sandwiched between them, just right for a comfortable read. Part of Cooper was embarrassed by all of this. He was, after all, the ripe old age of eight, and he wouldn't want anyone at school to know his *mommy* had to read to him every night so he could sleep. But he *did* need her to—and she did it, even though it meant going to bed later. Much later. This book was geared toward avid, "tweener" readers—it was funny, flippant, and illustrated with cool, edgy artwork, but it was also longer than picture books designed for younger kids. Cooper once heard his mother mumble, "Why couldn't you have become obsessed with something short, like *Green Eggs and Ham?*"

They both stared at the title on the front cover, as if they'd never seen it before. "*Once Upon A Moonflower*," Claire said in a tone so lonely one would think she had been abandoned in the Amazon without a machete.

"Written by Martin Baxter."

When she opened the book and turned the first page without speaking, Cooper shook his head. He almost said, "Nuh-uh, Mom, that's not how *he* did it," but instead he looked up at her with his dark brown eyes, where sadness had grown accustomed to settling, and waited for her to correct herself.

"Sorry," she said, "forgot."

But Cooper knew she hadn't forgotten. This page was always the hardest for her. She turned back and read the dedication without emotion, because if she slipped up and thought about the words on the page, she might have ruined bedtime. Again.

"Dedicated to my daughter Hope, the project I'm most proud of."

She then turned the page, and once again, Claire Payne began reading Cooper the story he needed to hear. The story that took them to another place—a place not of this world.

Once Upon A Moonflower

A Fairy Tale
(or A Tale of a Fairy)

*Due to its graphic (real) and cerebral (smart) nature, this story is not recommended for small children, unless they are really, really brave.

Written by Martin Baxter

Dedicated to my daughter Hope, the project I'm most proud of.

Dear Reader,

What you're about to read is my all-time favorite fairy tale, but that's probably because I'm in it. And you should know that I was totally honest in retelling what happened to me, except for the part about me being really scared of the dark. I wasn't that scared.

Anyway, enjoy the story. And remember, If You Can Imagine It, You Can Do It! Unless, of course, the thing you're imagining is absurdly difficult, and if that's the case, you always have your dreams. Unless you can't sleep. Then you should just rearrange your room or something.

Oh, yeah, almost forgot. Don't be afraid of the spooky parts, and don't worry about me (especially when the cranky jaguar tries to eat me) because I don't die. I live happily . . . well, you know the rest. It's how all good stories end. And you probably know how they all begin, too.

So here it goes.

Love,

Hope

*O*nce upon a time, there was a girl named Hope, who lived in the heart of the rainforest.

Oops. Let me start over. Forgot I was the star.

*O*nce upon a time, something really crazy happened to me: I woke up in the heart of the rainforest. And I mean the daddy of all rainforests—the great and magical Amazon. I'd say "amazing" Amazon, but that would be redundant. ("Redundant" means "superfluous".) (And "superfluous" means "extra".) My bad. I like big words.

Anyway, instead of waking up in our Portland house, like I did every other morning for the last nine years, I woke up in a fetal (baby-like) position, curled up on the forest floor in my purple, flannel pajamas. Very cute, by the way. Thank you, Santa.

"What is this place?" I said to a giant sloth clinging to the branch of a large kapok (very, very tall) tree.

The happy sloth spoke in a slow sloth voice. "It is home."

Honestly, I thought maybe he was, you know, "special," because he did everything in super-slow motion, but he was my only acquaintance (companion) in a strange land, which certainly wasn't like home at all. I didn't feel my soft bed, or see any of my books, or smell Dad's chocolate-chip pancakes. Where I came from, good days were welcomed by bright golden sun. But here it was dark and shady with only small slivers of sunlight peeking through the canopy of trees above.

"What do you do here?" I asked the sluggish sloth.

Still clinging to the smooth, gray branch, he turned his head slightly and said, "I hang on."

Duh. "Do you ever let go?" I asked, looking up at him from a pile of dead leaves where I now stood.

My new friend flashed a leisurely smile. "Only when I have to."

I looked up through the roof of tangled trees and wished for more sun. "Okay, funny little trick someone pulled, but I want to go back home now, to my home," I said.

"Don't be sad," said the sloth. "The forest will help you. It helps everybody." Still hanging on, he added, "But first you must find the treasure box—it holds all the magic of the forest. And then you must find the moonflower."

"Moonflower?" I said. The mere mention of the moon made me tremble. "But I can't be here when night comes!" I yelled. I couldn't be here in the dark.

The sloth slowly adjusted his grip. "It is the only way—the treasure box will give you what you need, and the moonflower will give you a home."

"I already have a home," I said, "away from here!"

The sloth's voice grew stern, like my dad's when he was trying to make a point. "Have some faith. First the treasure box, then the moonflower." I wasn't there five minutes, and already I had a list of chores. Maybe this place was home. "But beware of the Fierce One," the sloth continued. "He will begin to prowl at sundown, and for each one of his spots, he has taken a life. You must go now."

As soon as he said it, before I even had a chance to enjoy being lost in a horribly dangerous jungle, a giant water boa nudged her way underneath me until I had no choice but to ride sidesaddle atop her coils, and begin the next leg of my journey.

And suddenly the small amount of sun sneaking through the trees shrank to one tiny glimmer, and I began to shiver, thinking about surviving the night in this dark, scary place. It made spending the night at Grandma Margaret's seem inviting, meatloaf and all.

The facts were staggering (dismal) (bad). I had vanished into the jungle. I was riding a potentially lethal (deadly) (flippin' scary!) snake. And some spotted, fierce creature wanted me dead at nightfall. I wondered if I could dream my way out this nightmare, so I strengthened my grip on the snake's scales and closed my eyes. But when I opened them, the only thing that disappeared was the sun, and all I could do was hang on.

THREE

I f Phoenix was a jungle, Story Easton lived in the understory. Before she took up breaking and entering, you could say she lived on the forest floor—a microscopic organism hiding in the shadows, an easy target for the shit-droppings from those with higher positions. But now that she'd found a new passion, a nighttime habit more active than watching bacteria grow, she was ascending the layers, and now lived where shelter was provided, and everything around her enjoyed a nocturnal existence. Like a jaguar on the prowl, she lurked about, searching not for food, but for a new identity. She tried different branches of different trees to see how they felt, and when the sun came up, she went back to her sleepy life, going through the motions without intent.

And like most mornings, Story's Monday arrived like an unwanted dream, abrupt and loaded with bad omens. She tiptoed out of Martin Baxter's house in the dark, wee hours to avoid getting caught, but barely made it to her car without being noticed.

When she finally got there, the streetlamp highlighted a bright yellow park-ing ticket jutting out from under the windshield wipers—yet another reminder that no matter where she went, she was an interloper.

Before going to work, she stopped back at her own house to shower, change clothes, and work on Twenty-Nine Down, which had been giving her trouble. Thanks to a quirky home décor company, the ten-foot wall in Story's dining room was covered with special-order wallpaper printed up as a life-sized crossword puzzle. Each time Story used the chunky black marker to fill in an answer, literally scribbling on the wall, she giggled, knowing her mother would scoff at such un-civilized behavior.

Twenty-nine, as it happened, was also her age. She didn't dwell on that. In fact, she'd forgotten her birthday for the last three years in a row, remembering it only after the fact, when she was writing a check or looking at a calendar. But she was pushing thirty, the age at which you should have accomplished something in your life. Unfortunately, she could think of nothing she'd done thus far that could be considered important.

It'll last for days. Four letters. She stared at the four empty boxes awaiting letters. After a few seconds, it came to her. *Duh. WEEK.* She was happy she hadn't called upon the word she sometimes conjured up when she needed a little help in reaching a goal. "Abracadabra," she muttered under her breath. *Good thing I'm not counting on you.*

Ever since she was a little girl, Story Easton had secretly relied on her special word, a word that her mother thought was complete hogwash. And Story figured her mother was probably right, but it didn't stop her from trying it out on occa-sion. For Story, the Aramaic definition of "abracadabra"—*I create as I speak*—had given her a sense of hope, as it was not only a reference to God creating the uni-verse, but a promise that if you speak it, it shall be so. But during her lifetime, in the hundreds of times she'd used the word in hope of a real, magical result, it had failed her. Of course.

Story walked out of her humble bungalow, one she was renting because she refused to accept down payment money from her mother, who wanted Story to leave municipal Phoenix for a more acceptable locale, like Deer Run or Glendale. She walked through her brown and neglected yard to her brown and neglected hand-me-down Volvo.

If Story could at least pretend not to be disappointed in disappointment, her mother could not—Story was, indeed, a colossal disappointment to her mother, who was successful to an embarrassing degree. A year ago, in a futile attempt to please her, Story put her English major to "good use" and took a job as a writer. Sort of. She took a job writing annoying, well-wishing prose and verse (if you could even call it that) for Special Occasions, a greeting card conglomerate respon-sible for eighty percent of the market's need for optimism at any cost.

After arriving at work on that Monday morning, she assumed her usual position—that of a hostage in a dismal cubicle—and decided today was the day. She'd endured several months of spewing out bad, rhyming poetry and slinging empty slogans, and she wanted to design more honest cards. So on that Monday, she proposed her new greeting card line, *Life's a Crapshoot* the very spirit of which was cheeky and irreverent. Story pitched her innovative idea to her boss, Ivy Powers, when Ivy stopped by Story's cubicle.

Ivy loved having a boss-worthy salary, but hated being called *boss* because she wanted people to like her. Story called her *boss* every chance she could get, because it was fun.

On that Monday, Story explained how her new card line would appeal to realists, but Ivy Powers, always stoic and obsessed with the bottom line, stood in the cubicle doorway and retorted, "Realists don't buy cards."

In an effort to convince her that real life was no fairy tale, Story wheeled her chair to Ivy's side and handed her the first installment of the sassy new series. Ivy stared at the front of the card, which featured a picture of a little yellow chick, dirty and covered with hatchling droppings, and the words, *A Little Birdie Told Me Your Life's in the Crapper . . .*

And when Ivy opened the card, it said, *Don't worry. "Life is only a tale told by an idiot, full of sound and fury, signifying nothing."*

Ivy Powers stared at Story, and let out an irritated sigh.

Story chewed the last bit of her blueberry bagel and said, "It's Shakespeare, Boss."

"It's depressing." Ivy stared her down. "And don't call me that," she said, still staring. "Please." And then Story heard Ivy speak again. "Such ugly words," she mumbled, "from such pretty lips."

Though Ivy had turned down the *Life's A Craphshoot* series, Story knew some-one in the printing department (a lady who had handed Story toilet paper from the third stall a couple of weeks prior), and so, unbeknownst to her boss, Story had already had each card in her ten-card series printed up with crisp, matching envelopes, and decided to carry them with her as a small victory, proof that *sticking it to the man* (or woman) provided savory retribution.

Before exiting the cubicle, Ivy asked, with folded arms and a forced Monday morning smile, "How's the *Grief and Loss* series coming along?"

"It's hilarious, Boss," Story said. "Know anything that rhymes with *condolences?*"

"Less than a week," Ivy reminded her as she waved her makeshift wand—a bright yellow happy face on a stick—and made her way toward her next victim. Ivy often got nervous when deadlines drew near, but Story knew it didn't matter if she had one week or three months—she was beginning to take less and less pleasure in other people's grief.

The moment Ivy left, the phone rang, and as soon as Story picked it up, the other authority figure in Story's life said, "Darling, is this a bad time?"

"Actually, Mom, I'm kind of in the middle—"

"Great. Look, I expect you to . . ." She stopped herself and rephrased, but not before a long, irritated sigh. "I mean, I'd really love it if you could attend my gala party this Wednesday."

Story wanted to point out that using both "gala" and "party" was redundant, but remembering that her mother thrived on being redundant, she decided to let it go.

After a pause, Beverly Easton, the woman who gave birth to Story, said, "You *do* remember about the anniversary party, right?"

"Of course, Mom. It's the anniversary of you embracing your . . . greatness. What's it been? Fifteen years?" And after a snicker, she added, "Forever?"

But Story knew her mother was talking about another anniversary. Her mother's twenty-year-old company, Socra-Tots®, a little operation once run out of Beverly's basement, had become a household name, the end-all-be-all of early childhood educational products. The company, which was now a mega-corporation, peddled books, DVDs, CDs, and toys, and was rooted in finding clear, concise answers to lofty questions by way of Socrates himself. All products employed the Socratic Method, a model which focused on asking sharp, pointed questions like "What do you mean by that?" and "How do you know?" to promote discussion and debate.

"What do you mean by that?" Story's mother asked, as she had so many times before. Silence filled the next five seconds, but Story continued to conjure up the questions she'd heard since childhood. *What do you mean by "The doggie is sad"? How do you know the zebra is black and white? What makes you think the sun is hot?*

"Look, Mom, I'm not sure it's a good idea I come. I'm hardly the poster child for what a Socra-Tot should be when she grows up."

Calmly, her mother said, "How do you *know*?"

"Ugh!"

"Okay, no more questions," her mother promised. "Okay?"

"That's a question."

Another sigh. "How will it look if my only daughter doesn't show up to help me celebrate my life's greatest achievement?"

So there it was, finally, and Story laughed. "You finally said it," she said.

"That didn't come out right." But Beverly Easton's nerves got the best of her and she retreated to her comfort zone. "What did you mean by that?" she asked, and for good measure threw in, "And how do you *know?*"

"I *know*, Mom," Story sighed, "because I've always known."

It was true. In Story's eyes, Beverly Easton had always been disenchanted with her only child. Story had spent her childhood competing for the role of main character in her own mother's life, only to find herself overshadowed by grander, nobler protagonists. In fact, Story's mother had given her daughter the name *Story* in the hope of raising an interesting child, a child who would make a lasting impression, but if Story's life paralleled a narrative, her plotline might as well have been a flat line, devoid of rising action and suspense. And what was the theme of this *Story?* When you are expected to be extraordinary, and you turn out a disaster, you will cause chronic disappointment.

"What, precisely, have I achieved through you?" Beverly Easton mumbled.

Annoyed, Story hoped her mother would recant, change her mind, or at least lie, but Beverly Easton struck again, like a shark, always circling back for another bite. Story recalled another impressive fish: *The great fish moved silently through the night water, propelled by short sweeps of its crescent tail.* She wondered how Peter Benchley could have written a whole novel about her mother without having met her.

But when Beverly Easton came back for a second strike, it seemed as though she was trying to prod Story on—to greatness, to completion, to humiliation, perhaps. "You've never succeeded at one thing in your life. Seriously, name one thing that you've accomplished, that *meant* anything." Beverly paused only long enough to take a breath, as if there was a realization Story needed to make for herself. "Sure as the sun will shine tomorrow, you will have not accomplished—a thing."

After a moment of silence, Story exhaled, then mumbled, "The sun shone, having no alternative, on the nothing new."

"You think I don't recognize that?" Beverly said, adding, after a cackle,

"Samuel Beckett. I loaned you the book, darling. The rest of the world isn't quite as stupid as you like to think." She let out one, long controlled breath. "Another *first* line from the girl who focuses on *attempting* things rather than *achieving*. Bet you don't know the last line."

Hating that her mother, once again, was right, Story took a guess. "THE END!" she yelled into the receiver. When Story slammed the phone down, she considered the dial tone as much success as she could muster.

Story had often thought that each one of us, like Russian nesting dolls, has layers of stories inside. Her deepest layer's story had been *Curious George*; after hearing it at four, she longed for the man in the yellow hat to whisk her away for wacky adventures. Later, *Little Women* established another—oh, how she wanted to trade in being a little girl for being a little woman. And in college, Kate Chopin's *The Awakening* created yet another layer, showing her why someone might walk straight into the ocean and keep going until she found herself enveloped by deep, dark waters.

It was a fact that Story had failed at writing her own great American novel. Instead, she peddled commercial, spoon-fed slogans, which were far from literary and even farther from truth. So, in addition to knowing she was a failed novelist, she also knew she mass-produced shit for a living. But what she didn't know was that she was a fig fruit. It's true—the parallels are uncanny. In the rainforest, the fig fruit is a staple of almost every forest creature, but the fruit contains a laxative (which is highly acidic) that causes the seed to pass rapidly through an animal's gut. Thus, the animals act as seed dispersers. Story Easton and the fig fruit both used shit as a propagation method. Could a seed of hope survive a swim in a pool of poop? Special Occasions and Ivy Powers were banking on it.

Following a long afternoon of searching for upbeat sayings to adorn sympathy cards, the afternoon sun began its descent, and Story Easton began her own downward spiral into other people's dark sides. She left work, grabbed a burger, and headed home to tackle Ten Across, *Does the Wright thing.* Halfway through her glass of chardonnay, it came to her. *Flies.*

Two correct answers in one day was a new record. *Good omen?* Knowing it was the *Wright* thing to do, she initially resisted the compulsion to be someone else, but the longing overpowered her, and after changing her clothes, she soon found herself in her car, driving around, watching the sun retire. And once again, she searched for something, or someone, who would make her forget who she was.

She drove fifteen minutes on the freeway, long enough for stars to emerge in the Arizona night sky, until she saw an appealing sign—Paradise Valley. Paradise seemed like an improvement, so she took the exit and meandered around until she wound up on a hilly, rural road, a hundred yards away from paradise itself. Illuminated by several yard lights was a Victorian home, painted a robin egg's blue with white trim, complete with two ornate turrets and wrap-around porch. As one might expect from a fairy-tale scene nestled in the woods, a white picket fence enclosed a lush, green yard, but in the darkness, Story failed to see the patches of brown, dead grass.

Her parking spot was a small turnout hidden behind a hill, a quarter mile away. She began her trek to the perfect life in the perfect house. After an exhausting day, she was tired and therefore grateful when she saw how easy her entry would be—an open window in a back room on the first floor. Careful to make almost no noise, she extracted the screen, hopped through, and replaced the screen behind her.

Seeing no signs of life, she inspected the dark room, drenched in spots with moonlight. It was someone's office, but it was dusty and unused, with an un-expected sadness hanging thick in the air. A nameplate, displayed in brass and mahogany on a large desk, was highlighted by one vibrant moonbeam:

DAVID PAYNE, ATTORNEY AT LAW

(AT HOME, JUST *DAD*)

Story walked over to a closet's double doors and peeked inside. With enough moonlight in the right spots, she saw three boxes sitting on the floor. The one closest to her feet caught her attention. Having no lid, its contents overflowed onto the floor. One sheet contained a list of medical histories, and on another were handwritten names and phone numbers. But on another sheet, the sheet that explained how all the unorganized papers were connected, was an old, but beautiful, watercolor painting of a tree with exaggerated branches, each one containing a name written in black-ink calligraphy. And at the top of the parchment page was the title for this worn work of art: *Payne Family Tree.*

Jutting out of the box were other framed family trees, each one slightly different, but all related. When Story tried to shut the closet door, the box full of Payne lineage, as if in defiance for not having been properly tended to, somehow got in the way. Using her foot, she pushed the box back into the closet, and in doing so pushed someone's unfinished project farther away from completion.

At that moment, in a startling announcement, the only life in the room talked to, talked *at*, Story. "Miss you," squawked a green parrot in a silver birdcage hanging in the office corner.

Story stared at the bird's head, crowned with an orange, red, and yellow tuft of feathers, and wondered if she was hearing things.

"Miss you," it squawked again.

Story mouthed the words she knew by heart. *"A green and yellow parrot, which hung in a cage outside the door, kept repeating over and over: 'Allez vous-en!'"*

After wondering how the bird could already miss her, a complete stranger, Story walked closer to the cage and stuck out her finger. The bird then squawked, "Fuck it all!" in a very different tone, but it was obvious both phrases had been heard and practiced many times.

Story heard footsteps, so she hid under the desk.

The light came on, and Story saw a woman's feet with half-polished toenails shuffle across the floor. Story peered around the desk corner to see an attractive woman—actress-pretty, the kind of woman whose soft features and wavy blonde hair captured an entire room's attention. But her beauty seemed tarnished somehow. The woman shut the window, looked outside, and walked back over to the office door. She shut the door with authority, as if this was part of her night's routine, and approached the bird.

"Hey, Sonny," she said in a soft, melancholy tone. Story peeked out a little further from behind the desk, just enough to see a visibly upset Claire Payne take two pills from her pocket. Claire turned her head, so the bird wouldn't see, and swallowed them. After facing the bird once again, she said, "Well, Coop drew an inappropriate picture at school today, then refused to go to his baseball game, and I verbally assaulted one of my patients during a therapy session. So," she said, snickering, "it was a good day."

Her eyes began to well up. "I'm sorry about the door. I know how you love imperfection, but I called someone to fix it." She paused, and her voice cracked. "Every time it pops open and creaks, we think you're coming home."

Her hand trembled when she spoke again. "Friday's his birthday, and I don't think I can . . ."

Tears streamed down her splotchy face. "He's so angry, David."

Then, suddenly, she wiped the tears away, threw her fists in the air, and shouted, "Fuck it all!"

"Fuck it all!" the bird repeated as she walked toward the door.

Just as Story was about to get out from underneath the desk, the woman stopped in the doorway and greeted her raven-haired son.

The woman turned into another person, a pretend-happy person, for a split-second, and smiled like a good mom would. "I'm great, honey. Now, say good-night, and then it's bedtime. I'll meet you upstairs," she said, heading out the door.

Neither the woman nor the boy acknowledged the lie. Only the bird got the truth.

Small feet pitter-pattered over to the birdcage, and the boy seemed okay, until he spoke. "You promised," Cooper stated matter-of-factly, staring at the bird, now perched on a yellow mini-trapeze. "You promised you'd take me to find It when I turned nine." The bird stared back with black, motionless eyes.

After biting his lip, Cooper then made an all-too adult declaration. "Maybe you were wrong. Maybe there's no such thing as magic." He paused for a moment, and then his tone turned reckless. "If I don't find It by my birthday, I'm gonna do it," he said, his whole body tense and anxious.

Do what? Story wondered. *Run away?* But then Story's own muscles tightened, and she felt the boy's gloom pass over her like an invisible wave. A thought made her panic. *Shit, is this kid gonna kill himself? Okay, I get it. My life is not that bad.* Story was really starting to think she should break into more stable households, where children didn't make suicidal threats or talk to cantankerous birds. She envisioned this little boy's body sticking out of an oven. *Do eight year olds even know how to turn on an oven?* As Story pondered whether *broil* was a third-grade vocabulary word, she felt this boy's loss of innocence as her own, and almost shouted "abracadabra" in hopes of fixing the desperate situation. Between the bird, the boy, and the mother, Story had three different perspectives. *I had the story, bit by bit, from various people and, as generally happens in such cases, each time it was a different story.*

The boy walked away from the bird, but stopped halfway to the door and turned toward it. "Miss you," he said.

And then Story heard the bird squawk, "Miss you."

FOUR

For the first time in a long while, Story Easton knew other people more miserable than herself. She didn't know where all of the sadness came from, but she knew about unhappy families. *Happy families are all alike; every unhappy family is unhappy in its own way.* Still crouching beneath the desk, Story was alone now, but the mother and boy's grief felt like another, still-breathing person in the room. Story got out from her hiding spot and wondered if she should formally introduce herself to the bird, but when she looked at him, all she saw was a small but colorful parrot, preparing to be either sweet or belligerent.

"Fuck it all!" the bird shrieked as Story walked by. *Belligerent.* But this time, she forgave him.

Part of Story wanted to run out of that house and forget what she'd seen and heard, but another part of her, the authentic part that didn't want to fail, was drawn to these strangers.

After tiptoeing into the hallway, she made her way toward light—through the kitchen, where she glided her hand over cool granite countertops, through an unused family room, where life used to happen, and finally, to the base of the stairway that led upstairs, where she could hear them talking.

As Story climbed the steps, the mother, upstairs, surrendered a battle she couldn't win and, already tired, said, "Ready?"

The boy nodded as his mother reached for the book. By now, they were both snuggled up in their usual spots, and Story, having climbed the steps, was out in the hallway, barely out of sight. The boy clutched his umbrella and twirled it as his mother began.

"*Once Upon A Moonflower: A Fairy Tale (or A Tale of a Fairy)*." And then she added, "Written by Martin Baxter."

Of course, the mother and boy didn't know Martin Baxter, but to her surprise, Story did. By a strange coincidence, she'd spent the night before at his house, and had seen how sad and empty his pale blue eyes looked in the Phoenix moonlight.

After opening the book, the mother read the disclaimer on the first page. "Due to its graphic (real) and cerebral (smart) nature, this story is not recommended for small children, unless they are really, really brave." And then, as she always did, she read the dedication. "For my daughter Hope, the project I'm most proud of."

Story remembered the little blonde girl on Martin Baxter's shoulders, and then wondered what it would sound like for her own mother to say the word *proud* in reference to her.

After reading the introduction, Claire began the story. "Once upon a time, there was a girl named Hope, who lived in the heart of the rainforest."

The mother went on to read about Hope, lost in the dark jungle, embarking on a quest to find the magic treasure box hidden deep in the forest, but she didn't get far before the boy hung his head and said, "It's not gonna happen, is it?" He frowned. "He said when I turned nine, I'd be old enough, and when I was old enough, we'd go find the magic . . ." He didn't bother with the logistics. "*Together.*"

His birthday is Friday, thought Story. *He's supposed to find the magic treasure box on his birthday.*

His mother searched for the right answer, but it never came. "Honey, Dad meant well, but it's only a book, and Hope is only a—"

"Fuck Hope!" the boy cried.

"Cooper David Payne!" his mother scolded. "You're not allowed to say that word!"

"Fuck *fairies* then!"

Exhausted, the mother placed her hand on her son's leg, warm and sprouting small, soft hairs. "You're not allowed to say the 'F' word, Coop."

For just a moment, he stared up at her with an honest inquiry. "Fairies?"

And then the stress came crashing down on her as she pounded her clenched fists into her son's twin bed. "Fuck it all! *Fuck* is the word you're not allowed to say, goddamn it." She began to cry, mumbling "Sorry" and "Fuck" in-between sobs and hugging her son.

"See? You say it," Cooper said. "I've heard you say it to Sonny."

Sonny? It took Story a moment to realize the cranky bird had a happy, sun-shiny name.

A few seconds after the mother began crying again, she stopped, suddenly wary. "Did you hear something?"

"Nuh-uh," Cooper said, still teary-eyed, refusing to look at the pictures on the page.

Story left her exposed hideout and slipped into the last door at the end of the hallway. While Cooper and his mother finished their story several doors back, Story explored her new room, a guest room with very little in it save a desk, a bed, and a closet. In the closet hung two cocktail dresses still in dry cleaner plastic, and on the floor, Story found what she was looking for.

High-heeled shoes, beaded and shiny-black, called to her. She put them on, quietly prancing around in her very own pajama pageant, and after leaving her old self behind, she began to strut, emerging empowered and confident. Finally, Story Easton felt like someone else, someone who made things happen. In her mind, she sparkled with fairy dust, and flew through starry skies, bringing light to shadowy places. For a moment, Story was Hope, and she flew on fairy wings, found the magic box, and rescued Cooper from everything life had done to him.

And when she went to bed, she dreamed of an enchanted girl floating down an enchanted river.

TUESDAY

"Where exactly am I?" I asked my snake of a train as she slithered her way through moss and buttress roots.

She hissed her answer. "The greatesssssssst place on earth," she said. "Jussssssst look around. There isssssss life everywhere." Then she pointed her forked tongue toward a small hill abuzz with birds and insects.

"What do you do here?" Besides develop speech impediments, I thought.

"I sssssearch for sssssun," she said as her strong muscles contracted and she maneuvered us between tall grasses.

"Do you ever get lost in the shadows?" I asked.

She paused, then let out a brief hiss. "Ssssssometimes it's necessssssary to find onessssself in the dark."

I worried that her lisp might affect her forest reputation. "Have you considered using words without the letter 's'?"

To my surprise, she let out a small chuckle riddled with the letter "s," and then continued her hiss-lecture. "True happinessssssss can only be found when you let go of your fear and recognize the beauty of both light *and* dark."

I loosened my grip so I wouldn't hurt her, but I wasn't ready to see the glamorous side of darkness just yet. "If the forest is full of life, what about death?"

"Ah, death. The beginning of life."

I ducked my head to avoid a low-lying branch. "Beginning?" The lack of sun was impairing her judgment.

"Yessssssss, beginning. Death alwayssssss makessss room for more life. It issssss nature'sssss way," she said.

"Hey, is this about that spotted killing machine I'm supposed to watch out for? Are you trying to tell me something?"

"Sssssssshhhh. That's not until darkness comes."

"Geez, thanks," I said. "I feel much better."

She stopped, lifted her serpent-head, and turned back to look at me. "Remember, firssssst the treasure box, then the moonflower."

"Do they teach you guys that phrase in rainforest school?" I said. "You're all in on this together, aren't you?"

"Ssssymbiosissssss, my dear."

But before I could figure out what that meant, she flung me off her back like I was an annoying parasite, and as I flipped mid-air, I hollered, "You should know I have three library books due today, and if I don't get back home in time, I'll be sending the rainforest a bill!"

I landed with my face planted in a wild orchid, and when I tried to get up, I came face to face with another kind of bill, striped and multi-colored.

"Get up!" it squawked. "Get up! It's time to fly."

FIVE

When you wake up in someone else's shoes, it's hard to be yourself, which is why Story woke up that Tuesday morning feeling courageous. But when she undid the straps on the high heels and put them back in the closet, she felt like her old self again—a wayward, unwanted visitor. The night before, Story had conceived of the bold and admirable goal of helping Cooper Payne, not only because she really liked him, which was a rarity in itself, but also because she knew what it was like to lose someone you loved. But in the process of tidying the bed, it took Story one full minute to recall this ambitious goal, and then another five seconds to reject it.

She actually whispered, "Sucks to be you, Cooper Payne," as she put on her slippers and prepared her getaway. *The sooner you realize there's no magic treasure box, and the sooner you realize that life is one giant crapshoot, the better off you'll be.* After all, the shattered dreams of Story's youth had made her stronger—capable of not dreaming at all.

The digital clock read 8:33, which meant she'd overslept. A lot. On her *sleepovers*, she tried to be out before six. Luckily, Cooper and his mother had probably already left the house for school. She started walking down the hallway toward the stairs, but stopped in front of Cooper's open bedroom door. Something lured her inside, and within a few seconds, she was looking around his room at the things Cooper deemed important. There was a model airplane hanging from the ceiling, and in the corner was a ratty, stuffed puppy dog, too juvenile to be on display, but too special to be discarded.

Story snickered when she saw a Socra-Tots® collector's book set titled *Why Do Manners Matter?* sticking out from under the bed—there was no escaping her mother. On a white bookshelf sat a signed baseball in a clear plastic box, and next to it was a framed picture of Cooper and his father, laughing, his face turned to the side, trying to wipe ketchup off his son's. Beside that was an older, yellowed picture, Cooper's father in hospital scrubs, splotchy-eyed from crying, standing next to a clear bin and holding the tiny Cooper Michael Payne.

As Story continued to peruse the room's contents, she made frequent glances back at the picture of Cooper and his father, as if she were being watched. She approached a bulletin board with the word D-R-E-A-M hanging above it in big wooden letters. Tacked onto the corkboard were three things: on the top left, a foam cutout of a giant number one; on the bottom right, a banner which read, *If You Can Imagine It, You Can Do It*; and finally, at dead center, a ripped-out coloring-book picture of a pirate's treasure box lying underneath a palm tree.

On his bedside table sat a snow globe, an encapsulated winter wonderland foreign to the sun-lovers of Phoenix. Story picked it up and shook it until tiny white flakes flurried about, settling on the shoulders of the miniature Santa. When Santa was almost completely covered in snow, she tapped the plastic enough to free him, and Story found herself lost in a long-ago Christmas memory.

She was five years old, lying under her covers on Christmas Eve, her green eyes beaming with a sense of want and wonder. Two hours earlier, she'd placed a plate of warm cookies, a glass of milk, and a bundle of carrots by the fireplace, and she couldn't sleep thinking of Santa bringing her cherished and requested gift—her very own magic kit, complete with a shiny magic wand, a red silk scarf from which to pluck a goldfish bowl, a deck of cards, several mini-cups for concealing small objects, and finally, a purple, velvet magician's robe with silver stars.

Around midnight, she heard noise in the living room, so she snuck out to see if it had arrived. She tiptoed out of her room in her yellow footy-pajamas, down the hall toward what she knew would be the present that would change her life from ordinary to extraordinary. But when she got to the living room, the Christmas tree lights were off, and the treetop's bright star was dim and barely hanging on. Story's mother, with her perfect blonde bob and immaculate makeup, sat in a rocking chair next to the fireplace, not rocking, but instead chomping on Rudolph's carrot and dismembering a Santa doll with a seam ripper. And as Story watched in horror, her mother continued attacking St. Nick's seams, focusing on his stubborn groin. Without looking up, she said, "Young lady, you're supposed to be in bed."

With a gentle hand, Story placed the snow globe back down on the table, careful to preserve the fragile, innocent world inside, and walked over to an open closet. On the top shelf, Story saw several board games stacked on each other in a teetering pile. Without thinking, she lifted down the ouija board, the first in the stack, took the lid off, and crouched down next to it. As a joke, Story took the three-legged pointer in her hand, and asked it an important question: "Is Elvis really dead?"

With both hands clutched in a firm grip, she moved the pointer to *YES*. She laughed to herself, thinking of people who actually believed in this crap, and then asked another question high on her list of curiosities: "Does swallowed gum really take ten years to fully digest?" The pointer "magically" made an immediate move to *NO*, and she snickered some more, pleased with her little game.

Just as she was about to put the game away, she looked over at the picture of Cooper and his dad, and with a compulsion stronger than she'd ever felt before, asked a question that seemed to come from someone else: "What will save him?"

Then the pointer moved on its own. Story, shocked, first stared at the board in complete disbelief, and then turned around to see if she was alone. It appeared that she was, but the silence was unnerving, so she forced the pointer to a stop, cleared her throat, and closed her eyes. *Imagination's haywire today—too much damn sleep*, she thought. *When I open my eyes, everything will be back to normal. One. Two. Three.*

But when she opened her eyes, the pointer took her hands hostage and began to move on its own again. First it went to "S."

"Ah!" Story meant to scream, but it came out a whisper.

The pointer moved, in order, to "T," "O," then "R" and all the while Story repeated the mantra, *This isn't real . . . This isn't real . . . This isn't real.*

Finally, the pointer landed on "Y."

At first, she took a moment to catch her breath, wondering if it was finished, but shortly after, she had no choice but to try to decipher the message from beyond.

The rainforest story? she wondered.

The pointer then moved to "U." *You.*

She shook her head in defiance, trying hard not to look over at the picture that still seemed to be watching her every move. *Me?*

"No, no, no," she said.

But when Story looked at the coloring-book picture hanging on the bulletin board, she suddenly remembered sitting cross-legged on the shag carpet, coloring Scooby-Doo and sharing jumbo crayons with her dad. He had brought her a small bouquet of yellow daffodils from his garden out back, and tucked a perfect golden one behind her ear. Although she didn't realize it until that very moment, it was the last memory she had of him before he died. The smell of his aftershave flooded back, and as she recalled the way his gentle smile looked when he said, "It's okay to go outside the lines," she felt a pronounced change come over her.

She missed his voice. She missed his laugh. She missed feeling accepted, as if she had a place in the world. There had been no chance for goodbye, and no chance to finish anything they'd started. Lots of dreams were left blank, uncolored, dead. The rejection and hopelessness she'd felt ever since losing him now announced themselves as something far from okay—the kind of something no child should have to endure.

So now, when she stepped back from the bulletin board to examine the treasure box picture, it looked less like a cartoon and more real, as if she could reach out and touch the carved wood, as if it really did hold secrets. And when she held the number one foam tightly in her hand, she remembered the advice she'd received via fortune cookie: *Everyone gets one chance to do something great. Yours is coming soon.*

And that's when Story Easton knew that this would be her story. She would prove her mother wrong, and finally accomplish something that mattered. She took one last look at the picture of Cooper and his dad, and before she could leave them, before she could break her gaze, she made the promise she knew she had to make.

But mid-promise, she heard a loud banging sound coming from downstairs, which shook Cooper's wall of dreams, sending the giant number one and the ripped-out picture of the treasure box floating end over end, until they landed like feathers on the carpet. Story picked up both the giant number one and treasure box picture and promptly tacked them back up on the bulletin board.

And with a sudden sense of purpose, Story Easton tore out of the room a transformed woman, only to run into a solid man standing in the hallway.

"Shit!" she screamed.

"Shit!" he hollered. "You okay?" He extended his hands, as if to catch her.

Knocked back, Story took a good look at her victim. As it turned out, he wasn't a victim at all, but a thirty-something man, who managed to be handsome and scruffy at the same time. Dazed, Story caught herself staring at his strong forearms, his lean frame, and then, so as not to let him notice her ogling, his eyes. But they were no help. Pale blue, they were the color of the ocean on a gray day, beautiful and stormy.

"I'm fine. Hello," Story finally said, unaware of how flirty her inflection was until she heard the "o" stretch out and echo its way down the hallway. "Sorry, I didn't see you," she said, but when she tried to back away from him, she realized she had somehow snagged the waist of her pajama bottom around a tool hanging from his tool belt.

The two of them danced for moment in an awkward series of movements, until the man smiled, raised his eyebrows, and in a quiet voice said, "You're stuck on my big hammer."

She rolled her eyes but softened when the stranger said, "Here," and tenderly separated the two of them using the little claw of his much smaller hammer.

Story was still trying not to ogle. "You look just like . . ."

"That guy. I know."

Nice voice. Quiet yet confident. God, nice teeth, too, she thought when he smiled. *He's perfect. How despicable.* Secretly, Story hoped he'd burp, use a double negative, or act servile—anything to make him seem less attractive—but he didn't. Instead, his tall frame, unfaltering, stood still and attentive, his T-shirt calling attention to his lean biceps, strong from real work probably, not from fake workouts at a trendy gym. His Carhart work pants were clean and wrinkle-free, as if he wore them to do handiwork and then out to dinner.

Then Story raised her hopes. *Maybe he smells.* But no luck there either. When

Story subtly leaned forward and took in a breath, she inhaled a manly cocktail: part hardware store (complete with the slightly dirty smell of little drawers full of nails and screws), part freshly-showered clean, and part maple-cured bacon, which he probably cooked himself. *God, yummy enough to eat. And he cooks!*

And truth be told, he did look like *that guy*, if *that guy* was a Greek god with a tool belt. His light brown hair, cut short, lay close to his head in gentle swirls, and when bits of sunlight entered through the hallway window, specks of amber streaked his hair with gold. *What the hell am I doing?* she thought. *These are observations made by the predictable heroine in a cheesy beach novel. No wonder I can't make it as a real writer!*

But then she noticed something interesting and less clichéd. As he adjusted his tool belt, Story noticed what set this man apart—his hands. They were beat up, scraped, and chafed from his labors, but it was more than that—they seemed broken, like flawed companions for his eyes, which were bright but, now that she thought about it, vaguely wounded.

"Didn't mean to freak you out," he said. "I'm fixing a door downstairs . . . I heard something up here." He took a closer look at her as he rubbed one of his hands. "The homeowner said nobody would be home—"

"Right." Story let out a nervous chuckle. "Right! I forgot to tell her I was coming."

"Claire?"

"Yeah," Story said, swallowing. "She's my sister." Violating her personal rule of never reciting the oft-quoted Salinger because it was cliché, she thought, until the man spoke again, *If you really want to hear about it, the first thing you'll probably want to know is where I was born, and what my lousy childhood was like, and how my parents were occupied and all before they had me, and all that* David Copperfield *kind of crap—*

"Always travel in your pajamas?" He smiled again, but this time the smirk ended on a skeptical note.

She raised her eyebrows and took a step toward him. "Always entrap people with your big hammer?" she said, looking into his eyes. When he didn't laugh, she took a small step back. "Came late last night. Let myself in."

"People really should lock their doors," he said, nodding. "You could be a serial killer."

"I know! I totally could be!" Story said.

"If you're not a serial killer, what are you, then?" he asked, securing his hammers.

Story had already lied, so she continued her prevarication by pretending to be someone her mother would be proud of. "I'm a doctor," she said.

Impressed, he said, "Really? I've got this pain in my . . ."

"I'm a proctologist," she blurted.

". . . neck."

Story mumbled while the man, in a calm and thorough manner, described the aches and pains aggravated by his line of work. And then he glanced in Cooper's bedroom.

"That's my nephew's room—Cooper," Story said, lost in a dreamy stare, and when she said his name out loud, she felt more confident than ever about her decision. "He's turning nine on Friday. I'm here to give him a big surprise."

"If it's a free prostate exam, I'll be forced to call social services."

Story let out an awkward laugh, then said, "Nope, something else." She winked, shrouding herself in her noble endeavor, and whispered the words she wanted to believe, but didn't. "It's magic."

He perked up when he heard *magic*. "Good luck with that," he said, his smile returning. His eyes darted around a bit, looking first at her emerald eyes and her long, wavy auburn hair, and then his gaze fixed on her cupid's bow lips. "I'm Hans."

"Story," she said.

"Too bad," he sighed, shaking his head. "Not a big fan of stories."

Oh, my God, I'm such an idiot. I can't believe I used my real name. Trying to look calm, she said, "Let me guess, you're a realist," followed by a pause. "Do you buy greeting cards, by chance?" she asked, but when he gave her a puzzled look, she said, "Never mind. Look, I gotta go. Don't mention my being here to my sister, okay? I'm coming back at dinner to give him the—"

"Surprise, right." Hans covered his eyes. "Never saw you." But when he unveiled his eyes, Story saw a slight sparkle, a shimmering hint of almost-enthusiasm—which, like his voice, was just on the verge of giving a shit. "May you live happily ever after, Story."

And when the words came out, Hans looked a little shocked, as if he'd surprised even himself. Story wondered if he was teasing her, maybe to get her to flirt some more, but right when her mind wandered away from the dreamy man in front of her, and instead focused on the task at hand—her new quest to save Cooper Payne—Hans did something which seemed somehow genuine, and certainly notable.

He called her bluff and kissed her.

SIX

Having not been kissed, *really* kissed, in a long time, Story first went a little weak in the knees, and then stiffened, a self-conscious reaction to being caught wearing pajamas while suffering from un-brushed teeth and sleepy onion breath. It was like a post-coital morning-after kiss, but without the dinner-date protocol. She could have said, "That was nice," or at least "Thank you," but instead, she sabotaged yet another beautiful thing by saying, "What was that for?"

Hans could have given an elaborate answer, but he simply smiled and stared back. *Strong, silent type.* Story let out an audible, disgusted sigh. *Great. The clichés are free-flowing now.* "One kiss," Story blurted, "and you become a mute?" Out of character, she added, "A *cute* mute." And then she decided to stay quiet (and stop rhyming) when she recalled a first line in which being mute was attractive—at least, to one other person. *In the town there were two mutes, and they were always together.*

Hans studied Story's face, and finally said, with an air of magic and mystery, "Merry Christmas, Story."

She folded her arms and fought back a smirk. "It's not even Halloween yet." And then, in keeping with the weirdness—being in a strange home, getting kissed by a stranger, and deciding to help a little boy she hadn't yet met—she borrowed someone else's words and whispered, "All this happened, more or less."

Hans's voice was soft but definitive. "Vonnegut."

"Yes," she said, the brevity becoming contagious. "You're a Vonnegut fan?"

"Isn't everyone?" His pale blue eyes seemed to be getting bluer.

Mr. Rennaisance Man knows Vonnegut and *can fix a door? Damn it, these aren't even my cool pajamas.* Story envisioned beefy and glistening handymen sitting in a

Book Club circle, discussing extended metaphors and character believability, and wondered how she could get invited to such an event. Story watched Hans tighten his tool belt, and when he looked up at her, it seemed like goodbye.

Without thinking, she said, "This was a good time," revealing more than she wanted, and before the full embarrassment of her desperation could set in, she shut her eyes and hoped he didn't hear.

But he did. Hans stood tall, unmoving. "It was the best of times," he said.

Story figured she had nothing to lose, so she opened her eyes, and continued with the most recognizable and revered first lines in all of literature. "It was the worst of times."

"It was the age of wisdom," he said, convincing and proud.

Like a fool, Story continued to recite Dickens in her pajamas. "It was the age of foolishness."

"It was . . ." Hans began to laugh. "What the hell *was* it? I only read the Cliff Notes for this one."

"The epoch of belief," Story said, tucking her hair behind her ears.

"Ah," he said, "no wonder I didn't remember that line. It's stupid . . . What a hack." They both laughed. "I actually remember the *last* line of *A Tale of Two Cities* better than the first—it's much more memorable." He blinked slowly, folded his hands, and grew serious. "I can recite it in my sleep."

"What is it?" Story asked.

"Slips my mind," he said, smiling. But Story knew he hadn't forgotten. Something told her it was an ending that needed to be earned, and after all, he'd just met her. And Hans seemed like the kind of guy who never let his Dickens reach fruition on the first date, although his timing for kisses was odd.

"I thought you didn't like stories."

"I used to."

Hans wished her well with a warm smile, and Story could tell he was wondering about her. To Story, Hans looked as if he possessed a penchant for rescuing women in distress, not in a chauvinistic way, but in a real way, as if he somehow felt responsible. Several times during their conversation, when he was on the verge of talking, he instead offered her his hands. It was subtle, of course, but Story noticed how he extended them in a vulnerable way, somewhere between a peace offering and a safety net. And yet, other times, he rubbed them, as if they ached.

So when he presented his large, working-man hand to Story, and let her do the talking, she felt safe, but also bummed that he saw her as someone who might not be capable of helping herself.

"A pleasure," she said as she let his strong hands squeeze hers. After starting down the hall, she turned around for a moment to give one last smile to the beautiful stranger who would stay just that—a stranger.

Goodbye to the only real prince in Phoenix, the one who might have given me a chance.

Love,

Princess Failure

SEVEN

Many years ago, in a sun-kissed land, a young Hans Turner became a man too soon. Like most tales, Hans's is many-layered—story upon story stacked inside him like the hand-chiseled wooden blocks he could create to perfection. But just as every fictional fairy tale character has one defining moment—Cinderella's mother dying, Jack's run-in with a giant, Snow White's fickle dad marrying a murderous bitch—so did the very real Hans Turner. It happened in his childhood, and it carved into his life a dark groove that, no matter what he did to smooth it over, remained a deep, lifeless furrow.

Not that he didn't try to smooth it over, try to sand it out of his life for good. Ever since it happened, at the age of eight, Hans tried hard to wash his hands of it. But his hands were always, and are, the problem—they failed him once, long ago. To make up for it, he now used his hands as tools to fix and protect, certain that it is actions, not words, that save people—but there is an exception to every rule.

In stories, words often trump action. In stories, the things people say to each other breathe life into those in need of resuscitation. In stories, words can work magic. But stories lived only in Hans's past, where they existed on a flat, imaginary page, fixed in time, because any fool knew this: Compared to people in real life, stories always disappoint.

Though Hans never talked all that much, when people would ask him what his college major had been, he would answer, "I majored in wood," because it invariably conjured up inappropriate images of horny undergrads lusting their way through four years of school, and it always ended conversations he didn't want to have about why he wasn't living up to his potential. Hans was an artist, formally trained, with an MFA in woodworking, but with bills to pay, he gave up creating art to feed his soul, and became a handyman to fill his belly. That's why he'd been at the Payne house, to fix Claire's front door, and maybe, in doing so, help fix Claire, just a little.

Hans knew the difference between bloodwood and coast redwood. He also knew if a piece of wood was ring-porous or diffuse-porous. And he could tell, by looking at the inside layers of a tree, how it had become damaged—reddish brown streaks indicated injury by bird, and black specks suggested insect damage. But what Hans Turner could not do was apply this knowledge of trees and wood to the human realm, and therefore he could not tell, when meeting someone, whether or not he could fix her. So he gave up guessing and attempted to fix everyone. And when he felt he could not fix someone, his hands were the first to know—they ached.

But recently his hands ached the most when he tried to create true art, as he used to. The lively wooden sculptures he once carved held a story in each engraved curve, but now, if he tried to do anything more than fix damaged wood in a utilitarian fashion, or forge original creations for someone else's made-to-order vision, his hands throbbed. So Hans decided he'd focus his life on mending flaws rather than creating beauty.

So while Story scooted out of the Payne house and back to her own, Hans finished fixing the Paynes' front door and, in his mind, fixing Claire Payne. While talking—no, listening—to her to her on the phone, she'd sounded as off-kilter as that door of hers that would not stay latched. Hans did not know the reason for the frustration in her voice, but as he re-hung the door, pounding the doorframe with his carpenter's hammer and shaving off little pieces of the door with his planer, he did what he could to restore balance to door and owner alike.

Pound. A little stronger.

Pound. Pound. A little more solid.

Pound. Pound. Pound . . . balanced. And ready to withstand any shitty day. Lots of shitty days, perhaps, if he did his job.

Finally, when the planked, Hacienda-style door closed with ease and stayed closed, Hans let his hands glide over the recycled Douglas-fir, touching it with tenderness, as one would caress a delicate flower, or a lost love. After repairing Claire's door, Hans made a quick change of clothes, and left for his next appointment: not another handyman job this time, but an appointment for his *other* job.

When he wasn't fixing broken people's broken things, Hans made small rabbits and credit cards disappear. He locked rings together. He drew cards out of nowhere. A leftover childhood fascination, magic to him meant that some small corners of the world might still be enchanted.

Though quieter than other magicians, who liked loud *Presto-Chango* declarations and gaudy show voices, Hans won his crowds over without speaking. Ever. His mime-style became so popular in the children's party circuit, he had to give himself a name. He painted *Sleight of Hans* in a mysterious, whimsical font on a removable decal, and when he traveled to a magic gig, he used the decal to cover up his truck's permanent sign, *Fix-It-And-Forget-It Man*.

Today's magic gig was twelve-year-old Sarah Hartsinger's birthday party, which Hans thought would be like the others—Mylar balloons, bad sheet cakes, and a few beautiful but predictable moments of wonderment when he made things disappear. But when he showed up at the Hartsinger residence, he realized this was not to be.

The solid-oak front door opened and a petite, pony-tailed girl wearing a baby-blue hoodie greeted Hans. "Hey, hey, hey," she stammered, looking at Hans's retro tuxedo and his big, gun-metal gray tool box which held his magic tricks. In a frenzied flutter out of nowhere, her eyebrows danced up and down as she cracked her fingers and let out bullet-like utterings, seemingly uncontrollable, that sounded more like bodily functions than words. *KEECH. HOOL. URP.* And then she yelled, "Hey. Hey. Magician fuck-fuck-fucker!" which ended in an odd crescendo.

Strangely charmed, Hans gently shook her hand and wondered what the hell was wrong with her. His hands, acting as surveyors, throbbed in response.

The girl's face softened, and she gave him a warm, confident smile. "I'm Sarah. It's my party," she said, and then, laughing, sang, *"And I'll cry if I want to"* in a beautiful, angelic voice. After an embarrassed sigh, she added, "My mom likes that stupid song."

Hans smiled, still standing in the doorway, waiting to come in.

"Oh, sorry," she said sweetly, opening the door more and leading him into the foyer. "You really don't talk much, huh?" But then without warning, her eyebrows danced again, her fingers cracked, and the bullet-words returned. "Asshole. Bitch. Tit-tit-titties!"

A woman raced over to where Hans and Sarah stood, and after wiping her hands on a mini-apron tied to her waist, extended her hand. "Oh, geez," she grimaced. "I should've warned you. Sarah suffers from Tourette's Syndrome. She can't help what she says," she said in a kind, motherly voice. "Words that she wishes she never knew flow out of her mouth like a fountain of filth!" She threw up her hands with an awkward giggle.

Like an explosive sneeze, Sarah then screeched, "Dick penis!" but this redundancy came out in a sad, innocent, and sorry tone, as if she were unfamiliar with both words, and just trying them out the way most kids experiment with new vocabulary. Then she made eye contact with Hans. "Please don't leave," she said. "People always leave." And then, in a whisper, she added, "It's always worse when I get excited." Sarah smoothed her hair back and stood up straight. "Or when I'm trying really hard to be normal." Her eyes blinked in slow succession, and each time they opened, they revealed a different emotion. At first, embarrassment dominated, but then her gaze lightened, and shame evolved into wonderment, as if she knew a secret about Hans that he himself had yet to discover.

Hans closed his eyes for a moment, not sure if he should laugh or cry. *Jesus*, he thought, *there's got to be some way to fix this poor kid. Drugs? Therapy? Muzzle?*

Sarah and her mother led Hans down a hallway and into a large living room with a big banner on the wall that read *Feel the Magic—Sarah's Turning Twelve!* Sarah rolled her eyes and softly admitted, "I wanted an iPad instead of this party—magic is for babies." She smiled at Hans. "No offense."

Hans smiled back and shrugged at the same time, and thought, in a world where everything that can go wrong often does, babies needed magic the least. Broken people were everywhere: right there in the suburbs, with vaulted ceilings, oak doors, and nice mothers; in high rises; in crappy apartments; in grand estates, speaking different languages, loving other, different, broken people, all fighting the same urge to let their defining moment consume them.

And then Hans saw the motley crew awaiting him in the living room. *Whoa. We need some magic here*, he thought. He was greeted by six kids sitting on two poofy upholstered couches, and four others sitting cross-legged on the carpeted floor. One boy in overalls picked his nose without apology, another boy made ape noises and pretended to pick cooties out of another boy's wild black hair, and a chubby girl in a wheelchair was, for some reason, dressed in a too-tight spandex Wonder Woman outfit, while repeating in a slurred, spittle-laden voice, "Can you see me? I'm in my invisible jet! Can you see me? I'm in my invisible jet!"

As Hans set up his magic gear on a small card table in front of the room, Sarah brought her mouth up to Hans's ear, and he tried not to flinch at what she might say. "They're in my resource class at school," she whispered. "Mom said it's rude not to invite them," and then sat down on the floor, creating a front-row seat.

Hans nodded in acknowledgement, draped a large white linen cloth over the table, and began his first trick. After he made a shiny quarter disappear, the audience erupted with oohs and ahhs and overstretched smiles. Several kids clapped in a spastic, fast-forward motion, but Sarah's clap was polite, appropriate, and kind. At varied points in his act, Hans made eye contact with all the children, each with their own personal histories, but of all the stories in the room, Sarah's was the saddest. When she got excited, she showed visible restraint, trying not to speak. Once, she even covered her mouth, for fear another vulgar phrase would escape. But Hans saw her focus on his hands. Every move they made. Every conjure. Every summon. And with every new gesture, she sat forward a little more.

After thirty-five minutes of cards up sleeves, never-ending rainbow scarves, and hidden eggs, Hans prepared for his finale—pulling a white bunny from his black top hat—but Sarah raised her hand and interrupted.

When she spoke, her voice resonated both hope and desperation. "Can you make *me* disappear?" she said, blinking resignedly.

Hans stalled, not sure how to respond. The audience needed magic, and Sarah Hartsinger needed to not scream *cock and balls* at church.

After Hans motioned for Sarah to come up, he held a purple curtain hanging from a rod in front of her, hiding her from the audience. He then spoke quietly, turning to her so only she could hear. "I'm not going to use any fancy magic words here—"

"Words are overrated," she assured him.

With no real instruction, Hans began to count with his fingers, so the audience could see.

One.

Sarah's eyes widened when she whispered, "What am I supposed to do?"

Two, Hans indicated with his fingers.

Sarah's panicked eyebrows danced. "Gism whore!" came out as a mean whisper, as she looked to Hans for some direction.

Three!

And when the audience watched Hans fling the curtain in the air to reveal what was behind it, they began to cheer. One boy said, "She's gone!" and Wonder Woman cried, "She's invisible!" spraying saliva on the girl next to her.

Hiding underneath the tableclothed card table where Hans had, in the split-second before the reveal, sequestered her, Sarah looked up, disappointed. "I'm still here."

Hans thought about telling her, *Magic can't save everyone, but isn't it great how we made the kids in the audience believe in something enchanted?* But Sarah Hartsinger didn't need any more words.

Once the crowd dispersed, Sarah snuck out from her hiding place, and as the others mingled, she slyly made her way over to Hans, who was busy not eating bad sheet cake.

She stared at his calloused hands. "How'd they get like that?"

"Fixing things," Hans said, thinking of the difference between things that can be fixed, and things that can only be mended.

She nodded, and then smiled. "You're a bad magician."

"You're a bad *disappearer*," he said with a smirk. And for a moment, she disappeared into the wallpaper. "But you're an amazing singer," Hans said, delivering the words with his strong, flawed hands.

With that, Sarah Hartsinger took shape and came to life. "Once upon a time," she said, her soft voice employing mystery instead of vulgarity, "there was a girl who *almost* thought magic was *sorta* cool." She glanced behind her at the roomful of guests, making sure no one but Hans heard her confession.

Hans let his plastic fork fall onto the paper plate. Through a smile and a sigh, Hans said, "A story? I thought you said words were overrated."

He could tell Sarah wondered what he had against stories. And in that split second, he actually realized what it was. They're fixed. Stuck. Once they're written, they can't be changed. Fixed sorrow on the page. Closed books of despair.

Sarah did not deny what she'd said—instead, she displayed the same knowing look Hans had seen earlier. She then closed her eyes, placed her hands on her forehead in true psychic form, and said, giggling, "You're going to meet someone who makes you like stories again."

"Is that right?" he laughed, placing his plate on the table. "And how do you know that?"

She laughed back. "Magic, of course."

"So it's not just *for babies*."

Her smile was still there, but it softened, and when she raised her eyebrows, she became serious. "Keep your eyes open, Magic Man." But as she studied him, watching a smile subconsciously take over his face, Sarah knew Hans had already met that someone, even if he didn't know it yet.

"Yes ma'am," Hans said, grateful Sarah's instructive words had not devolved into an evil, semantic cluster of inappropriate body parts and fluids.

And as Hans Turner walked away, trying hard to keep his eyes wide open, the bright Arizona sunshine forced him to squint. For a moment, he switched his focus from the harsh, blinding beams to warmer, caressing rays, and he thought of a slightly broken woman living in her own slightly flawed tale. He thought of the artful curves of soft, cupid's-bow lips reciting other people's words, and wondered if she was living happily ever after.

EIGHT

"**Y**ou're late." Ivy Powers and her happy-face-on-a-stick greeted Story at her cubicle, spewing an onslaught of deadline reminders and a new suggestion for the *Grief and Loss* series. "You're including flowers in the design, right? Sad people like flowers."

"Sad people don't like flowers, Boss . . ." Guzzling her to-go coffee with beer-bong dedication, Story shuffled past Ivy to her desk. She'd just kissed a handyman, and she had only five days to figure out how to find a magic treasure box that didn't exist.

"Ms. Powers, please," Ivy said.

"They just say they like flowers to be nice, Boss. Because all of us stupid 'happy' people don't know what to say, and instead of just saying *sorry*, we bring them bushels of delphiniums, roses, tulips—all of which wither and die a slow death—so the recipient gets to witness the death of something they love. Again." Story's memories of the days following her father's death overflowed not with one indelible image, but with one overwhelming, offensive smell—death in the form of decaying bouquets from well-wishers.

Ivy flipped her happy face over like a pancake, and pointed to the other side of the cardboard cutout—a sad face with a slash through it. Bad attitudes were not welcome in her division. "Just because you feel like this doesn't mean you get to show it." She flipped sadness on its back like the cheap whore she thought it was, and showed, once again, the preferred happy face. "Now, *this* is where you need to be." She winked another scary reminder. "Happy equals profit."

"Cha-ching," Story said with an exaggerated smile as two-faced Ivy walked away. She hollered, "You're really growing on me, Ivy!" but because her pun was unappreciated, she knew the only *real* way to get back at her boss was to use company time for personal business.

So when all was clear, she Googled "Martin Baxter" to find out more about the magic treasure box, and how she could create one for Cooper. The first entry linked her to a fan's website about Martin Baxter, author of the popular children's book *Once Upon A Moonflower*. The next entry was an article in *The Oregonian*: "LOCAL PROFESSOR LOSES WIFE AND DAUGHTER IN FATAL CRASH."

Another entry led her to Arizona State University's official web site, with a link to Martin Baxter's background information on the Biology Faculty page. "Professor Baxter comes to us from Portland State," began the paragraph, which went on about Martin Baxter's area of expertise—tropical plants, specifically rainforest bromeliads. Learning he was "son of the late Abigail Baxter, world-renowned botanical illustrator" made Story curious if he had been close with *his* successful mother, and then she wondered if Mrs. Baxter's flower drawings could comfort a mourning widow.

Story found several other websites devoted to *Once Upon A Moonflower*, but none gave the specific location of the magic treasure box, nor did they explain what was in it, so it was time to ask the writer himself. After a successful Google search, she dialed Martin P. Baxter on Esther Drive.

A man answered, at last, on the tenth ring. "Hello." It was not a greeting—more like a warning not to bother him.

"Hello. Hi." Story fumbled, not sure where to start. "Is this Martin Baxter? Author of *Once Upon A Moonflower?*"

The man didn't answer. He took a couple of slow breaths, as if he was thinking. Story grew uncomfortable, so she began doodling a happy sunflower on her desk calendar, and when she could no longer stand the silence, she repeated, "Hello?"

The man remained silent, but Story heard him take a drink of something and clear his throat.

"Um, I'm sorry to bother you at home, sir," said Story, "but I'm doing a story about your children's book, and I have a couple of questions for you."

He grunted something that almost sounded like "Mmm-kay."

Story began scribbling the outline of a treasure box on the paper in front of her, hoping to fill the inside before the conversation's end. "What was your inspiration for writing a magical story that takes place in the rainforest?"

The man let out an unforgiving and disappointed sigh. He'd probably been asked that one a million times. Strike one.

"Um, how did this project differ from your academic writing—"

"Oh, for Chrissakes," he yelled into the phone, slurring his words a little. "It's a goddamned fairy tale! That's how it's different—"

"Right, sir. Sorry." Strike two. After a quick, desperate breath, she blurted, "I need to know what's in the magic treasure box."

After a long pause, Martin Baxter delivered four unexpected words. "It's just a book," he said. His voice had softened, though, and Story remembered the smile he wore in the picture with Hope on his shoulders.

"I know it's just a book, sir, but the story seemed to come from someplace pure," she said, "and I know it sounds crazy, but that treasure box is a source of hope for—"

"I'm sorry, I can't help you," he interrupted. "If you'll excuse me, I've got a lecture at ten o'clock, and I'm on my way out."

Story grimaced. Of all people, she should have known that sometimes even the mere mention of hope is an ugly reminder that you don't have any. "Of course, sir," Story said. "Thank you for your time." As she prepared to hang up, something urged her to stay on the line. After a pause, she said, "It's a lovely story, Mr. Baxter." In the brief moment between what she'd said, and what she said next, it truly was a beautiful moment between strangers.

But all beautiful things eventually die.

"I mean, I haven't read it all, but from what I've heard, it's clever, I mean, it's well-written, at least the bits I heard when I was eavesdropping." By now she was drowning. Being a colossal failure was Story's strength, though, so she pressed on. "I mean, if I was eight, this book would totally make me want to visit the rainforest . . . or at least recycle my plastic."

This is my favorite book in the world, though I have never read it. Ugh.

And then Martin Baxter did something he hadn't done in a long time. He laughed. "You're a horrible interviewer."

"I'm a horrible *everything*. Really. It's like a sport for me."

The silence was back.

"Well, thanks again," Story spit out, "and good luck with—"

"It has whatever you need."

Story was confused. "Pardon?"

He spoke in a deliberate and sincere tone. "The magic treasure box. Inside, it has whatever you need."

But before Story could ask him exactly what he meant, the sound of a dial tone intruded. She was left staring at her doodle of an empty treasure box, the white space on the page a glaring reminder of what she didn't have.

Strike three.

NINE

Claire Payne and *sorrow*, the constant companion that had occupied her passenger's seat for the last year, drove to work together, trying hard to keep *rage* from squeezing into the front seat. When she'd dropped Cooper off at school, a teacher had asked for, and received, an unexpected, impromptu parent-teacher conference regarding Cooper's angry outbursts over emotionally neutral things like right angles and cytoplasm, and by the time she left, Claire was late, pissed off, and ashamed she wasn't doing a better job with her son.

"What are you, fucking retarded?" she hollered out her window, honking loudly and swerving as a man, ambling through the crosswalk, kept her from speeding through the yellow light. When the light turned red and she screeched to a stop, the lumbering man approached her car window and reached for something in his back pocket. He was close enough for Claire to read his shirt, which said "Sunrise Manor"—the local mental hospital.

He might be an escaped axe murderer, she thought, there for a quick Tuesday-morning slaughter. She locked her door and whispered, "Oh, God, don't kill me, don't kill me. I can't die—I'm all he has now." She heard *Have a little faith* in her head, but ironically, it was her late husband David who had been good at seeing the best in people. In the past year, Claire had become accustomed to seeing the down side of things. She hadn't always been that way. In fact, she used to be the woman who "had it all," the perfect, together, working mother—the kind of woman nobody ever saw get flustered over hectic schedules or botched casseroles. Claire was never seen crying at the supermarket because something in the produce aisle made her sad, and she didn't shed tears over sentimental movies designed to manipulate your emotions. And she never used to swear at all. But recently she found herself saying things like "fuckballs" and "cocksucker" when life proved too much to bear, which, lately, was about every eight minutes.

The man motioned Claire to open her window, and with eyes shut tight, she pushed the button. But as it turned out, the man *was* fucking retarded, or as they said in Claire's line of work, "mentally handicapped with compromised social awareness and appropriateness."

The man's voice was lazy, inarticulate, and belabored, and at first, Claire thought he was deaf, but he managed to speak in a purposeful, almost command-ing tone in spite of it. He handed Claire a perfect silky red rose, its petals still closed tightly, defying the scorching Phoenix sun, and he uttered only two words: "Rise above."

What Claire didn't know was that these were words he had been taught by his social worker, as part of Sunrise Manor's new Rise Above community project, de-signed to alleviate the stereotypes and misconceptions of the mentally challenged. All she knew was that as soon as the man smiled at her, Claire Payne began to cry.

It began as a basic welling of the eyes, but escalated, in a matter of seconds, to a full-blown, sniveling sob-fest. This was the first flower she'd received since David's death.

With the light still red, she opened her car door and attacked the man with a bear hug, all the while dampening his custom-made, silk-screened T-shirt with tears and a small trail of snot. When she squeezed him, she was surprised he felt different than he looked. There was more to him than she'd expected—three layers to be exact. Far underneath his visible exterior was a musky layer of sweat, which wasn't gross, but the sweet smell of diligence and hard work. And next was a soft white undershirt, his contribution to acting like a grown-up. Over that, he wore the new shirt he was proud of, and Claire noticed a stubborn crease on his shoulder seam. He'd ironed it for good show.

As the light switched from red to green, he mumbled to Claire, "Like rose?"

"No. I hate flowers! Thank you so much!" Claire said in-between sniffles, running back to her car before oncoming traffic killed them both.

By the time Claire walked through her office door, she was a frantic heap of smudged mascara, topped with a healthy coating of humiliation.

"Good morning, Dr. Payne," Jessica said, just as she did every morning, but this morning Claire started laughing right in the middle of the waiting room when she realized *she* of all people was there to provide emotional advice.

"Do I look stable to you?" Claire said to Jessica, her twenty-five-year-old receptionist. "Who in their right mind would look to me for stability? Someone totally crazy, that's who."

Jessica gave Claire a look that said, *Shut up, there's a patient behind you*, so Claire shut up. After all, crazy people were her business. When Claire looked behind her, she saw the elderly Florence Dickerson, her nine o'clock appointment, having already waited for thirty minutes.

Claire gave her patient of five years a warm, "Good morning, Florence."

Florence Dickerson stood in a pool of her own silver-gray hair, which had cascaded down from her eighty-two-year-old scalp and piled up so high around her, she made Crystal Gayle's hair seem short. "Nothing good about it. Nothing good at all," she said in a formal, cranky English accent. "And I must kindly remind you not to call me Florence, as it is not my name."

"Of course," Claire said, directing Florence and her hair into her office. Florence Dickerson was convinced, with every strand of her six-foot long hair, that she was Rapunzel, from the Grimm Brothers' famous fairy tale. It had all started seven years ago, when she'd come across a picture of her former lover, a fallen World War II soldier, and for some reason, at the very moment she laid eyes on it, neurotransmitters in her brain exploded in a fireworks show fueled by sad memories, bad luck, and old age. From that moment on, even though part of her, buried deep, knew time had moved on, Florence Dickerson's subconscious redirected all her emotions toward the notion that she was still waiting for her lover to return from war. When she saw the picture, she recaptured that pining, incessant need to see him again by living in a metaphorical tower—being ready, at any miraculous moment, to unleash her locks on which her prince would climb. And thus, in her fairy-tale mind, she morphed into Rapunzel, the most patient woman in all fairy tales combined.

In medical school, Claire was taught not to fight the pivotal moments in her patients' pasts that dictated who they were. Her mentors said that if she did, she'd have to take up battle with not only World War II, but also burning infernos, neglectful parents, tuberculosis, and unrequited love—tragedies in people's pasts that forever dictated the paths of their futures.

"Here, let me . . ." Claire said, as she helped Florence step over her hair and settle in an overstuffed patient recliner. "How's your daughter, Karen? Did she drop you off today?"

"Yes. Yes, she did," Florence said, "but she's needed back at the tower."

"Oh?"

"Yes, it is in need of immense repair."

"Really?"

"The bricks are failing—it's old." She looked out Claire's office window with a longing gaze. "I'm getting old, too, you know," she said, looking more like a Florence now than a Rapunzel.

"How old are you, if you don't mind?" Claire asked from behind her big, polished desk.

"I don't mind your asking," Florence said. "How old I am—now *that* I mind." Both women stared at each other. "I'm tired of waiting," Florence said with authority. But then she looked to her psychiatrist for advice.

Claire called upon her extensive training, poring over a decade of education and volumes of information stored in her brain, looking for appropriate counsel, and then made the executive decision to borrow words from a rose-toting retarded man.

"Rise above," Claire told her, leaning back in her chair. Now, Claire had no idea what it meant, but she hoped Florence would have a meaningful interpretation of it.

Florence wasted no time interpreting. "I don't get it."

"Well . . ." Claire said, stalling. She then conjured up her high school drama club voice intermixed with a splash of cheerleader. "You're Rapunzel with a capital friggin' 'R'! You've survived imprisonment, abandonment, and bad tower food. You, my dear, are one magical, brazen bitch—"

"I am, aren't I?" Florence said, sitting up a bit straighter and holding her head a little higher.

"Damn straight. And you've been stuck, but it's time to move on. No more waiting. Rise above your comfort zone. Join the new millennium. Seriously, how old is your fairy tale? Nineteenth century?"

"Eighteen-twenties," Florence said, nodding. "But how am I going to rise above with all this hair weighing me down?"

"Get rid of it. Let him take the goddamned stairs!"

"The tower has stairs?" Florence asked, with a new twinkle in her eyes.

"Fuckin' A, it has stairs!" Claire said in a refined, professional voice. She stammered a bit, but said, "You don't see them because they're in back. A couple are cracked, but they're fine."

Florence looked over on Claire's desk at the big black scissors sticking out of her pencil holder, and raised her eyebrows. Claire picked them up and helped her patient at last cut away long lock after long lock.

Claire's post-session notes that day mixed the clinical with the emotional.

Tuesday, October 22nd, 10:24 a.m.

Florence "Rapunzel" Dickerson, after months of therapy, makes profound breakthrough in obsessive tendencies and grief-induced denial.

It was during that session that Claire stopped being a doctor for a moment and tried to remember what it was like to have faith.

Prognosis: Considering the remarkable evidence from her recent session, it is likely that Florence will make a complete recovery, eventually coming to fully understand the reality of the long, arduous altered state that has overtaken her life for seven years. Real change is not only highly probable, but inevitable.

But then she remembered who she was.

Prognosis: Regardless of the seemingly remarkable progress evident in the recent session, it is not likely that Ms. Dickerson will experience more than a slight respite from her grief-induced delusions, which have manifested themselves in a fictional form, and ultimately, real, lasting change is not only highly unlikely, but impossible.

Real people, after all, don't change.

Diagnosis: Life is not a fairy tale.

TEN

While Claire Payne climbed the fractured stairs back into her tower, Hans Turner delivered someone else's art. Custom doors he'd made with his hands, they were designed and commissioned by a very wealthy client interested in having an entryway that made an impression. In-between handiwork and magician gigs, Hans had put the final touches on these two oak beauties—massive double doors to be hung in the primary entrance of a home (mansion to most) atop a towering hill overlooking the elite Deer Run subdivision. The carvings of Apollo, the sun god, suggested a homeowner who ruled Phoenix—a king in the land of sun. Why he felt the need to be king, no one knew, not even the man himself.

When Hans arrived in Deer Run, he wondered how so many people could be so rich. Each yard, endless, lush, and green, might as well have been lined with dollar bills, because if you had green grass in Phoenix, it meant you could drown yourself in money as well as water.

His client, Judge Harold Stone, greeted Hans at the end of a long, winding driveway, while he pulled a couple of errant weeds from his flower garden. He looked good for a portly man in his late forties—folks who invest well and live in mansions usually do—and somehow, the Hawaiian shirt and flip-flops worked for him. Behind Judge Stone stood an expansive home, complete with a dozen Greek columns and a large, almost garish entryway.

"You're right," Hans said as he got out of his truck, "your current doors don't do it justice."

"May I?" said Judge Stone eagerly, walking toward the back of the truck.

When Hans released the tailgate and peeled back the tarp covering the doors, the judge was speechless.

"Are they what you—"

"They're stunning," Judge Stone said, leaning forward to touch the carved wood. "Even more beautiful than I'd hoped for."

When Hans asked which door he liked better, Judge Stone seemed bewildered. "I don't know," he stammered. "The one with the dragon is really intricate." Then he shook his head. "No, no. The dragon's beautiful, but the one with Apollo and the oracle is so lifelike. Sort of. What do you think?" Within seconds, he'd gone from confident verdict-maker to indecisive buffoon in flip-flops. He recovered enough to look grateful, and to keep his secret—that unless he had a gavel in his hand and a jury in front of him, he was unable to make a decision. "Either way, it's great work," he said. "I love them."

"Good, I'm glad. I've been working on them so long, I was starting to hear dragons in my sleep," Hans said, but at the sight of the indecisive Harold Stone, Hans felt a dull twinge in both his hands. But this was often how it started when he met flawed people—first he was intrigued, and then he cared, but he knew their stories invariably had a shitty ending, so now he rubbed the curiosity and Judge Stone out of his hands.

As it happened, Hans was right about Harold Stone, who knew what it was like to hear things in his sleep, although he'd spent a lifetime trying to forget it. It was exactly what Hans didn't want to hear.

On a fateful August night thirty years ago, Harry Stone had awoken to the sound of footsteps on the stairway outside his bedroom. He recognized the movement as his father's, and although he wondered why his father, clad in his work boots, would be up so late, he decided it must be nothing, and without weighing other options or thinking it through, he fell back asleep. The next morning, he awoke to his mother crying at the kitchen table, and in an instant, without ever having entertained the idea before then, he knew his father was never coming back.

The last words Harry said to his father should have been *Don't leave us, we're worth it*. Instead, they were *Pass the salt, please* at dinner. And so from that day forward, Harry Stone doubted himself whenever faced with any decision, big or small. His only respite from the constant state of fickleness was his courtroom, where he not only was decisive, but precise, consistent, and just.

Hans found Harold Stone staring into the cloudless Phoenix sky. "Sir?" he said. "You okay?"

Judge Stone, standing rock solid, looked around at his sprawling estate, threw his hands up, and said, "I'm great. How could I not be?" With the sun beating down on him, he peeled off his first layer, a Hawaiian shirt, exposing underneath a white T-shirt, crisp, pristine, and, for the moment, without blemish.

Lifting the first door, Hans said, "Let's make your neighbors jealous."

ELEVEN

While everyone else in Story's office sat in their cubicles, pretending to work, Story decided to go off-task in a much more obvious way—by leaving. As she walked past her colleague Jeff, feigning work on his *New Baby* series, she said, "Let me save you some time, Jeff. Picture a cute, screaming baby along with this tag line: 'When you're ready to take it back, you know it's really yours.' Now, take the afternoon off."

Without a word, he scribbled down what she'd said and left for lunch, as did Story. During her extended lunch, she planned on paying a visit to Martin Baxter in hopes that her tenacity would wear him down, and together, they'd come up with a plan to make Cooper forget how sad he was. She'd called the university pretending to be a textbook sales rep, and found out he had only a ten o'clock lecture today, and she was pretty sure he'd be at home by now, sulking.

She'd already been to his house, so she drove right to it, but this time she rang the doorbell. When he answered the door, Story said, "Hi, I talked with you earlier today—"

"I told you I couldn't help you," he said, shutting the door.

Story blocked the door with her foot. "See, that's the thing. I think you *can* help me, and that's why I brought this as a gesture of solidarity," she said, lifting up a native Arizona cactus wrapped in cellophane and a ribbon, picked up at a floral shop on the way over. "It's a cereus," she said.

"I know what it—"

"I'm serious!" When he smiled, she knew she was as good as in. She touched the tip of one of its sharp spikes. "Thought it might be a good example of how to grow a spine. Plus, I couldn't find a moonflower—obviously—and this was the cheapest nocturnal plant they had."

"You did your homework," Martin said. "Maybe you're not a bad reporter after all."

Story winked at him. "I think we both know I'm not a reporter."

"Well, you're much too friendly to be a reviewer, and way too available to be a publisher, so I'm stumped."

"Invite me in for a quick chat, and then I'll leave you to your stamen." She stared at Martin Baxter, still blocking the door. "That's the male part, right?" When he nodded, she said, "What's mine called?"

He wasn't sure if he should laugh or call the cops. "If you're referring to the female reproductive part of a flower, that'd be the pistil."

"*Pissed still*. A scorned man named it that, didn't he?" Story looked at her watch. "Come on now, invite a pistol in for a shot of bourbon already."

"What makes you think—" But he stopped himself when he realized the bottle was in his hand, so he opened the door and led Story Easton into his home. Drawings of various plants and flowers, some sketched on scratch paper, some on dinner napkins, were scattered throughout the living room. They walked past five abandoned TV dinners and several empty beer bottles, and when Story saw a crumpled up *National Geographic*, featuring a plethora of exotic shrubbery and foliage on the cover, she wondered if it was a botanist's alternative erotica—plant porn, perhaps.

"Okay," he said, after grabbing a glass, pouring her a drink, and inviting her to sit on the couch, "what do you want to know about the treasure box?"

"How big is it?" Story asked first.

Martin Baxter approximated the height and width with his hands, and it appeared to be about a foot wide and a foot deep.

She slapped her hands on her thighs right before her next big question. "Okay, where exactly is it?"

He said, quite directly, "It's in the heart of the Amazon rainforest," then followed with a vigorous gulp.

"Shit. That's complicated," Story blurted. "Isn't there a rainforest in the Pacific Northwest? Maybe Cooper wouldn't know the difference."

Martin Baxter sounded both elitist and jaded when he said, "Yeah. Most people can't tell the difference between a tiny field mouse and a giant capybara." After taking another drink, he asked, "Who's Cooper?"

Story ignored his question and moved on to more important things. "Fine. I'll just have to take him there. How do I get to the Amazon?"

"Very carefully," he said, taking another drink. "First, you fly into Manaus, and then you take a riverboat—"

"Help me plan my trip—and I'll pay you whatever you want. I'm loaded."

"It shows," he said, looking at her beat-up Volvo in his driveway. "I can't help you."

"Oh, Martin," Story said with a sigh, "we've already been through this."

He smirked. "No, really, I'm busy. Got a big trip of my own planned. Leaving in two days . . . and after that," he sighed, "the university's adding another class to my already busy schedule, and I just won't have any time."

She shook her head. "Let me get this straight, you'd rather go to the Hamptons than help a little boy reinvent himself? Where in the hell are you going that's so—"

"The Amazon."

"What?!" Story screamed. "That's awesome! We'll go with you! And Cooper can find the treasure box, and—"

"No. Absolutely not. Took me six months to prepare for this trip." Martin Baxter shook his head in an almost violent way. "First off, I don't even know you." He poured them both another drink. "Secondly," he said with a chuckle, "I don't even know you."

"Not in the biblical sense, no, but . . ."

Martin fought a smile, but continued, "Not to mention the fact that this magical treasure box is totally made up. It only exists in this mess of a brain," he said, pointing to his head.

"Not to him. To him, it's real." Story paused for a moment and, without trying, oozed sincerity. "It has to be."

He broke eye contact with Story and stared into nothingness. "You don't understand. This trip isn't just a trip. It's a journey," he said.

"Okay, I get it. It's an expedition with a purpose," she said. "We can help you. What are you after?"

He pointed his head in the direction of a large hardcover book written by Abigail Baxter, titled *Flores Amazonias*, sitting on his dusty coffee table. "Page eighty-seven."

Story flipped through page after page of beautiful hand-drawn flowers, but when she got to page eighty-seven, devoted to *Selenicereus wittii*, the tropical moonflower, there was no picture, just a blank box with the caption *No picture available.*

"My mother refused to draw a picture of a flower she'd never seen in bloom." Martin began to laugh. "Tenacious broad, my mom. She made twelve trips to the Amazon to catch it in blossom, but she never did." He held his index finger in the air, and with a flair that bordered on mysterious, he said, "One chance. That's all you get. It comes to life for one night out of every year, and as soon as the sun comes up, it withers away, and its life is over."

"So we're both looking for something that doesn't exist."

The professor said, "Oh, it exists."

"Have you seen it?" said Story.

"No," he said, "but it exists, it—"

"Has to," Story said with raised eyebrows.

"God, you're giving me a headache," Martin said, bringing both hands to his forehead.

"Just tell the university that we're your research assistants," Story said, realizing for the first time that, on the off chance that she'd actually get to go to the Amazon, she'd have to convince Claire and Cooper to go, too.

"The university isn't funding this trip," he said, sneering and staring into his bourbon. "After careful consideration, they think I'm a—"

"Suicidal drunk?"

"Never go into counseling." He threw a glare her way. "I have a sponsor."

"AA?"

He didn't look at her. "No . . . deep-pocket sponsor who, for some reason, has a particularly passionate interest in getting the world's first and only photograph of a tropical moonflower in bloom. I'd love to do research for the university, but since they're not on board, well, you go to the money." He put his drink down. "He's a local guy. Name's Judge Stone."

After that, Martin Baxter excused himself to the bathroom, and Story used her time alone to look at a picture hanging by the front door. The frame, heavy and silver, was made up of a series of flowers painted red, blue, and violet, interspersed with dark green, heart-shaped leaves. Inside the frame were two delicate faces, shining with smiles, and even Story, prone to cynicism, had to admit they were beaming with life.

"This frame was a birthday present," Martin said when he returned. He stood behind Story and looked at the picture as though he was looking through a window into another time. "They're all different flowers in the morning glory family. That's why she bought it for me. Morning glories are uncommon in art—everyone loves the rose." He pointed to each separate flower surrounding the picture. "This is a bindweed. This is a jalap. Scammony, below that. And this here is the non-tropical moonflower—*Ipomoea alba*—it's not the night-blooming cactus moonflower I'm hunting, but they're related. They're both nocturnal, they're both climbers, and they're both angiosperms." When Story looked to him for clarification, he added, "They flower."

He let out a short-lived laugh. "Kate always joked that if I had a choice between saving her or the ethereal moonflower in bloom, there'd be a moonflower, perfect and repotted, next to her tombstone."

But as Story watched Martin Baxter come to life when he spoke about his wife, she knew he would have done anything to save her. He placed his finger on the frame and caressed it as if he was touching the rare moonflower itself. "She didn't even like flowers—that's the funny thing." His face became more desperate and morose. "But she loved that I did. That's the kind of person she was."

Story felt his sadness in her gut. "I read about your wife and daughter, and I'm so sorry—"

"Everything I loved was in that car." An intense Martin Baxter stared at the photograph as if he could will them both back to life if he tried hard enough.

Underneath Kate and Hope's picture was another one of Hope, taken at what looked to be a kindergarten production of "Three Billy Goats Gruff." The picture showed Hope wearing a whimsical, mischievous smile and a cardboard cutout shaped as a big cloud. "She played the part of the wind," Martin said, staring at the picture and smiling. Without breaking his gaze, he said, "It wasn't a speaking part, but she stole the show," and then he laughed a little. "She practiced for weeks. At first she was just a whisper of a breeze, but then the whisper became a blustery gust, and finally, one night, she raged through the house, whisking away everything in her path." He replaced the smile on his face with a pensive stare. "Everything she touched, everything she did, retained the very essence of her.

When you were around her, you felt . . . alive. She could make you fall in love with the wind."

The next picture frame was empty, except for a piece of paper, folded into a small square, stuck in the center of the frame. Story figured whatever was on that paper was either too private or too painful to be in full view, yet was important enough to be put on display.

Martin swiped his finger over the glass, daydreaming about the first time he told Hope about the moonflower. He and Kate had taken Hope to a local botanical garden after she'd asked how greenhouses worked. When her dad told her how the sun was involved, Hope listened with a focused curiosity. Though the sun was an infrequent visitor in Portland, Hope had always been a fan, and she was enamored of the very idea of the radiant ball of fire.

Thanks to her dad, and several books he'd given her, Hope knew facts about the sun that most eight year olds did not. In fact, when asked, Hope could draw a diagram of energy flowing through the sun's seven layers. With a red crayon, she'd draw the core, then the radiative and convention zones, then the photosphere, chromosphere, transition region and, finally, the corona with its blistering loops. And that night, after spending the day inside a botanical greenhouse, a giant solar collector in which Hope got to observe the power of the sun's heat and the plant life it produced, she asked her dad, "Does a person have a core like the sun?"

Sitting cross-legged on her bed, she looked up at a picture of the sun hanging above her headboard.

Martin thought about it, sat down next to her, and put his arm behind her small shoulders. "Like the sun, people have layers—skin, muscles, bone—but the closest thing to a core would probably be a person's heart. Some believe that's where the soul is, and hopes, and dreams, and fears—"

"Fears?" Hope asked.

"Sure," Martin said, strengthening the hold he had on his daughter. With a smile, he said, "What's my brave Hope afraid of?"

When she stared up at him, he could tell she didn't want to say it, but he figured it out anyway. That's what dads do.

"If you're afraid of the dark," he said, "that's quite common."

"Seriously?" Hope said.

"Oh, yeah," he assured her. "I know plenty of grown-ups who sleep with nightlights."

Hope sighed. "I wish I were older. I wouldn't be afraid of anything then."

Martin laughed at that, until he realized that a perfect, organic teachable moment had presented itself. Martin was surprised it hadn't come up before. "You know that flower Grandma hunted for so long but never found? The same one I tried to find when I went to the Amazon last June?"

Hope nodded. "The nocturnal one?"

"It's a tropical, night-blooming moonflower, and Grandma wanted to draw it because it's very rare and very beautiful. It only blooms once every year, at night, and the moment the sun comes up, it shrivels up and closes its petals."

Hope scrunched her nose. "This isn't part of a riddle, is it?" Hope hated riddles.

Martin raised one eyebrow, and said, "What's white, alive, and dead all at the same time?"

"Let me get this straight," said Hope. "It actually likes the dark?"

Martin looked into his daughter's eyes. "It *loves* the dark, because it needs the dark." It was something he and the moonflower had in common. "Maybe at night, you should pretend you're a moonflower, soaking up the darkness, basking in the moonlight, and then you won't be scared anymore."

"Hmmm," she said, "I guess. That might be apropos," she said, looking slightly embarrassed. She smiled. "Am I being verbose again?"

"You, verbose?" Martin teased, smiling.

Hope blurted, "Wait, Dad, I've got it now. Let me start over." She let out a young-girl giggle. "Oops. My bad."

Martin always envied Hope's ability to start over, because the idea of Hope growing up and leaving him to start over without her left him feeling empty. It was years and years away, but Martin prematurely mourned her absence. "Okay," he said, "start over."

Hope beamed. "I will be the fabulous fairy that sleeps deep inside the moon-flower bud!"

Martin wondered, at that moment, what it must be like to be Hope, full of possibility and magic, and he longed for the ability to walk in her lavender Converse sneakers for one moon cycle. He laughed, and then he said, "Okay, but you'll be waiting a long time for it to open. And then when it does, it might be hard to get out. You'll be stuck."

"You'll come and release me," Hope said. But then Hope, suddenly serious, seemed to change her mind. "I'll figure it out, Dad," she said, looking into her dad's eyes. "In case you can't find me, you know, like that time at the mall when I found my way back."

"Of course you'll figure it out. You always do," he said. "By the way, how do you become a fairy?"

"Magic." Hope gave him an incredulous look. "Duh."

Martin nodded. "Duh. The Amazon is full of magic."

"Yeah." A sense of mystery seemed to consume her, and Hope's eyes lit up when she said, "I will wake up in the middle of the Amazon, and I will have to find a magic treasure box, which will turn me into a fairy—and I'll be able to fly!—and when I get scared at night, I'll find the moonflower and it will teach me to love the dark."

Martin kissed his daughter on the forehead and whispered, "I love you."

She smiled and said, "This much?" holding her arms out as far as they would stretch.

Normally, this was when Martin would stretch his own arms out, but that night, he said seven little words that came to him like a dream. "I love you more than the moonflower."

"Really?" Hope said.

He nodded, and then he said, "I have an idea. I'll write a story. It'll be educational—it'll teach about the rainforest—but it'll be an adventure, too. I'll write it, but I'll write it like I'm you." *One moon, one story in her sneakers.* "Stories are important. It'll be about you, and the moonflower—"

"And a magic treasure box!"

"Yes! And you'll live in the Amazon rainforest—"

"Where exactly in the forest?" she said.

A confident answer rolled off his tongue as if it had always been there, right on the tip. "Where hope lives."

Martin still touched the glass of the empty frame, and the folded-up picture of the sun that Hope had drawn with a jumbo yellow crayon, but then he changed the subject, or seemed to. "Did you know that even though the moon is the brightest object in the night sky, it gives off no light of its own? It actually reflects light from the sun." A smile fought to form on Martin's face. "That's what Hope used to remind me when my moon did battle with her sun."

When Martin finally released his hand from Hope's sun, Story said, "No offense, but what makes you think you can find one of these elusive moonflowers in bloom, when so few others have?"

"Mother came close several times," he said. "She kept a detailed diary for each trip—locations, water levels, temperatures, lunar positions—and I've been studying every entry. All the data points to four days from now as my best chance at seeing one in bloom."

"I see," Story said.

When Martin Baxter set his drink on the table, Story could tell the bad news was coming. She felt a hint of a shadow descend over them both as a big cloud enveloped the sky. This was the beginning of what would be a short-lived October afternoon storm, and as the tension surged, so did the power. The lights flickered once, and when they flickered a second time, it seemed to fuel Martin's impatience. "Look, you seem like a real stand-up person," he said, "and I wish you the best in your endeavor to help your friend, but this journey is a solo one for me—always has been." He stood up and walked Story to the door.

Story said, "Good luck," in a quiet voice, right before the door shut behind her. For the second time, she walked away from Martin Baxter's house, but this time, she did so in daylight. She looked up into the one part of the darkening sky where sunshine still lingered. There, amongst the encroaching clouds, she witnessed the grand Phoenix sun, the one thing that united them all, and she said a secret prayer for those counting on their one chance.

TWELVE

When Story returned to work, she found Ivy creeping around her cubicle, preparing her customary stranglehold. "Have a nice lunch?" she said, looking at her watch. The workday was almost over.

It was a bright cold day in April and the clocks were striking thirteen.

Story's beautiful, full lips spouted off an incongruous, ugly reply. "Yeah, Boss. It was a working lunch. Had soup and salad with a bunch of realists wanting to buy cards, and several sad people who hate flowers—"

"Have you been drinking?"

Story scoffed. "It's four in the afternoon. What do you think I am, a drunk?" Story got away with snide comments to her boss for two reasons. One: Since Story had been at Special Occasions, she'd designed more top-selling cards than any other writer. Though she repeatedly missed deadlines and, in general, was untrustworthy, her end product always resonated with people. Two: For every five unpleasant comments Story hurled Ivy's way, she always threw in one decent and superficially sincere one, just when Ivy didn't expect it, thus making it hard for Ivy to hate her for extended periods of time.

Ivy folded her long, lanky arms. "How's *Grief and Loss* coming along?" she asked, but all Story could think about was whether or not Martin Baxter would classify Ivy as a weed. "Lindsey's almost got *Wedding Bells* finished, you know."

Definitely a weed, she thought. "How's Lindsey's divorce coming along, Boss? That's sure to inspire a hell of a romantic greeting card," Story said.

She figured that would send Ivy on her way, but like any successful weed, Ivy sprouted right back up. "Story, you know that splendid feeling you get when you've won?"

"No, actually, I don't."

"It's glorious." Ivy beamed. "That feeling . . . that's what we want for people when they read one of our cards."

Story thought about it for a moment. "What if they haven't really won?"

Ivy Powers swatted Story's desk with her happy-face-on-a-stick, as if she was murdering an invisible fly. "Then you make them *feel* like they've won."

And so came divine inspiration, without warning, from an unlikely source. *That's it*, Story thought. That was how she'd buy some time with Claire and Cooper. Story hugged her slave driver boss and said, "Boss, you're not a weed, you're a genius." Ivy Powers repelled the embrace, and Story dashed out of her cubicle. But after several paces, Story turned back to Ivy and winked.

"You're not a genius, Ms. Powers," Story said with sincerity. Then she told her what she needed to hear: "You're a winner!"

THIRTEEN

ooper stared at his dinner plate, pushing his meatballs around with disdain. "I hate meatballs," he mumbled, resting his chin on the table, looking at a giant pile of spaghetti. "Dad was the one who liked—"

"Please, Coop, just . . ." she started, but the doorbell saved them both from another unhappy meal in the house of Payne. "Are you expecting anyone?" Claire asked her son.

Cooper was never expecting anyone, and he gave her a look that said as much. He jumped up from the table and ran to the door. When he opened it, Story Easton greeted him with a wave and a smile. "Hey," she whispered, as if the two of them shared a secret.

"Hey," Cooper said, defying the don't-talk-to-strangers rule. He stared at Story for a moment, and said, "Tell me you have a pizza."

Story laughed. "Nope, no pizza. Something better." She smiled, raising her eyebrows. "Way better."

Story still didn't have the details of her plan worked out, so when she heard Claire Payne's footsteps approaching the door, she looked around the entryway, for something—anything—to help her formulate a believable story. She spotted an umbrella stand acting as a stand-up vase for a giant bouquet of wood-handled umbrellas, unusual for an Arizona residence, and next to it, on a small table, sat a big stack of junk mail and some magazines. On the top was the same *National Geographic* magazine she'd seen at Martin Baxter's house, except this one was crisp and unopened.

"Hello? Can I help you?" Claire was still in her work clothes, a gray suit jacket and skirt, and Story found her more intimidating than when she'd seen her last. "We're in the middle of—"

Cooper looked at his mother and widened his brown eyes. "She has something, Mom."

Tired and distracted, Claire looked at her watch. "Is it a package or something? I didn't realize the mail came this late."

Cooper gave Story a knowing look. Story had never liked children much, even when she was a child, but Cooper didn't irritate her as other kids did. He was smart. He had a future in sarcasm, she felt. And he was the kind of kid who might buy one of her cards when he grew up, or at least make fun of one of Ivy's. Not to mention, he seemed to be on her team at the moment.

But Claire was going to be more difficult. All moms have built-in bullshit detectors as a result of always being short on time, and from living with men for so long. Story had to act fast, so she mustered every ounce of enthusiasm she could, threw up her arms, and hollered, "You won!"

Cooper's face lit up. He didn't care whether they'd won a free car wash, a lifetime supply of popsicles, or the Arizona state lottery.

Claire Payne blurted, "Um, I'm sorry, but we don't want any—"

"No, no, I'm not selling anything," Story said, placing a gentle hand on Claire's arm. "This is real." Story searched deep for truth, and when she couldn't find it anywhere, she settled on something better than truth—necessity. "I'm a representative from *National Geographic* . . . here to deliver your prize."

Out of patience, Claire said, "Look, I don't even read it—it was my husband's." Claire had spent the last year answering phone calls and accepting packages for a dead man, and it never got any easier. "If he signed up for something, I don't know—"

"It's a random sweepstakes," Story blurted. "Your name was drawn from thousands of subscribers. You're Claire, right?"

"And I'm Cooper!" Cooper said, squirming his way toward her.

Story smiled and crouched down to shake Cooper's hand. *Call me Ishmael.* "Story."

"Like the Once-Upon-A-Time kind of story?" he said.

"Yeah," she said with a wink. "But not nearly as interesting."

Turning his smile into more of a smirk, Cooper looked up at Story, pointed at her, and spoke in a commanding, life-or-death tone. "You . . . should have some meatballs." After a stern glare from his mother, Cooper smiled again.

"Oh, I'd hate to impose," Story said while performing an invisible victory dance.

Cooper took Story by the hand. "Come on, Mom always tells me we should share with those less . . . What's the word, Mom?" he asked, looking in the driveway at Story's very humble-looking Volvo.

"Fortunate," Claire said, giving him a *you're-in-big-trouble* look.

"Everyone's a critic," Story said as Cooper Payne led her into his house.

As Cooper watched Story inhale an entire plate of spaghetti, Claire, uncomfortable with the weirdness of it all, said, "So, you couldn't have just called?"

"Mom!" Cooper said.

"No, she's right. We usually do call first," Story said. "But this is a very special prize, a special promotion—"

"I knew you were selling something," Claire said, shaking her head.

Acting nonchalant, Story twirled more spaghetti on her fork while conjuring up some drama in her voice. "Well, if you consider getting the greatest adventure of your lives for free *selling*, I guess you're right. I *am* selling something." She looked at Cooper. "I'm selling the chance of a lifetime." Maintaining her stare, she raised her finger. "One chance."

The thrill was too much for Cooper, and he got so excited he actually froze in his chair, mouth agape.

Claire looked at Story with a clear, maternal message designed to protect her already fragile son: *Don't make promises you can't keep.*

But Story had never felt more confident in her life. There she was, sitting in a house she'd already broken into once, having dinner with two broken people who couldn't afford to get more broken, faced with breaking a promise which could lead to the destruction of the one non-annoying child in the universe, and yet, she'd never felt more together. She had to pull this off.

Story put down her fork, looked at both Claire and Cooper, and folded her hands. "It's a trip. To a magical, faraway place."

"Like Neverland?" Cooper asked, leaning forward.

"Sort of," Story said, "but less Michael Jackson, more Peter Pan."

"Will there be swords?"

"Yep."

"What about alligators?"

"Definitely."

Then Cooper glanced at his mom. "What about fairies? Magical places are always dark. Fairies give you light."

"Yes, there'll be at least one fairy." Story wanted to give him a little nugget of what she'd come for, so she turned to Cooper. "But the best thing . . . is the treasure."

The whole table fell silent for a moment until Cooper yelled, "Mom! We're going to find It!"

Claire Payne looked into Story's eyes. "Okay, I get it. This is one of those panoramic nature movies. We've already seen all the IMAX films. And we took a family trip two years ago to Cairo and saw all sorts of buried Egyptian treasure."

"It's not a movie. It's a real place, a destination our magazine's been covering, in depth, for the last six months. Your family's been chosen to help deliver a firsthand account of the region's—"

"It's the rainforest, isn't it?!" Cooper said, barely in his seat. "It has to—"

"Coop, it's not the—"

"It is," Story said, feeling like Willy Wonka, Ed McMahon, and Santa all at the same time. Cooper's excitement only fueled her as she entered the Zone, that creative place she always entered right before she penned the perfect greeting card catchphrase and tricked people into believing they were special. "We named the sweepstakes 'It's Your Forest, Too,' to highlight how we're all connected to the rainforest, and by inviting a regular family to see its beauty, readers will get a more real look at what the rainforest has to offer, instead of the usual scientific, photosynthesis, global warming crap."

As soon as she said it, Story realized she didn't sound very professional. "I mean, science is great—we've based a whole magazine on it—but there's something magical about the rainforest that the common observer rarely gets to see."

"Which rainforest?" Cooper asked with trepidation. Under the table, he crossed his fingers and toes, hoping it would be the right one.

"The Amazon, of course. Is there any other?" Story said, channeling Martin

Baxter's moxie for the moment. "But there's a catch."

"I knew it!" Claire said. "All for the low, low price of ten thousand dollars, right?!" She hung her head and mumbled, "*This* is why I don't believe in people."

Catching a nervous glance from Cooper, Story said, "No, we pay for everything, ma'am, and take care of all travel arrangements. The catch is . . . we leave in three days—"

"We'll be there for my birthday!" Cooper jumped out of his chair and ran to his mother's side.

"Just a minute!" Claire yelled. "Everyone just wait a goddamned minute!!" she screamed.

"Mom, are you gonna say the 'F' word?"

Claire started clearing the table, crashing dishes together. "We can't leave the country in two days." Until that moment, Claire had thought the whole trip idea was ridiculous, even a bit eerie, but when it was time to give the reasons why they couldn't go, she couldn't think of any.

Story and Cooper waited.

"I'm a doctor!" she finally remembered. "My patients need me."

"She's not a real doctor," Cooper scoffed. "She just asks people questions." He began mimicking his mother. "How do you *feel* about that? How is that working for you?"

Can I go anywhere without my mother? Story wondered.

A calmer Claire asked, "Seriously, I've never heard of winning a prize with a deadline. Why can't we just postpone—"

Story screeched, "Postpone?! No offense, Claire, but this a cutting-edge voyage. Some very smart people have worked out an innovative idea here—it's never been done before—and they don't want a stale, planned trip. They want to see your spontaneous reaction to a world that thrives on adaptability." On a roll, Story continued to pull rainforest-type words out of her ass. "You don't catch the . . . poison dart tree frog hopping around with a scheduled itinerary. He *adapts*. And that thing that looks like a pig . . ."

"A tapir," Cooper interjected.

"Thank you. You don't see a tapir planning out his afternoons. Why? Because he doesn't know whether he's gonna take a crap, take a nap, or get ripped to shreds by a jaguar!"

"Awesome!" Cooper yelled.

"So, Claire," said Story, "the field crew thinks impulsiveness is paramount here. They'll be capturing it with their cameras, in interviews." And then, caught up in her performance, she looked over at the door for effect. "I'm surprised they're not here yet."

Claire Payne, trying to look as if she didn't care, smoothed her hair down and moistened her lips so she'd be camera ready.

Then, Story borrowed words from someone who really knew what he was talking about. "It's not a trip, Claire. It's a *journey*."

Just then, the doorbell rang. "Is it them? Is it the camera people?" Cooper asked, while Claire peered out the window and saw a workman's truck.

"No," she said. "It's the door guy from this morning. What's he doing here?"

As Story sank in her chair, the meatballs rebelled against her stomach and came dangerously close to coming back up.

Shit.

FOURTEEN

"Sorry to bother you, Dr. Payne, but I think I forgot my planer," Hans said to Claire as Story and Cooper listened from the kitchen table.

"What's wrong?" Cooper whispered when he looked at Story, wide-eyed, her hot seat getting hotter.

"Think I might have left it on the kitchen counter when I was packing up." Hans's voice trailed off as Claire followed him over to the kitchen table. When Cooper said hello, Hans shook his hand, and then, to Claire's surprise, asked Cooper to check his own pants pocket. When he did, he pulled out a long, silk scarf, first red, then yellow, then green, until finally, four feet later, purple.

"Cool! How'd you do that?" Cooper said.

"I didn't do it. You did," Hans said. Without missing a beat, he gave his attention to Story, pretending to look surprised. "Hey, Story, nice to see you again," he said with a wink only Story could see.

"You two know each other?" a confused Claire asked. "I thought you were from out of town—"

Story's meatballs rebelled again. "I am. We don't—"

"We met this morning," Hans said, smiling. "Spending some quality time with your sister?"

All eyes were on Story. "I dropped by to give you your prize this morning," she said, "but you guys had already left, and I ran into him instead."

"Technically, you ran into my hammer—"

I'm gonna shove your big hammer right up your . . . "Yeah, and then we talked about how, while I'm in Phoenix, I'm gonna visit my sister."

Hans kept up his warm smile, but it took on a sinister slant. "What's her name again? Your sister?"

Story scratched her head and spewed out the first name she could think of. "Ivy."

Claire said, "How nice you have family here. Ivy's a nice name."

"Not really," Story muttered, grabbing her purse. "Look, I feel bad I've imposed. I'll come by tomorrow to discuss the particulars, and we'll begin making our arrangements," she said, dashing out of the kitchen, past Hans.

But he touched her shoulder as she walked by. "Wait," he said, looking her in the eyes. "Don't you think it's cool that we have two doctors in one house right now? I mean, if I were ever gonna accidentally pound a nail in my—"

"You're a doctor?" Claire asked Story, who now looked very much like a deer caught in bright, unforgiving headlights.

Hans said, "Yeah, she specializes in p—"

"Plants," Story said, before Hans had a chance to whip out his big hammer and ask to have it examined. "I'm a botanist. That's why they put me on this assignment," Story said, now unsure and awkward. "The Amazon has a lot of crazy plants."

Hans laughed. "Oh, those *crazy* plants. You're very scientific, Dr. Plant Lady."

"Am I missing something here?" said Claire.

Again, all eyes turned to Story for an explanation, and just as Story was about to experiment with honesty, her cell phone rang. For once, she was thankful it was her mother.

"Mom?" Story said. On her way out of the kitchen, she motioned to Claire and Cooper that she'd be right back, and then scurried down the hall toward the den. When she flipped on the light, Sonny greeted her.

"Fuck it all!" he squawked.

"Oh, fuck you, you mean bird," Story said, flipping the bird the bird.

Story's mother gasped. "I beg your pardon, young lady—"

"Sorry, I was talking to someone else."

Beverly Easton sighed, then asked the first of her many questions. "What exactly is your malfunction, Story Thyme Easton?"

"I told you never to call me that, Mom."

"You mean, your *name?*" Beverly said.

"Seriously, Mom. *Story Time?* Am I a person, or a monthly event at the children's library?" And then she muttered, *"There was a boy called Eustace Clarence*

Scrubb, and he almost deserved it."

Beverly scoffed, "Easy. C. S. Lewis," and then added, without missing a beat, "Your middle name is a tribute to your dear grandmother Harriet. She was very fond of herbs. Thyme is known for its *bitter* taste, you know." She waited a moment, and then employed, once again, the Socratic Method. "Story Thyme—how does that name make you feel?"

"I feel like a kiddie-porn star!" Story screamed into the phone, no doubt loud enough for Cooper, Claire, and Hans to hear out in the kitchen. "There are other herbs, you know. Sage is cool, and Rosemary—that's actually a real name that doesn't make me sound like a circus sideshow freak."

"But Story Thyme is unique," Beverly said with a scoff. "You have to admit that it's pretty special."

Story thought about it for a moment, and spoke in calm, quiet voice. "Names don't make us feel special, Mom. People do."

Beverly Easton paused. "Why do you think that is?"

This time, Story didn't get angry. She just answered, "It's the way of the world, Mom."

"I see." After a long pause, she said what she called to say. "Do you need a dress? For the gala party?"

"Um," Story stammered, "I, uh . . . Something's come up, Mom, something really important. I mean, it's important I don't screw this up, so I don't think I'll be able to make it to your party."

Beverly Easton gave up asking questions for the moment, and switched from the interrogative to the declarative. "Just because your name is bitter doesn't mean *you* need to be."

"I'm not trying to be bitter, Mom. I'm just trying to do something decent."

"So am I."

"I'll try to make it, Mom," Story said, hanging up just as Hans walked in.

"You all right?" he asked, walking toward her. "If it's any consolation, you don't look like a kiddie-porn star. Adult porn star, maybe, after some work."

"Thanks," she said, swiveling in the desk chair, maintaining her glare.

As Hans walked past Sonny, the bird squawked, "Miss you."

Story shook her head. "You have a way with birds."

Hans was now standing in front of Story. "What can I say? The ladies love me."

"It's a boy," she said. After a pause, she added, "Are you trying to bury me out there or what? I know it looks bad, but I'm doing something right for once, and I'm sure you're a really great guy, but . . . I need you to get out of my way."

Hans just stared. "Face of an angel, mouth of a truck driver. You remind me of a girl I met today."

"Are you listening to me?" she asked, and he nodded. "Look," she said, "I don't expect you to understand, but just play along. If you give me away, everything will be ruined, and . . ." She waved her hands in front of Hans's face. "He *needs* this."

All Hans really heard was the last bit. "Yes, Cooper is a fine little fellow. He was telling me about the trip he won. The trip you seem to be giving away for free, for some reason."

Story sighed. "Look, they're probably getting suspicious. We'd better get out there—"

"Yes, we should. We should also tell Claire that you slept in her guest room last night—"

"What do you want?"

"It's more like what I *need*."

"Okay. What do you need?"

Hans Turner raised his eyebrows. "A vacation."

FIFTEEN

"This is blackmail, you know," Story said, shaking Hans's hand.

"I do know. And thanks for playing, by the way."

Story rifled through the desk for anything that would make her look more legitimate to Claire. She saw dozens of pencils, pens, and paper clips, but left them all untouched. When she opened another drawer, she saw a stack of old *National Geographic* magazines and grabbed a few.

She opened one last drawer. "Perfect," she said, as she took a small camcorder out from behind a bunch of hanging file folders and stuffed it in her bag.

"Hmmm, a thief, too," Hans said. "You suddenly got more interesting."

"Don't get your hopes up. I'm just borrowing it."

Hans stood up tall, swept his hands through the air in elegant, fluid gestures, and said in a phony magic-show voice, "Ladies and gentlemen, boys and girls, the nice family *once* had a camcorder, and then, *presto*, it disappeared!"

"Can you make yourself disappear?" Story sounded sincere, and a little snotty.

Hans softened, and gave her a look that made her almost feel bad. "You'll regret saying that someday."

"Really?" she snickered, surprised by her own crankiness. Hans was indeed fabulous—funny, wicked-handsome, and literate—but the timing was all wrong. Story was about to embark upon a journey that could produce her first taste of success, and a cute handyman-magician was only going to complicate things.

Mr. Complicated answered with confidence. "Really."

Story grabbed his hand and led him toward the door, exhaling the whole way. "Let's go tell them the good news."

When everyone was back in the kitchen, Story explained that her boss, the project coordinator for the "It's Your Rainforest, Too" sweepstakes, had called to let her know one of the crew members had fallen ill, and wouldn't be joining them.

"We need to replace Shawn. He was in charge of carrying our gear. So Hans here has generously offered to come with us," Story said.

"Just glad I could help—"

"Shhh," Story said with a slight smile. "Sherpas don't talk. They just carry." She took the camcorder out of her bag. "I brought this with me, so we could start the filming ourselves, in case the crew was late. Which they are," she said, pretending to be dissatisfied.

Claire stared at the camcorder. "Wow, that looks just like our camera."

"Weird. We must have the same one," Story said.

Hans focused on Story, who was fidgeting with buttons. "Pack mule, huh?" he said. "Okay, I guess. If that's really what you—"

"Zip it, Sherpa Boy," Story snapped, herding all three of them together to record the happy moment. "Okay, everyone," Story instructed from behind the lens. "Give us your first reactions to your upcoming trip. What do you know about the rainforest?"

Exhausted, Claire Payne fake-smiled at the camera for a moment, and then, having had enough, took herself out of the shot. "Look, I've got an early day tomorrow, and this is all . . . too bizarre. I'm sure the trip would've been wonderful, but the timing isn't right. We should wait," she said, thinking briefly of scissors and a long-haired old woman.

"Mom?" Cooper said, looking at her with a desperation that was unprecedented even for him. What he said next didn't come out as a complaint or a whine—in fact, he didn't sound like a child at all, but rather like someone delivering a truth that only he knew. "It's gonna happen. Just like Dad said it would."

Overwhelmed, Claire Payne walked out of the kitchen. Dead silence fell over the room just as Story turned the camcorder off. "Is she gonna be okay?" Story asked Cooper.

He pulled a stool up to the counter to finish his milk. "Yeah. She just needs to talk to Sonny."

"Let's hope he's in a good mood." Story sighed, mumbling, "Fifty-fifty chance."

"I need to tell your mom one thing before I go," Hans said. When Cooper confirmed she was in the den, Hans went to tell Claire he was giving her a discount on the original estimate, because the door had been a lot easier to fix than he thought it would be. The door to the den was shut, so he cracked it open, and when he did, he saw a side-shot of Claire Payne with her suit jacket off, white button-down shirt wide open, exposing her shiny, ocean-turquoise bra and liberal cleavage to Sonny the bird.

Claire didn't immediately see him, which gave Hans a chance to avert his eyes and gather his thoughts. *Damn the poor lighting. Damn my conscience for making me look away. And damn that lucky bird.* And then he caught himself wishing it had been Story standing there, exposed and vulnerable. Her oversized pajamas had left a lot to the imagination.

"Oh, God!" Claire gasped, closing her shirt when she saw Hans. One minute she was asking Sonny about the trip, and the next . . . the next, she was apologizing for not showing him her breasts more often, when he was alive.

Hans covered his face. "Sorry," he mumbled under his hands. "Just wanted to let you know I gave you a discount on the door."

Mortified, Claire kept her back to him. "Um, thanks. You did a good job. I'll tell all my friends about you."

"I'd appreciate that." Just as he was about to walk away, he said, "You know that trick I did for Cooper?"

"Uh-huh," Claire said, still buttoning, and still mortified.

"I never wanted to learn that trick. It ended up being my favorite, though. It's the one that inspired me to perform for people." By now, Claire had buttoned her shirt and put on her jacket. "Sometimes it's the thing you think will never work that actually . . ." He abandoned his thoughts when he realized words were getting in the way, and he walked out the door.

"Were they okay?" said Story when he returned to the kitchen.

"They were both very nice," said Hans.

"Cooper," Story said, "I'll be right back. I'm gonna help Hans carry his gear to his truck." She grabbed his only "gear," the small planer, which was so light

Cooper could have carried it with two fingers, and left Hans empty-handed.

"I'll need your cell phone number," she said quietly, pulling a piece of scratch paper from her bag as he trailed behind her. As they both came to the door—the front door, the very door Hans had repaired earlier—Story opened it wide, exposing a black canvas sky splattered with millions of glimmering stars. With one foot on the tiled entryway and the other on the porch outside, Story gripped the door handle and thought, *What am I opening here?*

Without speaking, she looked back at Hans, who looked happy to have a door opened for him for once. A stream of moonlight connected with him, and as naturally as breathing, Story recalled Martin Baxter's words: *Did you know that even though the moon is the brightest object in the night sky, it gives off no light of its own? It actually reflects light from the sun.*

Breaking her gaze at the moon, Story fixed her sights on Hans, whose hands reached out to her, even when they were by his side. And when Hans's eyes met Story's, she felt something crazy. Something totally inane. Something that made her feel as if she could, quite possibly, find success. And deserve it.

Though she had no idea how this journey would turn out, she was certain of one thing: Story Easton wanted the handsome stranger to come with her.

None of it made sense yet. And all of it was surprising.

But it felt comfortable.

It felt a lot like a great first line.

SIXTEEN

Claire Payne, now a lot more dressed and a lot more grounded, walked into the kitchen to tell Cooper there would be no impromptu trip to the jungle.

"Babe," she said as he drank his milk at the counter, "I know you think this trip will fix—"

"Can Story read it to me tonight?" Cooper interrupted. He knew what was coming, but when you're eight, delaying the inevitable is still better than experiencing it.

By now, Story had returned, and when she heard the tail end of the request, she gave Cooper a thumbs-up. Claire delivered a reluctant okay. "But then it's goodnight for you," she said, "and goodbye for Story."

Story froze. They both knew what she meant. *Goodbye, Amazon. Goodbye, hope.*

When Cooper started to run toward his room, Claire called to him, "You can go get the book and the umbrella, but let's read it in the living room tonight, sweetie."

While Cooper ran upstairs, Claire took Story by the arm, looked her in the eyes, and held up a firm index finger. "One: Let him open the umbrella. I know it doesn't make sense inside the house, but just let him. Two: He'll probably want to arrange the couch pillows in some sort of special way. It's okay. Three: Read *every* word on the page, and don't diverge from the story or try to embellish. It makes him sad."

She wanted to tell Story this would be the last time she'd be reading, or even talking, to Cooper, but she didn't, and let Story go into the living room, where Cooper was now waiting.

When Story sat down next to him, he'd already fixed the couch pillows and was opening the green umbrella. "Here it is," he said, handing her the book.

"Cool," she said. "You like this one, huh?"

He just stared back, gave her a half-nod, and folded his hands.

"Okay," Story said, getting comfortable. *"Once Upon A Moonflower: A Fairy Tale (or A Tale of a Fairy).* Written by Martin Baxter." She paused, then looked to Cooper for validation.

Cooper's eyes widened, indicating she should open the book for something important.

"Oh," she said. "Sorry." She opened the book and read from the title page. "Due to its graphic (real) and cerebral (smart) nature, this story is not recommended for small children, unless they are really, really brave." She then read the sentence below that. "Dedicated to my daughter Hope, the project I'm most proud of."

Cooper smiled. *"Now* you can read the story," he said, but Story, distracted, stared at a photo sticking out of the book's pages. She recognized the picture because she'd seen it earlier in Cooper's room. It was the one with Cooper and his father at a baseball game. As Story stared at the photo, she thought about her own father, and imagined him with David Payne, laughing, at some baseball game far, far away.

But Cooper didn't, and wouldn't, comment on the picture. It was there to remind him of the dad he once had. For him, it was proof that the man who could hit a baseball farther than anyone he knew—a man who could read every big word and who smelled like aftershave and green apple Jolly Ranchers—was, in fact, the man who loved him more than anything in the world.

Story turned the page, read the introduction, and then began. "Once upon a time, there was a young girl named Hope, who lived in the heart of the rainforest." As soon as she said it, Cooper was in another world, a world he clung to as tightly as he clung to the green umbrella handle in his hand. Story went on for several pages, using her best little-girl voice, but when she got to the part where a talking capybara described the magic treasure box that Hope would need to find, Cooper sat up a little straighter and twirled his umbrella a little faster. As Story read the description of the box, she tucked it away in her mind for future use. "'It will be hidden underneath leaves and roots, and on it you'll see an intricately carved kapok tree, the tree of life," she read. "Its lid will have a curvy, inviting handle made of several woody vines called lianas, interwoven in an arc.'"

"A *braided* arc," Cooper said, interrupting Story's reading. When she gave him a confused look, he said, "The woody vine lianas are interwoven in a *braided* arc."

"Oops, sorry," she said, accidentally in Hope's voice. That sounded silly, so she repeated "Sorry," in her own voice. Story continued, and by now, Claire Payne, more attached to the ritual than she thought, found herself standing just outside the living room's entryway, unbeknownst to Story and Cooper, and sat down on the hallway floor to listen to and mouth the words as Story read the advice everyone in the rainforest kept giving Hope: "First the treasure box, then the moonflower."

Story noticed Cooper smiling, so she looked up at him and smiled back. "What?" she said.

"Dad said when we found the magic treasure, we wouldn't become fairies or anything, 'cuz we're boys, but we'd become Rainforest Superheroes, and instead of lanterns, we'd carry his grown-up flashlight, and show everyone the way out of the jungle." Then Cooper looked up at his umbrella.

When Story asked Cooper about it—why he'd need an umbrella, because it never rained in Phoenix—he remembered what his dad had told him when he gave him the umbrella. He remembered the words because it was something his dad had said often. And just as Cooper delivered the familiar words to Story on the living room couch, Claire Payne mouthed them from the nearby hallway. "Because it's unexpected. That's why."

As Claire sat alone, wiping a lone tear from her cheek, Cooper explained how the umbrella would be their other superhero tool in the forest. "My dad said umbrellas protected people from lots of things besides rain—that's why me and mom started collecting them." He then flashed an embarrassed, little boy smile. "Plus, he said all the girls would stand next to us if we had one."

The timbre of Cooper's voice, which so approximated happiness, made Story ache for him. *I am doomed to remember a boy with a wrecked voice.* Story felt more sorry for Cooper Payne than she'd ever felt for anyone, including herself. She wanted to say something to him, to comfort him, but she'd never been good at that, so she turned to the written word. It was time to put her *Life's a Crapshoot* collection to good use. After reaching into her bag, she chose the perfect card for this imperfect situation, and handed it to Cooper.

It was blank inside, but the front said everything she wanted to say. In fact, it said the only thing that can be said to someone who's endured true tragedy.

𝕷𝖎𝖋𝖊 𝖘𝖚𝖈𝖐𝖊𝖙𝖍.

𝕾𝖔𝖗𝖗𝖞.

With the start of a smirk forming, Cooper softly said, "Life sucketh," feeling less alone than he had in a long time. And then he replaced his almost-smirk with a passionate reiteration. "Life *does* sucketh!" He looked up at Story, and stared at her for a long time, as if he'd known her forever. "I heard someone on TV say that nothing good lasts forever," he said.

She snuggled a little closer to him. "But nothing bad lasts forever either," she said, hoping he would believe it. As she watched him try to wrap his little mind around the big, elusive idea of hope, she shoved her inner cynic aside and said her silent prayer. *Abracadabra. Abracadabra. Abracadabra.*

"So what do you do?" he finally said.

Story thought of advice she'd heard a long, long time ago. "Ten percent of life is what happens to us, Coop, but ninety percent is what we *do*." As Cooper absorbed the concept, Story said, "So . . . we'll *do*. Magic doesn't happen to those who wait. It happens to those who go get it." She took his hand in hers. "So let's go get it. Your birthday's Friday?" After he nodded, she said, "Well, we have a lot to do. We have to pack, and—"

"Convince my mom to let us go . . ." He laughed.

"Yes, among other things," Story said. "Let's finish the story, so we can get some sleep. Tomorrow's a big day."

As Story picked up where they left off, Cooper lifted his head high, took the book in his hands, and closed it with gusto.

Story wondered if she'd pushed him too hard. "What's wrong?"

"Nothing," he said. "We don't need to finish it." He smiled. "I know how it ends."

Out in the hall sat a stunned Claire Payne. She had tried hundreds of times to wean Cooper from the book, and now as she listened to her son divert from the story on his own terms, she sat up straight, proud, and grateful.

"I wish Dad was here," Cooper said in a dreamy stare.

Story resisted the urge to say, "He is here, in spirit," because sometimes the truth hurts.

Then Claire Payne resisted something as well—the urge to be sensible, predictable, and faithless. She resisted the urge to *wait*. At that moment, she prescribed for herself a change that seemed not only possible, but necessary. She dove head-first, waving at Florence Dickerson mid-dive. And instead of entering the living room to deliver a rational and prudent "no," she did the unexpected. She said "yes."

SEVENTEEN

Claire and Cooper walked Story out of the living room and down the hall to their newly repaired front door. They made a meet time for the next day, and after Cooper said goodnight to Story, Claire gave her one last look. Story knew it was a look of warning, a friendly reminder not to mess with a mother and her offspring, and in response she mouthed, "Trust me," right before she went to her car.

But Claire had no idea how untrustworthy Story really was. Her mother's infectious fear of not achieving perfection made success difficult, and thus, her past was riddled with how *not* to do things: how *not* to win your seventh-grade spelling bee by spelling "discotheque" correctly, how *not* to find the secret code in your Wheaties box, how *not* to get your lab partner to ask you out, how *not* to get an internship at *Glimmer Train*, how *not* to write a book. *That's it!* she thought. *That will be my new book title.* How Not to Write a Book, *by Story Easton. Step One: Be a complete failure of a human being. Step Two: Have nothing interesting to say. Step Three: Instead of writing, spend your time eating cheeseburgers and contemplating the up-sides of suicide instead of writing. Step Four: Replace potential plotline ideas with fantasies about kissing sexy handymen, saving heartbroken eight year olds, and completing unrealistic journeys filled with nonexistent magic.*

Now that Story had Claire and Cooper on board, she realized for the first time just what she'd done. As she left the Paynes' home and drove away under a starry Arizona sky, she tried to focus on the confident stars instead of the unending blackness before her. What *was* magic, anyway? A false hope peddled by those who either didn't need it, or were so desperate to get it they perpetuated the lie? Was she as bad as they were? How could she, of all people, really believe this could work?

On that Christmas Eve years ago, Story had found her mother ripping the crotch out of Santa. She looked at the already eaten cookies, empty milk glass, and the Santa doll, which had become a massacred pile of arms, legs, and not-so-jolly torso. Her mother, uncomfortable with the stare, said, "I need some extra stuffing for my pillow prototype." That year's Socra-Tot brainchild was the Learn-While-You-Sleep educational pillow—a serious, rigid pillow designed with hands-on activities like tying shoelaces and telling time. Each activity came complete with Socrates-inspired philosophical questions to haunt small children in their sleep: *How Do You Really Know What Time It Is? Why Is It Important To Tie A Double-Knot?* In the months after Story's father's unexpected death, her mother had put all of her energy into their *future*—Socra-Tots®.

"What are Santa and the reindeer gonna eat, Momma?" Story asked her mother, covered in Santa's white, fluffy innards.

"Grow up, Story."

Story recognized the phrase as the first line of a story she'd heard about a wonderful place called Neverland. *All children, except one, grow up.*

Her mother let out a long, controlled sigh. "Okay. I might as well tell you. You're six now—"

"I'm five—"

"The Santa legend derives from stories about a real man, Saint Nicholas, who most historians believe was from Patara, which is now Turkey. Anyway, he helped some girls get dowries so men would marry them, and over the years, willing participants in the mythology of Christmas have him flying through the air with reindeer, which can't be done, and bringing presents to billions of people in one night, which is impossible." She threw her hands up. "The wind chill at the North Pole would induce hypothermia before he even got out of the damn toy shop."

"So he's not bringing me my magic kit?" Story asked, envisioning subzero Santa and his reindeer dying miserable deaths, frozen and facedown in an unrelenting blizzard.

"Magic is rubbish. It's a whole lot of waiting around for things to happen," said her mother. "Let me tell you how life breaks down, in terms of percentages: Ten percent is what happens to you, but ninety percent," and here she took Story's little face in her hands, "is what you *do*." She reached beside the rocking chair, picked up a wrapped present from the floor, and invited Story closer. "Here."

Story opened up the very flat present, revealing not magic, but the latest Socra-Tots® publication, a large, hardcover children's book, titled *Knowledge Is Power: The Debunking of All Things Magical and Mystical*.

"Thanks."

"You're welcome, Story," she said sternly. She then raised her voice and her eyebrows, looking and sounding like a maniacal kindergarten teacher, and asked one of her favorite questions: "And what do you and I know to be true?"

Story raised her head in an expected robotic movement. "That it's better to be a smartass than a dumbass."

"That's right, sweetheart," she said. "Knowledge is power."

With that, Story returned to bed, and as she was falling asleep, she knew she was no longer waiting for Santa, nor her magic kit. "Abracadabra," she whispered, to will away the desire for magic in her life.

And after a few hundred repetitions, it worked.

EIGHTEEN

A s Story made her way home, Cooper snuck into the den to say goodnight to Sonny, and to see the newspaper article hidden in his dad's bottom desk drawer. Claire didn't know Cooper knew about it, but kids have a way of finding what their parents don't want them to discover. He couldn't read all of the words, but what he really wanted to see was his dad's name in print. Cooper liked the way it looked on the page. It was only three words, but the letters were clear and bold, as vivid as Cooper's memories of his perfect, strong dad.

He pulled it out from the bottom of the drawer, unfolded it, and read the headline that had made that day's first page. "LOCAL ATTORNEY-TURNED-HERO SAVES THE DAY BUT NOT HIS LIFE." And then came the words he was looking for: *David "Sonny" Payne* called out to him in the first sentence, slapping him with the reality he needed. Cooper didn't know all the details of the "tragic incident," but he did remember that morning.

David Payne had taken the day off to spend with Cooper, but not before he made a couple of stops—to the bookstore to pick out something brand new, then to McDonald's for a big breakfast to go. After finishing their hotcakes and sausage, they retreated to Cooper's room, and David read the title of the book—*Once Upon A Moonflower*.

Cooper raised an eyebrow. "Is this a girl book?"

David asked his son, "Does surviving all by yourself in the rainforest sound like a girl book?"

Cooper, intrigued, shook his head and grinned. "Let's pretend we're in the rainforest!" With anyone else, Cooper wouldn't have said it, but with his dad, it was different. Cooper always smiled when he thought of those games. Some were silly—*Let's pretend the coffee table is a life raft and the living room carpet is a stormy ocean*—and required a footy pajama-wearing Cooper and his dad to sit, cross-legged, on top of the sturdy walnut table. Others were sillier—*Let's pretend these wooden spoons are swords*—and required man and boy to duel each other while Claire made dinner. And other memories made his heart hurt—*Let's pretend we're superheroes, Dad*—which required Cooper to become larger than life. All his dad had to do was be himself.

"Totally," David said, pointing to the green umbrella in Cooper's closet. "We'll need that in the rainforest."

They snuggled next to each other on Cooper's bed, underneath the opened umbrella, cracked open the crisp binding, and breathed in the new-book smell. After the title page, when the actual story began, David Payne didn't use a girl voice, but instead created this strangely believable, animated persona. As he read to his son about Hope's predicament, Cooper soaked it up like other stories he'd heard before, but when he heard the part about the magic treasure box, Cooper listened with genuine intensity, marveling at the concept of a magic box in the middle of the jungle. "Is it really magic, Dad?" A little embarrassed, Cooper added in his best adult voice, "I mean, it's like, cursed or something, right?"

David scooted closer to Cooper, and when he said, "Of course, it's magic," he put his arm around Cooper, looked him in the eyes, and made the notion of magic not only acceptable, but desirable.

"Cool. Can we get one?" Cooper asked, sitting up.

"There's only one, Coop," he said, "and it's in the middle of the Amazon." David Payne used his serious voice. "Do you know how to use a machete?"

When Cooper said he did not, David shook his head, and said, "Wow. It's gonna be a lot of hard work then." And then, David Payne raised a finger, turned to his son, and said, "Maybe we'll go find it together—"

"When?" Cooper blurted.

"Um, when you're older," David said.

Cooper asked, "When's *older*?"

"Uh, when you're . . . nine." As Cooper stared with wonder, David said, "Yep. On your ninth birthday, we'll go find it together."

"Promise?" Cooper said, wide-eyed.

David Payne answered with a confident nod. "Promise."

And so, one year later, everything in Cooper's life hinged on that promise.

The irony was that David Payne had been known for following through on his promises. Cooper had listened to him tell stories about clients he'd defended, and because his dad had once explained it this way, Cooper thought of what his dad did at work in baseball terms. Here's what Cooper knew. He knew that outside of baseball, it wasn't right to steal, but if someone steals a loaf of bread for his family, it's different than stealing a TV. He knew that his dad didn't defend true bad guys because it was wrong, even if the bad guy was some sort of Most Valuable Player with an amazing record. His boss got mad at him for that. He knew that players who had struck out had used up their chances and needed, without question, to be benched for a while—sometimes forever. But he also knew—and this one seemed to be the most important thing—that his dad believed that a real home run was giving someone a second chance.

So on that ill-fated Monday morning, after he'd finished reading to Cooper, David Payne slipped out to a convenience store for an unexpected mid-morning ice cream treat and found himself face to face with danger. He didn't see a man with a gun. He saw a boy with nothing to lose. And when the boy pointed the gun at the clerk and demanded money, it was a calm David Payne who convinced him to let everyone in the store—the clerk, two other women, and a mother and her son—go to the back room, where they'd be out of danger.

As the boy bagged the contents of the till, David, facedown on the floor, spoke to the boy of second chances, and how he could help him get one. After bagging the money, the boy called someone on his cell phone and had a disjointed conversation, all the while keeping the gun pointed at David, who was telling him the sentence would be much less if he gave up the gun. And it seemed as if the boy was listening, so David tried to get up with hands raised. He looked at the boy, who was red-faced, angry, and empty-eyed, and when David mentioned something about faith, the boy shot David Payne, point blank, in his heart.

After seeing his father's name in newsprint, and touching it with his finger, Cooper put the article back where he found it and approached Sonny the bird. "I knew you'd do it," he said. "I knew you'd keep your promise." Sonny pecked at a hanging cluster of birdseed dangling from the cage top. Cooper smiled when he thought of him and his dad, together, running around the jungle, hunting for the magic treasure box. "And I know you'll be there." He put his finger up to the cage. "Somewhere."

Sonny the bird hopped over to Cooper's finger. He could not hug Cooper, nor could he leave his cage to accompany Cooper to a ballgame, so he did the only thing he could.

"Miss you," Sonny said.

NINETEEN

When Story arrived home, it was after ten o'clock. She put on her pajamas, poured herself a glass of cabernet, and stared in amazement at the clue for Thirty-Eight Across. *Cooper's mission.* She'd seen it before, but that was before Cooper, and she decided that seeing Cooper's name on her crossword was uncanny, and beyond coincidence. So she downed her glass of wine and poured another. "Hmmm, *Cooper's mission* . . . nine letters," Story said aloud to her big, hard crossword puzzle—the best date she'd had in years. *What* is *Cooper's mission? To avoid meatballs . . . to let go of his umbrella . . . to find the magic treasure box by his ninth birthday . . . to find Hope.*

She took a break from her puzzle to watch the short footage she'd taken at Cooper's house. When she sat down on her couch with the borrowed camcorder, she must have hit rewind by accident, because when it finally played, she didn't see Hans, Cooper, or Claire, but a handsome man with dark hair and large, sapphire-blue eyes like Cooper's.

As she let the replay run, the camera moved back and forth in sharp, abrupt motions, recording random shots—first the ceiling, then the den's hardwood floor. And then she recognized Cooper's giggle. "Stop tickling me, Dad!"

The camera then landed on David Payne, the interviewee, in his desk chair as he folded his hands and tried to look serious. On the desk in front of him sat two glasses of milk and a tower of Oreo cookies. "Okay. I'm ready. I don't want you to flunk," said David. "Go ahead. Ask me anything you want."

Recording, Cooper said, "Question number one: Where were you born?"

"Chicago, Illinois."

"Question two: What is your father's name?"

"Michael Anthony Payne." David smiled. "Gramps to you."

Story could almost hear Cooper's smile behind the camera. "Three: What is your profession?"

"I defend people who make mistakes."

Taking a break from the interview, Cooper moved the camera for a moment and said, "Is that what Gramps does?"

David said, "Not exactly. Gramps, Uncle Peter, and Uncle Steven are prosecutors. They—"

"Get the bad guys," Cooper interrupted. "That's what Mom says." Cooper focused the camera back on his dad. "When you get the bad guy, you're a hero. Right, Dad?"

David Payne paused for a moment, but then said, "Right. Heroes get the bad guys."

"Okay, question four: What is your favorite thing to do?"

"Eat Oreo cookies with my son," he said without hesitation.

"That's me!" Cooper said.

"Yes. You are my son," he said, handing Cooper a cookie. Cooper's hand emerged to grab it, but the camera stayed steady. "You are my favorite son."

Cooper giggled, and then said, "We're dunkers, aren't we, Dad?"

"Yes, we prefer dunking our cookies. But not before we do this," he said, dismantling his cookie by removing the top and eating the creamy middle. "See, it's all about balance. In the beginning, we had dark and light, and now all we have is dark. But," he said, with the dark cookies sandwiched between his thumb and index finger, "we must unite dark and light once again." He dipped the small, black circles into the milk until they disappeared in a pool of white.

"Light," Cooper said, "and dark." His hand appeared again to dunk the cookie in his glass.

"Yes. Light and dark," David said. "Each makes the other seem sweeter."

"Last question," Cooper said. The camera shook a little. "What is your favorite part of being a dad?"

Cooper experimented with the camera, pushing the zoom button until his dad's faced filled the screen. David Payne looked straight into the camera, pointed, and mouthed, "You."

Then the image turned to static.

Just as Story was about to turn it off, more footage appeared—footage maybe no one else ever saw. Story watched as David Payne, at his desk, stared at the camera lens, which was about five feet in front of him.

He ran his fingers through his hair, then leaned forward, and said, "I just came from upstairs, watching you sleep, and it occurred to me that maybe you didn't get to ask all the questions you wanted to. And I know I could just tell you tomorrow, or the day after that, but this is more . . . unexpected. So I figure I'll give you my best advice about life, while it's still fresh in my brain—"

But then, right in the middle of a sentence, the battery died, and Story was left staring at a black screen. Story knew she'd uncovered something important, but she was more interested in David Payne's message. He wasn't peddling hope—he was selling faith. Anyone can hope for the best, but only the true superheroes can actually muster up faith, and when Story watched him look at his son, this is what she saw him saying with his eyes.

After walking over to her crossword wall, and staring at *Cooper's mission* again, she decided she wasn't going to figure it out, so she consulted the Internet. She spent fifteen minutes searching the name "Cooper" for anything that might fit, and on the twenty-fourth entry, she got her answer, and a chill crept through her body. Leroy Gordon Cooper, Jr., American astronaut, circled Earth twenty-two times in 1963 in a Mercury spacecraft. The name of the mission summed up two important things for Cooper Payne. The first word was something he needed, and the second was, simply, an inevitable event.

FAITH NINE

WEDNESDAY

I addressed the toucan in front of me. "Fly?" I said. "If you haven't noticed, I don't have any—"

"Hang on. We'll be your wings." And with that, the toucan, plus three other birds—a parrot, a green aracari, and an emerald toucanet—introduced themselves and, using their large beaks, latched on to my pajama shirt. Within seconds, they took flight, and so did I.

Flying in and out of trees, I said, "This place is growing on me!" as a gentle breeze wisped through my hair. The forest floor beneath me now looked like a mossy green carpet, and as we flew in between branches and giant leaves, ants raining down on me—gross—I asked the birds where we were going.

"What do you want?" they screeched in unison.

I actually had no idea. I missed home, and I worried about the nighttime that was surely on its way, but I was having an adventure, an authentic adventure I only ever found in books, and I wasn't ready for it to end. "I need to find the magic treasure box," I told my feathered friends.

The toucan shrieked. "I didn't ask you what you needed. That is for the forest to decide. I asked you what you want."

This was one fastidious (picky) bird. I gave him the answer I thought he wanted. "Uh, I want to see this beautiful forest, and all of the animals who live here, and—"

"Nonsense!" The toucan slowed down, and the others followed suit, circling above a small, meandering creek full of floating water lilies. "Let me refresh your memory," he said. And when he spoke next, he imitated my voice. "I'm sick of being eight! I want to be eleven so I can get my ears pierced!"

So this bird was not only picky, but also psychic. How could he have known I'd said that?

The birds began flying again, but the toucan continued his clairvoyant (telepathic) diagnosis. "And what about the time you told your dad you wished you weren't afraid of the dark?"

"Hey, that was a moment of weakness!"

"Or when you said you wished you could fly?" the toucan screeched.

"I meant on my own." Realizing they could drop me any second, I added, "No offense."

We kept flying for a long time, and then suddenly, they picked up speed and my peaceful flight turned into some sort of death race. We weaved in and out of large, unforgiving branches, and when a dragonfly splattered in my face, I decided to close my eyes and pray I didn't have a mid-air collision with a squirrel monkey.

"First the treasure box," the toucan yelped at top speed, his words disappearing behind us as we soared faster and faster.

"Then the moonflower," squawked the toucanet.

With my eyes still closed, I felt an abrupt stop, then a quick descent, and finally, I heard no more birds, but beneath me I felt the ground—furry and moving.

TWENTY

Hans Turner loved George Harrison because he was a man of his word. Every morning, when he sang "Here Comes the Sun," the big, bold Phoenix sun streamed through Hans's bedroom window, defiantly sneaking through the blinds. When a stubborn ray reached in and touched his face, Hans soaked it up.

Like a good conjurer, Hans had spent many years growing skilled in the art of distraction, training both his hands and his mind to forget the past. But each day, Hans did allow himself to remember one thing—a song. Every morning, at exactly 7 a.m., "Here Comes the Sun" played on Hans's clock-radio/tape-deck. And this Wednesday morning was no exception. This morning, when the clock read seven o'clock, the guitar intro began and Hans swung his legs toward the floor. By the time George Harrison sang, "Little darling, it's been a long, cold, lonely winter," Hans felt ready to begin a new day. Even though he would begin his Wednesday with George Harrison's hopeful sun on his mind, if you looked closely, you could see he was still hanging on to a yesterday when the sun was brighter.

On that Wednesday morning, the day after meeting Story Easton and blackmailing her into taking him to the Amazon, Hans sat up in his bed, scratched his head, and thought about what he'd done. As he pondered the scenario—accompanying a strange female with an affinity for breaking and entering, maybe even with a past in kiddie-porn, into a dangerous jungle—the whole thing seemed preposterous. Absurd and preposterous.

And he couldn't wait for it to begin.

Deep down, Hans knew waiting for anything was a sign of weakness. Waiting until you retire (or expire) for life to begin was his definition of an oxymoron, yet without admitting it, he had one thing in common with inert observers of life—like them, Hans only pretended to live, because under his solid oak exterior was a diseased center, a sick core fed by regret that polluted his mind into thinking he could avoid the very thing that was rotting him from the inside out.

So instead of confronting the demon from his past, Hans focused on safe, secret mantras in his life. *Measure twice, cut once. Putty and paint, make it what it ain't. Always sand with the grain.* And he'd thrown away emotionally charged objects that reminded him of his childhood—his worn baseball glove that smelled like leather oil and reminded him of sunny, carefree days, and a delicate, orange-blossomed poppy flattened into a book and into his memory, given him by someone he'd loved very much.

But there was one thing in his home that did remind him of his past. In fact, it represented the one thing in his past that made him who he was, twenty-seven years later. Unlike the other things in his house, this one was not simple, and in it lived the story of Hans's life. This object, a yellowed and cracked photograph that Hans hadn't looked at in years, was tucked away in a box on the top shelf of his bedroom closet, and when he dug out his passport for his upcoming trip, there it was, underneath, and he was forced to come face-to-face with the thing he tried to avoid—but the thing he'd kept just the same.

The very second it came into view, he picked it up without thinking, rescuing it from its dark, lonely box. And as soon as he looked at it, as soon as he looked at *her*, with her strawberry blonde pigtails and apple-green T-shirt, the day started all over again for him. Twenty-seven years earlier.

That Sunday, the whole family had eaten chorizo and eggs before church, and ended up enjoying a sunny day at their home in the small town of Crystal River, Florida, a town whose motto boasted of a snowflake-like uniqueness: *Crystal River, no other town like it!* Hans's father chopped wood in the backyard, while his mother husked a basket of sweet corn on their porch, all the while singing along to the blare of the radio coming from the kitchen window. "Here comes the sun," she wailed, her enthusiasm so infectious that soon, the whole family was singing. Violet was a quirky woman who fabricated the world around her into an enchanting romp, designing her home and her life to be one giant gingerbread house complete with polka-dots, lemon drops, and infinite possibilities of mystery.

Violet Turner lived inside a story, and on a daily basis she invited her family to live in this fairy tale world by maintaining a running dialogue of storytelling. At breakfast, while placing shiny-silver serving spoons in each bowl, she'd welcome in the day with a *Once upon a time there lived a magic cloud who lived in a magic ocean of a sky*, and Hans and his sister sat on their seats' edges, anticipating Cloud-love or Cloud-anarchy, depending on their mother's mood. During chores, Violet taught her children to tell each other stories in which they'd change the mundane parts of their day into extraordinary events, thus rewriting what they knew to be true into what they wanted to be true.

Her two children embraced her eccentricity because it was all they knew. She was their mother—the one who dyed all of her aprons violet to match her name, the one who used her flair for language to make up new words for ordinary objects, and the one who named her twins Hansel and Gretel, to ensure they'd take care of each other for life, or at least always leave a trail of pebbles to guide the other out of any dark forest.

Around noon that day, Hans and Greta, as they called themselves, went for a walk on the riverbank of the Crystal River, which ran straight down the center of their state and skimmed the outskirts of their home.

"Be careful—take care of each other," Violet said to her nine-year-old twins, who had made this journey together many times before. They knew to watch for cars across Peters Street, they knew not to talk to strangers, and they knew to be careful by the water, especially because, swollen from excessive rains, it was higher than normal.

They took turns singing, "Here comes the sun, doo-doo-doo-doo." With full bellies under clear skies, they skipped along the trail to the riverbank, and when they got there, they played games all their own, acting out several different fairy tales at once, layering one story atop another until it was impossible to tell where one began and another ended. Greta, chatty and sassy, found it difficult to stay quiet as she pretended to be a slumbering princess asleep on a pea-sized pebble, while Hans, the designated quiet prince, spun gold from the straw-like riverside weeds.

Sprawled out on the grassy riverbank, Greta, eyes still closed, lifted her head and whispered, "See if the shoe fits. It's part of the story."

Hans said, "The one you're wearing?"

Greta scoffed. "Take it off, and then put it back on. If it fits, it means I'm queen of Crystal River!"

"We know it fits, so——"

She dramatically laid her forearm on her forehead. "Please, I'm not well," she said. "Put the slipper on fast. I must leave here in my magic coach and escape my evil stepmother."

"I'm telling Mom you said that, and I'm done playing the princess and the prince. I wanna go look for frogs," Hans said. "Or cool stuff like this!" he said, as he leaned over a bird's nest hiding in the brush to see one perfect speckled-blue robin's egg. Hans reached out to touch the beautiful egg, and hold it in his hand, but then stopped, because it wasn't his job. Greta, his only sister, was his family; the egg had its own.

As he looked back, his sister stood up and stomped her foot in protest, and Hans laughed. But right as he began walking away, he heard her gasp, then shriek. When he turned around, he saw Greta fall backward, tumble down the embankment, and plunge into the water.

At first, he howled with laughter, holding his belly while he thought about the wet walk home, but then, as she slipped farther into the engorged river, he realized she really couldn't get out, stopped laughing, and ran toward her, down the steep decline of rocks and sand.

"Greta! Grab my hand!" he yelled, extending his right hand as he ran. When he reached the water, he ran parallel with it, following Greta, now bobbing up and down, arms thrashing in-between gasps.

Hans sprinted as fast as his nine-year-old legs could carry him, moving a few yards ahead of Greta, and leaped out onto a small rock, then onto a larger one. Perched and poised for her to float by, he knew this would be his only chance to grab her. Just a few paces ahead, the already deep water swelled even more, white rapids emerging in mean swirls. Hans stretched out his hand, caught Greta's eyes in his, and leaned his whole body over the rock, waiting for her.

Greta, still flailing, now mustered up the strength to keep her head above water, and extended her hand as the current hurled her toward Hans.

"Grab on, Greta!" Hans cried, drowning in his words. "Grab on!" And it must have worked, because when her hand reached his, he grabbed hold tight and felt her squeeze back. Using his other hand to grab her forearm, he pulled hard, and thought he'd done enough to help her onto the rock, but then the unthinkable happened.

His hand gave out.

Not entirely, and only for a second, but by the time he regained his strength, he'd lost his grip. One knuckle—slipped through. Another—gone. And finally, one tiny pinky finger with a pink-painted nail slid through his grasp, leaving his hand empty.

With his other hand, he clung to her little wrist, but it, too, slipped away. His hand seemed so big next to hers, and even before it was over, even before anyone else in the world beside Hans and Greta knew what had happened, Hans felt betrayed by his hands. He was supposed to take care of his only sister, but he'd failed her. His hands had failed her. And now, as she looked back at him one last time, he thought he saw a tired but contented smile, as if she were grateful and satisfied for their time as prince and princess.

She disappeared under the water, and he dove in, struggling to find her and bring her back up, but the water tried to suck him under, too. When he surfaced, choking and exhausted, he realized she was gone, sinking deeper and deeper into the darkness with no pebble trail, no guide, to lead her out of the shadows.

That was the end of that story, and for Hans, the end of all stories.

Hans lay breathless on the riverbank and, within moments, his hands began to throb with pain—not with sharp, shooting pains, but dull, deep aches. And when Greta's face flashed through his mind, the aching intensified and stayed with him all that day and the next, and the day after, when his twin sister's funeral was held, and the pain would return to him throughout his life every time he thought of her. And though that was every day—when he looked at his hands, when he looked at his own reflection—her picture was something he rarely had the courage to view.

Hans held the tattered photo in his large hand, careful not to drop it and, once again, let her down. He put it back in the box, on top of five years of tax returns, and when he put the lid back on, he made sure it was askew, letting in light, if only a little. He then looked out the window at the sunshine drowning the Arizona horizon, and as he let some of the arid warmth of the desert-heaven, with canyons instead of rivers, touch his skin, he pretended they were together, safe, on dry land, and reminded himself why he'd moved here.

And while still in his desert-heaven, he remembered the women in his life he'd tried to save, but couldn't. In high school it had been Nicolette, the beautiful girl who didn't think she was. And in college it had been Whitney, too preoccupied with her bright future to live in the present, and of course, long before that, it had been Greta, the dreamer. Hans's hands, now saturated with memory, pulsed with the familiar, painful throb that never let him forget.

Was Hans a bad fixer, or could all of them simply not be saved? Every time he'd said goodbye to one of them, his hands ached, and all he could do was ask, *Why am I here?*—why, when he couldn't save any of them?

TWENTY-ONE

As Hans Turner relegated stories to his past, Story Thyme Easton rolled into work late, imagining ways to "accidentally" feed Ivy weed-killer. She'd already made her rounds with the other writers, and now stood in Story's cubicle. In her dark green power suit, she blended in with the evergreen carpet in a perfect camouflage. "Nice you could join us," she said, her long fingers wrapped around Story's favorite pencil, devouring it with a twisty clench.

"That's my lucky pencil," Story said, trying to free it from Ivy's tight grip. "That pencil's made you a lot of money, Boss."

"Yes, it has." Ivy let it go and inched her way over to the cubicle entrance. "I expect it to continue to do its job." She gave Story a direct look. "Is that going to be a problem?"

Story lifted her head high and scratched it. "That depends. Is the community pencil sharpener working?" Ivy cut office supply costs by having only one pencil sharpener, a source of contention for all the writers who preferred to use pencils for first drafts. Ivy scoffed and let out a sigh, which couldn't decide if it was irritated or just bored. Story touched her unsharpened pencil and observed her boss, as nondescript as her sigh, and said, "You know how I hate dull things."

Ivy tugged at the fake handkerchief peeking out of her suit pocket, trying to look more interesting, but ended up walking away, uttering her usual commentary—lame and empty. "Sharp tongue, Little Lady," she said, "sharp tongue."

Story sat down with her lucky pencil, held it tight, and hoped it would help her do the impossible. In the next forty-eight hours, she needed to plan a trip to the Amazon for herself, Claire, Cooper, a nonexistent camera crew, and one door-maker/magician who'd blackmailed his way into coming. And according to her preliminary research, planning a trip on such short notice would cost about twenty-thousand dollars, which was twenty-thousand more than she had.

She squeezed the pencil and thought of Cooper's face when he found out he'd be in the Amazon for his birthday, seeing the greatest promise of his life come to fruition. She smiled as she saw flashes of Cooper's future, after discovering the treasure box at such a crucial juncture in his life. She saw Cooper as a grinning young man, faith intact, having lived a childhood full of baseball games, sleepovers, and Valentines from girls who saw light in his eyes.

But as she tightened her grip, she saw a different life, a *what if* life. *What if* she failed? *What if* she didn't come through on her promise? What if she failed to lead Cooper to his destiny in the rainforest? She saw a jaded Cooper on the verge of manhood, sitting in a cubicle like hers, too empty to even entertain his dreams, the hole left by his dead father still gaping and neglected.

And then, an even more depressing thought—*what if* the second version of Cooper's life was, in fact, his destiny? Who was Story to meddle? Maybe not everyone could be saved. Maybe some people aren't supposed to be saved. Maybe magic is a false hope for most, and real only to a select few. Maybe Cooper, like Story, was doomed to live in nighttime.

Maybe.

But maybe Cooper's fate didn't rely on magic at all. Maybe it relied on one person to follow through on a promise David Payne could not fulfill. And who else was going to try?

Story suddenly saw the big number one from Cooper's bulletin board everywhere she looked. *One* on the giant wall clock, tick-tocking to the next deadline. *One* on an old to-do list. *One* on the first page of the newspaper on her desk. *One* lurked in her memory to remind her that everyone gets one big chance in life. She formed a number one with her index finger, trying to find one reason why she should abandon her impossible quest.

When her office phone rang, she knew it was her mother—the woman was so powerful she could even affect the sound of her ring. It exploded into the series of repetitive, shrieking bleeps heard from most office phones, but with the Beverly Easton sense of urgency.

"So? Are you coming tonight?" she said, more demanding and awake than Story thought anyone should ever be before noon.

Shit. Gala parties were not part of her trip-planning agenda, but she knew her mother would not take no for an answer, so she decided to put her off. "Sure, Mom, I'll be there."

"Okay . . ." Beverly said, clearly unconvinced. "Seven o'clock." She paused. "I'm counting on you, Story."

"Join the club, Mother," Story said. "I'll even put on mascara and try not to embarrass you."

Most mothers would have denied their own daughters ever embarrassed them, but Beverly Easton ended their conversation with, "Good."

An exasperated Story hung up the phone, picked up her pencil again, and began drawing on her desk calendar in hopes of doodling her way to a solution. Feeling as though she was losing a race that hadn't even begun, she scribbled *Ready, Set, Go* over and over until she was reminded of her destination. *To . . . the jungle. To . . . the moonflower. To . . . the treasure box.* She then focused on what she needed. *Money.* The paper in front of her was riddled with goals, hopes, and obstacles, and as she stared at the words, they danced around a bit, but when they settled, three of them stood out. *Go* popped out first. Then *To.* And finally, *Money.* Then she remembered what Martin had said the day before. "Go to the money."

Judge Stone.

After finding the address for the man Martin had mentioned, she grabbed her purse and tore out of the office. When Story looked back at the maze of interlocking cubicles, she saw Ivy's head and green suit collar emerge from the middle of the maze. Ivy remained silent, but gave Story a deadly glare.

Story raised her hands, and said, "I have no choice, Boss."

"Where are you going *now*?" she hollered in a bossy tone.

Story hollered back, "To the money!"

TWENTY-TWO

Martin Baxter crammed himself into a third-grader's desk chair at West Hills Elementary School, gave himself a gold star for attendance, and waited to begin his presentation. He sat in the rear of the classroom, watching the backs of small heads bob back and forth as the rosy-cheeked teacher smiled and gave directions in a slow, drawn-out cadence.

As she instructed her students to put away their crayons and paper, Martin felt an indescribable sadness come over him. It felt incongruous. Nearby was the fun fake castle in the corner, and the cheery drapes painted to look like a piano keyboard. Despite the hint of happy adventure, Martin felt sad, and therefore alone—the only one in the room who, no matter how hard he tried, could find only sorrow. It all reminded him of her—the waxy smell of the Crayolas, the little Levis worn by small, shiny-haired girls, the sun flooding through the windows.

The university had made him a mandatory volunteer for its new outreach program, in which faculty members presented their published work, in layman's terms, to area grade schools. Exposing local children to pro-rainforest tenets would help promote an environmentally conscious community, they were told, but what the university really wanted was to facilitate Martin's healing process. On hiring him, they had no idea how much his past would affect his work, and they were eager to help Martin become a world-class scientist again.

But sending Martin Baxter to a grade school to forget about his grief was like sending a fat man to a fudge factory to forget about his hunger. When Martin placed *Once Upon A Moonflower* on top of the little desk, it occurred to him that Hope should have been sitting there with him, coloring, learning new things, and smiling as her father read the book he'd written for her. This was Martin's last engagement before beginning, in just two days, his quest to see the moonflower, and he decided to do his best and get it over with.

"Dr. Baxter? We're ready for you," Mrs. Olson said, after she'd assembled the seventeen cross-legged third-graders in three rows on the floor. Some folded their hands, two whispered in each other's ears, and one picked his nose, but most looked at least somewhat intrigued. Martin had no cookie treats or free giveaway prizes, so he'd have to offer something interesting. The last guest speaker, from the local bakery, had brought five dozen donut holes and free baby-whisks for everyone. And they still complained about not getting chocolate cake. Nine year olds were a tough audience.

Martin took his place in front of the class, book in hand, and said, "Um, I'm Dr. Baxter, here from—"

"Are you a *real* doctor?" one of the boys blurted, "or are you just one of those guys who reads a lot, so we have to call you a doctor?"

"Joey!" the teacher said from the back of the room. "That's not how we talk to our guests."

Martin, shaking his head, said, "Actually, I can't read. It's been a real bitch, too, going to school for eight years, and not being able to read. But I make enough money to hire someone to read everything to me, so that's nice."

All of the kids covered their mouths, not because he'd uttered a swear word, but because he'd denounced the holy concept of reading, which was the focus of all seven posters hung in the room. The teacher wasn't sure how to respond to Martin's strange comment, but there was one little girl in the room who got the joke, and she began to laugh. When Martin smiled at Hillary, she tucked her shiny hair behind her ears and smiled back.

"Okay," Martin said, opening his book. *"Once Upon A Moonflower*, written by—"

A polite Hillary raised her hand. "Actually, Dr. Baxter, we already read your book yesterday, and Mrs. Olsen explained it to us so we wouldn't look stupid," she said.

"Now, Hillary," said Mrs. Olsen, "it's his book, and I'm sure he'd love to read some of it to you."

"Nonsense," Martin said. "They already know what's going to happen. Where's the fun in that?"

After an uncomfortable pause, Mrs. Olson said, "Maybe you could take some questions from the class, Dr. Baxter."

He nodded, and called on the first hand he saw, that of James in the back row. "Did you bring cookies?"

Skipping that question altogether, he called on a brown-haired girl. "Go ahead . . . ?"

"Kirsten," she said.

"Go ahead, Kristen."

"No, not Kristin, *Keeeerston*."

"Sorry. *Kuuuurston*."

"No, it's—"

"Just call her K-Something. That's what I call her," Hillary said, smiling. "Tell us about your job. It sounds cool."

Joey struck again when he laughed and said, "Yeah. Really cool." And when he added, "He studies *plants*," the class laughed.

"So, Joey," Martin said, "ever had a cut or scrape?"

Joey, the slow-eyed, chubby mouth-breather, laughed, riling the crowd, and said, "Yeah, I took a giant digger on my skateboard last week. So?"

"So . . . more than likely the medicine you put on your wound had *plants* in it. Ever heard of the cocoa tree?" Martin looked at Joey's doughy middle and said, "Looks like you're a chocolate-eater, but if you're unfamiliar with the cocoa tree, you should know it contains over 150 different chemical compounds in its bark, seeds, and leaves, which heal everything from emaciation to cuts and burns and poor immune systems." Martin Baxter stared out the window, and his unfaltering gaze, coupled with his terseness, unnerved the kids. "Know anyone with cancer, Joey?"

"Uh, my Grandpa Louie has—"

"Rosy periwinkle, only found in the rainforest, treats several types of cancer, and since its discovery, childhood leukemia survival rates have risen from ten percent to ninety-five." Martin continued to gaze out the window. "Ever used bug repellant? Then you've used a product containing sap from the annatto, or lipstick tree, found in the rainforest. Did I mention that half of the world's plant species exist in the tropical rainforest?" He stopped to take a breath, and asked, "Know anyone taking birth control pills, Joey?" and when he got a dirty look from Mrs. Olson, he decided not to explain that the oral contraceptive would not be possible without wild yams from the Amazon.

Martin focused his attention on the kids. "Look, the cool thing about plants is that each one, like a snowflake or a fingerprint, is unique. Take the moonflower, for example. Not one is the same. That's why it's so hard to find one. It blooms differently under different circumstances. Its signature sweet smell attracts a very specific moth which pollinates it to induce its death." The kids' eyes were starting to glaze over, so he decided it was time for a hands-on experiment. "Could I have a volunteer?"

Hillary popped up from the middle of the crowd and squirmed her way through little bodies to get to Martin. "I'll help," she said.

Martin nodded a thank you, and said to her, "If Mrs. Olson doesn't mind us using them, would you give everyone in the front row a different flower from that vase?" He pointed to a large bouquet of fresh flowers sitting on Mrs. Olson's desk.

After Mrs. Olson nodded her approval, Martin turned his back on the crowd, and Hillary handed each student in the front row a different flower, keeping one for herself. Still turned around, Martin said, "Flowers use their scent to attract insects just as humans use perfume to attract other humans. And each flower has its own smell, its own molecular story, lurking underneath, letting us know who it is. There are between fifty to a hundred different chemicals making up any particular scent." Martin turned around with his eyes shut tight and said, "First person on the left, come up and put the flower in front of my nose. I've become pretty good at this."

A mousy little girl in a denim jumper walked to the front and held her flower in front of Martin's face as he crouched down to her level. "Okay," she eeked out, "it's in front of your nose."

After taking a whiff, Martin said, "Easy. Two-phenylethanol, the most recognizable chemical compound in the most recognizable flower scent—the rose." He took another whiff. "A red-orange Fragrant Cloud, to be exact—a hybrid tea-rose."

Even Joey was wowed, and as the students murmured, Martin called the second student up for his next challenge—a tall stalk with bright pink flowers. After a brief inhalation, Martin said, "*G. hortulanus*," and everyone laughed. "Not that kind of anus," he said, smiling. "It's the scientific name for a garden gladiolus." They all looked to Mrs. Olson to confirm this. She nodded—it was indeed a gladiolus—and all of the kids clapped.

Without prompting, the next student jumped up. "This is a weird one," the little boy said. "Bet you can't guess it."

Martin breathed in the flower's scent like a sommelier breathing in a wine's bouquet, but grimaced at the height of the inhale. "Hmmm, stinky. Voodoo lily—one of the few flowers that uses the smell of rotting meat to attract flies."

The boy holding the lily said, "Gross. Why would it want to attract flies?"

"It's complicated," Martin said, "but it needs the flies to move the pollen from the male part of the flower to the female part."

"Sounds dirty!" Joey hollered, suddenly more interested in flowers now that they conjured up images from his prepubescent imagination.

"Any more flowers?" Martin asked.

"One more." Hillary brought over the biggest flower of the bunch, its color as bold and radiant as her smile, and the moment she put it near him, it seemed as if he'd been covered in warmth and light.

"It's a sun-lover," he said, taking in the prairie sunflower. "Her head turns and faces the sun until she's had enough. It nourishes her . . ." he said, but when he said *her*, a small ache formed deep inside his core. He began speaking in a dreamy tone. "We've tried to duplicate flower scents by making man-made ones, but it's never been successful." He opened his eyes and turned to Hillary's, then glanced away. Her eyes were bright and full of hope, but he couldn't bear to look. "Some things are not meant to be replaced," he said, sending Hillary and her sunflower back to the classroom floor.

TWENTY-THREE

When Story entered the upscale Deer Run subdivision, she realized how long it had been since she'd come into a stranger's home without the intent of breaking in. Somehow, in the bustling madness of the past couple of days, she'd forgotten about pretending to be other people, and had accidentally been living as herself.

After driving up the long, winding driveway, she got out of her car and approached Harold Stone, who was standing near his new double-doors, watering his desert marigolds. He wore his signature carefree ensemble of Hawaiian shirt and flip-flops, but as he sprinkled water on his flowers, he did so with a delicate and nurturing touch.

Story raised her hand to say hello, and he waved her over. As she walked toward him, she was blown away by the remarkable front doors. "My God, they're exquisite," she said.

"I've got a hell of a door guy," said Harold Stone.

"I actually know a guy," said Story, surprised at herself. "He's really good—"

"Come on. Who could outdo that work?"

Drawn to the doors, Story let her hands caress the fine curve on Apollo's wavy locks, and in a silent admission, she decided Judge Stone was right. No one could outmatch the artistry she saw before her.

She outstretched her hand. "Story Easton," she said, putting forth a strong handshake to match his, but as it turned out, his wasn't strong at all. It pulsed in a series of mini-squeezes, all of which were inconsistent and hesitant.

"I'm, uh, Harold Stone, Judge Stone," he said and, as if he still weren't sure, he added, "Harry Stone."

Story took a deep breath and put on a confident face. "Sorry to bother you, sir, but I was wondering if I could talk to you about an upcoming trip I'm planning."

He broke eye contact and shook his head. "I'm not interested . . . there's a sign out front about solicitors," he said, turning to go inside.

"It's about the moonflower," Story said.

Harold Stone stopped in an instant, turned around to face Story, and looked her over. "How about a glass of lemonade?" he said.

Story and Harold walked into the grand entryway, complete with marble floor and massive chandelier, and he led her into the kitchen. While Harold squeezed lemons he'd picked himself, he asked Story how she knew about the moonflower.

"We have a mutual acquaintance—Martin Baxter. I work for *National Geographic* Magazine, and I met him in preparation for a promotional trip we're planning to the Amazon," she said.

By the time the glass was full of lemonade, he handed it to her and said, "You're lying." After a cordial smile, he added, "Does it need more sugar?"

Story said, "Yes, it's a bit tart." As he sweetened her drink, she said, "How did you know?"

He sat down on the barstool next to her and rested his hands on the high granite counter. "When you mentioned the magazine, you looked up and to the left, a dead giveaway for a liar. I was a judge for almost twenty years."

"Was?"

Harold Stone stared into his glass when he answered, "Yes. Gave it up about a year ago."

"Why?" Story asked. "Did Phoenix run out of bad guys?"

Story had expected him to smile, but instead he answered, solemnly, "I let one of them go." He folded his hands, then unfolded them and laid them out flat. "And I shouldn't have."

What Story didn't know, and what Harold Stone didn't want to talk about, was that this event had exacerbated his already pronounced problem with deci-sion-making. That one wrong decision had polluted the one place where he'd al-ways found confidence—the courtroom. And now he found himself in a constant state of uncertainty. He'd abandoned his usual ability to rationalize, and now flip-flopped his way through each day, desperately grasping onto anything that might help him feel confident and powerful again—eating vitamins, basking in past victories, and even mimicking his former, confident gait. In the interim, he'd traded in the spotlight for a less showy job, caring for his intricate garden, which was more forgiving of mistakes.

Story gulped down her lemonade and her pride. "I need your help."

"Okay?" he answered.

"I need to accompany Martin Baxter on his expedition to the rainforest." Before the next sentence even came out, she knew how high-maintenance it must have sounded. "And I need to bring two other adults. And one eight year old."

"Martin's the expert—that's why I sought him out," said Harold. "As long as the mission gets accomplished, I don't care who goes. He can run the expedition however he wants."

Except Story and company weren't part of the expedition Martin wanted. Story pressed on. "Mr. Stone, this trip isn't just a trip," said Story. "It's a journey for this little boy. He's already lost his father and if he doesn't take this journey, he'll lose his innocence, too. Cooper needs to believe that some promises can be kept."

Judge Stone looked perplexed and torn. He fidgeted, and then voiced a strange and random thought. "Maybe I need to learn how to answer questions again . . ." he said. "Maybe I need someone to ask the right questions."

Do I have the perfect woman for you, Story thought.

Then Harold Stone looked up at her with a sense of urgency. "Did you say Cooper?"

"Yes, he's the little boy—"

Harold Stone's face turned pale. "What's his last name?"

"Payne. Why?"

Harold Stone took a deep breath and remained silent.

"Sir? Do you know him?"

"No," he said, "but the bad guy I let go . . . murdered his father."

TWENTY-FOUR

S tory and Harold stared at each other for a few moments before Story said, "Are you sure?"

He nodded. He was. After the shooting, they informed Judge Stone that the young man awaiting a hearing for auto theft, whom he'd let out for one night on bail, had shot and killed a man named David Payne, who had appeared in Judge Stone's courtroom on occasion. During the weeks that followed, Harold Stone found out everything he could about the family David had left behind. He learned that his wife Claire was good at listening to other people's problems, and that she liked the ocean and the color blue. He learned that his son Cooper loved baseball movies, big books, and sausage pizza. And his dad.

Story began talking about the promise David Payne had made to his only son, but Harold Stone blankly walked through the kitchen to the veranda, which overlooked an expansive half-acre flower garden. Meticulous and stunning, it intersected with several brick paths, which were all connected and led back to one giant circle in the center.

"Sometimes I stand in the middle," Harold said, taking in the garden's beauty, "just to remind myself how many different paths there are to choose from." But what he didn't mention was how many times he'd retraced his own steps, thinking how things might have been different had taken a different path on that fateful day in his courtroom.

"You couldn't have known," said Story. "How could you possibly have known what he would do? Some people are just plain criminals, they're sick—"

"Are they?" he blurted. "Or are they simply products of pivotal moments in their lives that turned out wrong?" He stared at the circle that united the garden's pathways, and said, "Maybe if I'd listened to him, tried to help him." His gaze looked past the garden, out to the horizon. "Then maybe David Payne wouldn't have tried to help him and . . ." Harold Stone started to cry, hid it, pretended to clear his throat, and changed the subject.

"It's all connected, you know. Those flowers," he said, pointing to the back of the garden where tall desert sand verbenas stretched toward the sky, "those bees, that hummingbird, the ants you can't see, the fungus you don't even know exists."

He laughed a little when he said, "I never used to care. They call it companion planting—putting tarragon by the vegetables keeps the pests away, putting anise by the roses repels aphids while improving the strength of the flowers. Sometimes it takes a long time . . . I planted those Spanish daisies months ago, but they're thriving now that the creeping thyme has taken hold."

Story wondered if Harold Stone had a companion beyond his thyme. "If you help me get Cooper to the rainforest," she said, "I can make his moment turn out right."

Turning back to her now, Harold smiled sadly and said, "Why do you think I'm watering my own flowers?"

"Because you like gardening?" a confused Story said.

"No, because I had to let the gardener go after I lost all my money."

"What?!" Story sounded like a disgruntled toddler.

"I know it doesn't look like it, but I'm broke," he said. "Right after I quit my job, I was in quite a state—I sold all my properties, cashed in my other investments, and went to Vegas, thinking I could make enough money to justify not working, and then I could travel and forget my worries."

As they watched from the veranda above, a homeless tabby cat sauntered into Harold's perfect garden and took a perfect, steamy crap near his catnip, which he'd planted there as a companion to his other mints.

"Shit, Harry," Story said as she hit the top of the elaborate veranda guard rail, "how is it possible to lose that much money?"

"Easy. A full week of one bad decision after another, and poof!" he said, stretching out his fingers, "it's all gone." He turned around to look at his mansion. "Thank God this was paid for. The front double-door was the last purchase I made as a wealthy man—that, and Martin's expedition."

The cat covered up his dirty little secret with sandy Arizona soil and ran off for his next exploit, just as Story came to the realization that she was back to square one. "So you can't help me."

Harold Stone became a stammering explosion of indecision. "Maybe I should call Martin, tell him to take the kid . . . but maybe I shouldn't intervene . . . The last time I followed my gut . . . I don't know." He stared straight ahead, and as Story looked at and through him, she realized failure wasn't all she'd tried to convince herself it was. *He was an old man who fished alone in a skiff in the Gulf Stream and he had gone eighty-four days now without taking a fish.*

Story could tell he wasn't going to do it, and she felt the disappointment as he continued his tentative declaration. "Afraid not. Not in two days, anyway." He did look sorry. "For Cooper's sake, I hope—"

"Hope is for fairy godmothers and pansies, Harry. We need money."

The two of them, too poor to buy their way out of their problems and too smart to hope for the best, leaned on the railing and let the sunlight try to warm their dampened spirits.

Harold felt grateful for his flowers, shining in the sun, and was satisfied to have a less glamorous role than his mariposa lilies. "At least that's free," he said, of the ball of fire in the sky, born as a star, ninety-three million miles away.

Before Story departed, she asked him the only question left to ask. "Why the moonflower?"

He remembered the first time he'd read about the decisive moonflower, blossoming just once in its lifetime, but blooming with resolute determination. And finally, Harold Stone answered with authority, "It lives and dies without regret."

TWENTY-FIVE

lueless as to how to get twenty-thousand dollars in twenty-nine hours, Story Easton moped her way to her car, but at that same moment, Claire and Cooper Payne skipped around their house with a newfound sense of joy. Joy had been gone from the Payne house for a full year, and they were happy to welcome the stranger back into their lives by playing hooky from work and school, and by eating chocolate cake as a late breakfast.

When Claire called her office to explain her upcoming absence, Jessica snapped at her, shocked. "What you mean, you're leaving? You never go anywhere."

"Cancel my appointments, Jess," Claire said, smiling at a giggling Cooper.

"The Carls are going to have a fit, you know," said Jessica. Carl Daniels, a long-time patient, suffered from multiple personality disorder and saw Claire four times a week, showing up as a different Carl each time. Jessica needed to keep track of them for scheduling, so she gave each of Carl's personalities a different name: Anxious Carl came on Tuesdays, Show Tune Carl on Wednesdays, Mute Carl on Thursdays, and Horny Carl on Fridays.

"Well, I suggest telling him on Thursday when he can't talk back," said Claire. And then she laughed. "Otherwise, be prepared to show some serious affection and major cleavage on Friday."

Jessica was still miffed. "And what am I supposed to tell Rapunzel?"

Claire wiped chocolate frosting from Cooper's bottom lip. "Tell her not to wait up for me," she said.

TWENTY-SIX

nce upon a time, there was a woman who discovered she had turned into the *wrong person.* Story couldn't get that line out of her head. As she drove away from Judge Stone's house, she let the line bounce around, aimless and lost in her mind, and she decided that the annoyingly successful Anne Tyler was a fraud; she didn't write fiction, she wrote about Story's disappointing existence, and Story wanted a percentage of her earnings for exploiting her mistaken identity.

Perhaps she's spying on me, she thought. *Perhaps Anne Tyler is actually watching me from afar.* She pictured Anne Tyler wearing a brooding black turtleneck, smart glasses, and a chic, writerly scarf, putting last-minute touches on already perfect metaphors, and felt sick. She looked down at her ratty, second-hand T-shirt adorned with a faded Sex Pistols silk-screen decal—a shirt once cool in a thrifty, *I don't care* way, but now easily found in the juniors department at every major clothing store.

Having struck out with Harold Stone, Story retreated to her house instead of going back to the office to be interrogated by Ivy. She sat on her couch, daydreaming about the money she needed, and thought about potential stick-up lines for a bank robbery. *Give me twenty-thousand dollars or four tickets to the Amazon, suckers!* And when she realized what a horrible bank robber she'd be, she thought of the most successful person she knew. She figured her mother could probably rob a bank, conduct a conference call, and receive a pedicure all at the same time. And her stick-up line, or lines rather, would be a series of annoying questions designed to stun the clerks long enough for her to steal the loot. *What is money, really? Isn't it just a bunch of germ-infested paper? How do you really know what it's worth? How do you feel about being zealots of greed?*

Her mother's gala party was only a few hours away, she had no date and nothing to wear, and she felt more like a failure than she ever had before. At least when she screwed up in the past, it was only her own life. Now, she'd have to face her mother's mountain of success having just completely failed to make one lousy dream come true for one poor kid who desperately needed it. On top of that, she'd have to break the bad news to Cooper, who was probably packing at that very moment for the adventure of his life. But the bad news would have to wait until tomorrow—she just couldn't deal with it today—and for now, she could fulfill at least one promise by going to her mother's party.

She'd been to one other Socra-Tots® function in her past, and it had made a *Star Trek* convention seem normal. The giant convention center's main floor overflowed with ultra-happy vendors, each peddling Socra-Tots® products and singing the praises of the *Knowledge Is Power* motto and its ability to change children's lives. The event was so large and involved that Story had gotten lost among the bustling consumers, who waved checkbooks as they dreamed of Ivy League educations for their lazy toddlers who they were sure could be fixed with one more set of flashcards. By the time her mother took the podium to vocalize her vision of the company's next fiscal year, Story had set up at the children's table, in a tiny chair, coloring outside the lines—a disappointment even among her four-year-old peers.

According to her mother, tonight's event at the Gurston Library and Museum was going to be more formal than prior Socra-Tots® functions, "less commercial and more celebratory." Story hoped she'd be able to disappear into the crowd, free to hide from questions about her accomplishments as a Socra-Tots baby, all grown up. Most of all, she wanted to hide from her mother. Though Story knew her mother was a taskmaster with a glaring intolerance for imperfection, deep down, she couldn't help but feel Beverly Easton deserved a more vibrant daughter than her, someone who lived up to the Easton tradition, someone who lived up to her own name by weaving an interesting yarn of a life.

Story held her head high, trying to convince herself she could pull this off with a bit of grace, but then, realizing she couldn't do it alone, she picked up the phone and dialed Hans.

"Story. Hey," said Hans.

Story took a deep breath and swallowed her pride, again. "I called for two reasons: to ask you for a favor, and to deliver some bad news." She envisioned Hans massaging his hands.

"I'm all about giving," he said. "Ask your favor first."

After a frustrated sigh, she said, "Okay, I feel dumb having to ask you this, because you barely know me, and normally, I wouldn't be going to one of these stupid, pretentious parties, but I promised—"

"I'll go," Hans said.

"Oh," Story said, followed by a pause. "Great. Pick me up at six?"

"Tux or jeans?"

"Um, tux," she said, starting to worry about her own wardrobe. She gave him her address.

"So what's the bad news?"

"The trip isn't going to happen." When Hans didn't say anything, she added, "And if you want to tell Claire Payne I'm a liar, and have the police arrest me for breaking and entering, then have at it."

"That sounds more like a second date." Hans remained quiet for a moment. "What happened to *doing something right for once*? What could possibly be holding you back from that?"

"Twenty-thousand dollars."

"I see," Hans said. "It's only a trip, right? It's not like someone's life depends on it."

Story let out a sad, defeated, "Right."

"See you at six," he said.

"See you at six."

As soon as she hung up, Story heard a knock at her door. When she opened it, no one was there. Instead, she found a white box wrapped with a red ribbon. She picked it up, held her ear close to the box to check for a ticking sound, and then untied the ribbon and lifted off the lid. A gold sticker held together two edges of carnation pink tissue paper, and inside, folded in perfect symmetry, was a black, beaded cocktail dress, way too beautiful for Story's budget. And next to it were a pair of black Dolce & Gabbana pumps. Underneath it all was a hidden envelope and card with a handwritten note: *Have you shaved your legs today?* As soon as she saw the annoying question mark, Story knew who'd sent the package.

The answer to the question was "no," so she showered and shaved her legs, for her mother, and for her date—just in case. She then tried to look presentable by putting her hair in a French twist, applying mascara, and glossing up her lips. After dressing, she looked in the full-length mirror at her shaved legs, made-up face, and cleavage framed by the sweetheart neckline on the form-fitting dress. The newness of Story's dress felt good as it connected with her skin, as if she could get used to its freshness as opposed to her usual used, worn, and stale garments. But though she was pretty, she still felt like a failure—a failure dressed expensively.

While she waited for Hans to show up, she poured herself a glass of wine and sat down at her dining room table, observing her consistent, daily companion—the ten-foot tall crossword puzzle. Thirty-Nine Across. *Hughes's dream.* Eight letters. With money on the brain, she contemplated Howard Hughes's possible dreams. Eight letters. *AIRPLANE.* No. *MILLIONS.* Neither fit with the "R" she already had.

After another glass of wine and another hour of trying to figure out the puzzle, a knock broke her concentration. When she opened the door for the door-maker himself, Hans Turner stood in front of her in the crisp, black tuxedo he wore for magic performances. It looked like a normal tux, in that it fit him well and seemed to be made out of decent fabric, but unlike the run-of-the-mill suits she'd seen, his had something unexpected—the pocket was stuffed with some sort of scarf, much more exciting than Ivy's fake pocket-cloth. What she could see—the purple end peeking out of the pocket—was just the beginning. Purple would become red, then green, then yellow, and then continue in a rainbow of options, all from the magic hands that opened doors of possibility.

It was love at first sight. It troubled Story that this line, a joke meant to highlight the absurdity of the very notion of love at first sight, was occupying her brain and polluting a decent moment.

"You shaved, too," Story said. She felt wobbly.

"You . . ." he said. Taking in all of her, from her long, smooth legs to her shiny, kissable lips, he forgot to finish his sentence. "Beautiful." And then he pulled a quirky bouquet of plastic flowers out of nowhere and presented them to her in one fluid, charming movement.

"Mmmm," she said, smiling as she took a whiff. "Waxy."

Confident in his answer and in his choice, he said, "They'll last forever."

TWENTY-SEVEN

When they arrived downtown, Story and Hans walked across Park Street, and up the two flights of cement steps that led to the Gurston Library and Museum. The front of the building—hundreds of windows nestled in a wall of brick—seemed unusually dark for such a big event. "My mother's probably showing footage of her twenty years of success," Story said with a laugh. "And knowing how much my mother likes to witness success, the lights may never come back on."

They walked down a long corridor toward the main reading room. The journey down the brick-lined hallway reminded her of the walkway leading to the Royal Table in Cinderella's Castle at Disney World. She'd seen it on television when she was little, and though she'd resisted it, she remembered secretly wondering what it would be like to live as a princess.

Hans moved to open the door, but Story felt the need to do it herself. She turned the doorknob and prepared for a long evening of boredom, humiliation, and more phonics and building blocks than anyone ought to see in one location. She figured she had the wrong room, because when she opened the door, all she saw was black. But just as she turned to leave, she heard a roomful of people yell, "Surprise!"

When the lights came on, Story saw a cocktail party, not a Socra-Tots® convention. The beautiful octagonal room—the same one, full of rare art and special-edition books, used for special events with high-brow Phoenix officials—felt both regal and cozy. It was aglow with a warm light and abuzz with roving waiters carrying appetizers and green apple martinis, Story's favorite. The vaulted ceiling went up two stories, and all eight sides of the room were connected by wall-to-wall bookshelves, extending all the way to the skylight at the top, interrupted here and there by framed artwork. Attached to the bookshelves were three polished mahogany ladders fastened by way of a metal track, which traveled the circumference of the room, and made available any unreachable book. To the left of the door was a four-string quartet playing a refined and lively instrumental version of "(I Can't Get No) Satisfaction."

As Story looked around the room, she spotted some familiar people, but most were only vaguely identifiable. After taking in the scene, Story's gaze came full circle, and ended up focused on one person who, at that very moment, Story realized was her true center, the person who'd always acted as Story's vantage point—even when her point was shrieking and unbearable. There stood Beverly Easton, center stage, in front of several rows of other standing guests.

Beverly Easton walked over to Story and Hans, who still stood at the threshold. "Happy thirtieth, honey," Beverly said, with a hug that seemed strangely maternal. "I knew you'd forget—you always forget your birthday."

Story braced herself for *Why do you suppose you're so forgetful?* but it never came. Duped by her own mother, a dumbfounded Story faced her, shocked. "How did you . . . What about the gala . . . anniversary party?"

Her mother kissed her on the cheek and said, "It's next week . . . I still want you to come, and after this, you can't say no." Beverly Easton took in the stunning venue, and then looked at Hans with raised eyebrows. "Maybe he can come, too."

"Uh, Mom, this is Hans," Story said, leading both of them out of the doorway and into the party. Hans shook Beverly's hand, and the moment she said hello, she looked down to see a small and shiny hand-painted wooden egg in her hand. Story let out a nervous giggle when she said, "He does it all. Fixes doors, repairs . . . um . . . broken things . . ." With a flush traveling up her neck, she was careful not to say, *Seduces unsuspecting women with his hammer.* Smiling warmly, she finished, "Performs impromptu magic tricks." When Story said it, she gave her mother a look that said, *Please keep your Magic-Is-Rubbish lecture to yourself.*

"How nice. Let's go mingle," Beverly Easton said, taking Hans in one arm and Story in the other. After getting a good look at Hans, she said, "Good Lord, you're gorgeous. You look just like—"

"I know," Hans said, nodding. "That one guy."

"You are a *dish*," she said, taking him in. "Really. You're a prince. Do you want marriage? Children?" Giving Hans a playful squeeze, she strolled toward the crowd.

"Mom!" Story shook her head, then mumbled an Austen-tacious line: "It is a truth universally acknowledged, that a single man in possession of a good fortune must be in want of a wife."

While Hans shook his head and declared he did not have a fortune, Beverly Easton fired back, "Oh, don't be a brat, Story. Is it so wrong for a woman of my age to want grandchildren?" She didn't wait for an answer, but instead began introductions in the form of a quiz. "Story, do you remember Fred Harrington?"

Story stared, trying to place him, but had no idea who he was.

The old man, hunched over and cranky, said in a raspy and scraggly voice, "Let me refresh your memory." In a turn for the worse, he yelled, "Sit down in back! I know you're writing on the seat again!"

"Oh, God," Story mumbled, realizing it was her middle-school bus driver. In seventh grade, her mother decided it would be good for Story to attend a year of public school (to build character, she said), and in defiance, Story wrote inappropriate limericks on the bus seats.

Hans laughed, Beverly flashed a fake smile, and Story said, "How nice to see you again," in a loud voice.

"I'm not deaf! Happy damn birthday," he scoffed, scooting off toward the nonfiction stacks to hide until his "time" was up, he said. Story figured if he planned on dropping dead right there in the library, it was better to die surrounded by truth than perish in fiction.

Story barely had a chance to recover from the Fred Harrington encounter when her mother pulled her and Hans over to three bubbly, grinning girls Story recognized. "Hey, Story!" they said in unison.

"You remember the Turlington Triplets. You used to play together when you were little," Beverly said, inspecting them. All three had flipped-up hair, the perfect shade of blonde, not too platinum and not too brassy, and their figures were perfect, too—athletic but feminine. They all wore knee-length red dresses, which were not exactly the same, but three variations on a theme. V-neck. Spaghetti straps. Strapless.

Her recollection of them came in bursts. The first thing she remembered was how they secretly wanted to be Story's sisters so they could live with and learn from the incomparable Beverly Easton, mentor extraordinaire. So there they were, the evil stepsisters in the flesh. That is, if the evil stepsisters were supermodels instead of big-nosed monstrosities.

Story conducted three handshakes with the ladies in red as she recalled the *play* her mother had referred to, which was really endless hours of boot-camp role-play practice with the oh-so-cute triplets. They had been the official poster-children for Socra-Tots® for five full years, providing pig tails, effervescent smiles, and hope for parents suffering from high expectations for their own children. They adorned millions of brochures, and starred in hundreds of videos, all of which helped Socra-Tots® Inc. make millions. As Story observed their predictable smiles and shallow exchanges, she felt a twinge of joy come over her. They hadn't turned out that great after all.

"God, what's it been? Twenty-five years? What have you been up to?" Story asked.

"I work for the UN. UNICEF Division," the first one said. And when she delivered a loud, "Save the children!" her eyes looked a little crazy, but the other two nodded in harmony with her melodic declaration.

The second of the trio said, "I'm the head developmental geneticist for the leading cancer research center," and put her thumb and index finger together to show she was *"this* close to finding a cure!"

The third-let finished with, "I teach music." Story breathed a sigh of relief. That didn't seem so impressive. "To quadriplegics." *Christ.* "From all over the world—my company just went global and we're giving ten percent of the proceeds to charity! You know, your mother taught me that in life, ninety percent is what—"

"Oh, shut it, Samantha," Story said, grabbing an envious green-apple martini off a roving waiter's tray and gulping.

Samantha, unaffected, said, "And thanks to Socra-Tots®, I've been fluent in six languages since toddlerhood!"

Story turned her head to avoid her mother's look—she was oozing with pride—and, averting her eyes, she thought about how hard it must be to teach someone without arms how to play the piccolo. She couldn't even get a full-bodied eight-year-old boy to the jungle.

"Girls, this is Hans, Story's friend," Beverly said. She raised her eyebrows and whispered, "He makes magic doors—"

"The doors aren't magic, Mother, he's a mag—"

"Some of my doors turn out to be quite magical, actually," Hans said.

But Beverly Easton ignored Hans and moved on to the next guest, shaking his reluctant hand and saying, "Story, say hello to Shawn." Beverly pretended to fan her face with her hand when she announced, "Old flame," then extinguished a fake ember on Shawn's shoulder. Just as Story was thinking it was a nice gesture for him to come, she saw him hold up five fingers and mouth something to Story's mother, who whispered back a scolding, "No, the deal was four hundred, not five."

"Mother!" Story hollered, softening her voice when she said, "You paid him to come to my party?!" She took a moment for the horror to set in, as she watched Fred Harrington take two hors d'oeuvres for the road to help him celebrate his "time" being up. "Jesus, Mother. Are they all on paid, rotating shifts?" she said, looking over the many guests who were posing as friends.

Hans did the math. "Hey, I deserve *six* hundred, then. I drove her here."

Beverly Easton brushed Story's bangs out of her eyes with one nurturing sweep. "Darling, no offense, but you've never inspired a very loyal social circle—some of your acquaintances needed a little incentive to show up."

With that, Story took a direct route to the first roving cocktail tray she could find, and after placing her empty glass down, grabbed two drinks and a crab cake, another of her favorites that she didn't think her mother knew about. She handed Hans a drink. "This martini's just the first installment of your date fee. I'll send you money when I have it." She sipped furiously, ate the green apple wedge hanging off the glass's edge, and recalled her checking account balance. "On second thought, you better enjoy the martini."

Hans took Story's hand and led her through a roomful of people, all of whom seemed rather oblivious to her presence. "I think this would be a great opportunity," Hans said, "for you to tell me about yourself, Story. Without lying this time." They walked through French doors, out onto a small terrace overlooking the Phoenix nightscape. When Story looked unwilling to participate, Hans turned away from her. "I *could* just go ask your fifth-grade teacher," he said, pointing to a woman in a denim jumper talking loudly and shaking her head in disapproval. "I overheard her saying something about you being a smartass with a bad attitude and bad penmanship. Or maybe I'll have a chat with your gynecologist, yucking it up with the musicians over there. He's sure to have some juicy tidbits about you—"

"Fine," she said, "but nothing about me is very interesting. My name is Story Easton. I write bad advice on greeting cards for a living, because the good advice doesn't sell. I'm an only child—unprecedented disappointment, if you couldn't tell. Lately, I've been breaking into decent people's homes so I can pretend to be someone else besides my boring, miserable self. Let's see, my mother secretly rules the world from an underground lair. I like an occasional greasy burger. I hate questions. And I haven't had a date in over eight months because I'm not particularly charming or forgiving. Is that enough to send you running?"

Hans thought for a moment. "How often, exactly, do you crave a greasy burger?"

Story smiled.

And then, they talked—about burgers, about politics, about unbelievable magic tricks. All the while, Story watched Hans's hands dart back and forth, like a cat intently watching the thing it desired. Sometimes he touched his face, and when he did, she imagined his fingers on her own cheek. And just when things were getting cozy, Beverly emerged from the party and came out onto the terrace. "Sorry to interrupt," she said, "but may I have a moment with my daughter?"

Story promised not to be long, and Hans left them, mother and daughter, alone under starry skies. Story turned to Beverly. "Thanks, Mom, it was lovely."

"The crab cakes were shitty," said Beverly. "I told them how you like them, but they didn't turn out right. And I told our little orchestra to play *only* Rolling Stones songs—I heard you say you liked them once—but I could've sworn I heard Bob Dylan five minutes ago. And those Turlington Triplets! . . . dreadfully servile." She shook her head in disgust. "Factory-made cutouts." She looked at her only daughter. "You, Story, are one of a kind," she said, glancing inside the building at the exclusive collection of exceptional art.

"Stop it, Mom," Story said, smiling and using every ounce of energy she possessed to not look stunned, or worse yet, cry.

"I think I may have been a bit hard on you, Story Thyme," she said, staring off into the Phoenix night sky. "Your father was such a nurturing man. When he died, I was solely responsible for you, and I knew I had to do whatever was necessary to make a life for us. But I was so busy teaching you to survive, I didn't teach you how to live."

"Are you feeling all right, Mom? You're not going to try to convince me Santa Claus is real or anything, are you, because I don't think I can—"

"You can do anything you want, Story," she said with unfaltering resolve. Story waited for the words to fall flat, to become unbelievable or insincere, but they remained strong, pure, and true. "You just have to believe you can."

Out of nowhere, Story Easton said, "Mom, you work so hard, you need someone to be your gardener."

"Don't be silly. I have ten gardeners," she said, her perfectly groomed eyebrows arched as high as they would go.

"No, you need a partner. A man who acts like your gardener. Like Dad did." Story hesitated, thinking about the dad she'd grown up without, the dad she'd missed every day of her life, and for the first time, she understood that while she'd gone without a dad, her mother had gone without a husband. "You're so busy being the perfect flower. And you've worked so hard trying to get *me* to bloom." The moment she said it, she realized how true it was, and wondered how she'd never noticed it before. "But who takes care of you?"

So what if the plant-gardener analogy referred to Paul Simon and Carrie Fisher's failed marriage? (She'd heard it once in an interview—Paul referred to himself and Carrie as two flowers without a gardener.) It still worked.

"Well, I guess I could be friendlier to Miguel when he's watering," said Beverly. "He does seem to have a tender touch."

In a moment of weakness, Story clung to the notion that her mother believed in her, and tried to savor a feeling that might not come again. "So, I've got this thing going on, Mom. It's important, but I think I've screwed it up."

"Nonsense. Is it a worthy cause?"

"Yes. Very."

"If you think it is, then it is, so make it work, look within yourself. Good for you. It's not a chance unless you take it."

"Too bad my insides aren't lined with cash," Story mumbled.

"Is this about money? Because if it is—"

"No, no, no. I won't take your money." She became flustered. "I don't need the prince," she said, growing more agitated, "and I don't need a fairy godmother to wave her little wand—"

"Don't be ridiculous. Magic is rubbish. Real fairy godmothers carry checkbooks—"

"No, really, I'm not taking your—"

"Shut up, will you? It's not mine, it's *yours*," Beverly said. "All I ever wanted was for you to have doors of opportunity wherever you looked. Did you really think I forgot to get you birthday presents for thirty years? What kind of mother do you think I—"

"What you are talking about, Mother?"

"Your trust fund," she said, simply.

"I have a trust fund? How much?" Story asked.

"Twenty thousand."

"I have twenty thousand dollars?!"

"No." She paused just long enough for Story to become depressed. "Not exactly. I put twenty thousand in on every one of your birthdays, starting when you were seven—that's when the company really took off—and then I gave you retro-pay for the birthdays I'd already missed, so that makes six hundred thousand, plus interest, which is well over two million now, and that's nothing compared to your percentage of revenue from all Socra-Tots® merchandise." After calculating, she added, "The real party begins when I'm dead, my sweet, rich only child."

"Why didn't you tell me?" Story said, mouth agape.

"First off, you never asked," she said, "but mainly, I was waiting until you were motivated to see something through. I was waiting until you gave a shit about something." She kissed her daughter's forehead. "Looks like you give a shit about something now. Right?"

Story could have explained the plan in detail, reassuring her mother of her laudable plan, but Story's eyes told a truth that was big enough even for Beverly Easton. Confident, Story said, "So what happens next?"

Beverly Easton paused, then did what she did best. "What do *you* think happens next?"

Story thought about it. *Talk it out*, her mother used to say. *Think it through, now.* "Okay. What happens? No, not what *happens*." She was so excited, she could hardly speak. *Ninety percent of life is what happens . . . ten percent is what we do.* She looked her mother straight in the eye and, for once, felt she was looking straight ahead. "I'm going to *do* it." Story's face became serious, determined. "I have a very important birthday party to plan."

"Don't pay the guests to come," her mother said. "Upon further reflection, I suppose it's in poor taste." She tested Story one more time. "Am I invited?"

"I'm afraid not, Mom," Story said, with a hint of genuine regret. "This is a solo effort—gotta stay on my game. I made a promise."

Beverly Easton could have spewed out her *Knowledge is Power* motto. She could have asked a question. But instead, she said something she'd never said to her only daughter. "Proud of you," she whispered in Story's ear. And then she walked back inside to relieve the next shift.

Hans came back to Story's side when her mother left, and watched her stare out into the distance. "Nice chat?" he asked.

Story felt the weight of the night tighten in her chest, and didn't answer, but nodded as she filled up with something foreign—something that was, at first, unrecognizable, but then evolved into something she'd desired her whole life. Was it *pride*? She made a silent introduction—*Pride: me. Me: pride*—hoping they'd see each other again.

Hans touched his pocket to make sure his surprise was still there, hiding behind his magic scarf, but not before he stretched his fingers, trying to relieve the ache without Story noticing. Before he knew it was Story's birthday, he'd already decided to make her a small gift to say he was sorry her plan wasn't working out. So nestled somewhere between green and blue silk was a tiny wooden machete to remind Story that if she couldn't get to the jungle, maybe the jungle could come to her.

Reaching for the gift, he said, "So, since it's your birthday—"

"The trip's back on!" Story exclaimed.

Disappointed he wasn't the one who fixed the problem, Hans moved his hand away from his pocket. "That's great."

But when she looked into his gray-blue eyes, they seemed stormier than usual. And suddenly, she figured out *Hughes's dream*. It wasn't Howard Hughes, but *Langston* Hughes. DEFERRED.

What happens to a dream deferred? Does it dry up like a raisin in the sun?

No one's dreams would be shriveling on Story's watch, so she grabbed Hans around his shoulders, pulled him into her, and kissed him without apology. For a long time. And when things escalated to that beautiful place where both kissers forget where they are, and who they are, she whispered in his ear, "I really, really, really, *really* want you . . . to be my sherpa."

"I really, really, really, *really* want . . . to carry your bags," Hans said. He paused for a moment. "Wait. How many bags will you have?"

"See?" she said, kissing his neck. "The dream wasn't dead, just interrupted."

"Story Easton, I don't know what the hell you're saying, but I like the way you say it." Still tight in his embrace, Story slipped off her expensive right shoe and, without even thinking, played tender footsie with Hans. Instinctively, Hans got down on one knee and placed the right shoe on the right girl.

After getting back up, he returned more kisses and said, "Where should we go on our second date? Maybe Fred Harrington will let us make out in the back of his bus . . . or maybe those Turlington Triplets need some help saving the world—"

"The jungle. Isn't that where most people go for a second date?"

"Only if I get to dress like Tarzan. And I'll buy you a . . . Hey, I made you a little something. Or are you one of those princesses who wants the box with the big red ribbon?"

Story thought about what she really needed, what Cooper really needed, and as the clock in her mind struck midnight, she caressed Hans's strong, skilled hands, and said, "Actually, all I need is the box." How long would it take, she wondered, for a magic door-fixer to carve a magic treasure box?

THURSDAY

Too scared to open my eyes, I explored what I was sitting on with my hands. Coarse hair. Warm flesh. Slow, easy gait. Snort.

Snort?!

Now, this startled me, so I did something I suppose one should never do while riding a strange animal in the jungle—I pulled this snorting thing's fur, which sent it running, all the while snorting, "Don't touch my fur! I have enough to worry about! Don't ever touch my fur!" When he heard a noise behind us, he barreled, fast as his squat legs would go, toward a riverbank.

"Gosh, sorry," I told him. With my eyes wide open now, I said, "Since when do pigs have fur?"

This time, he let out a timid, embarrassed snort. "I. Am. Not. A. Pig."

But before I could ask him what he was, we both plunged into the river, and I found the world and the water around me swirling in slow motion. Bright-colored fish darted about in an excited frenzy, but tall plants swayed, unhurried, and danced amongst themselves. Just as I was beginning to enjoy this underwater realm, a thick, shiny fish swam over to me and smiled a mouthful of razor-sharp teeth.

"Ahhhhhhhhhh!" My muffled scream let the river water pour into my mouth. I yanked the non-pig's fur again and kicked him in the side like an incensed (exasperated) (mad) cowgirl.

"Okay, okay," he gasped, exiting the water and lumbering back onto the riverbank. "Had to get to the water. Heard a noise. Got scared. Had to get where it's safe."

"Safe? I almost got my left cheek torn off by a piranha!"

"Oh, they don't mess with me," he said, finally sounding confident. "Fur's too hard for 'em to chew."

"And you are . . ?"

"I'm a capybara. No relation to swine." After a snorty breath, he added, "Rats and mice are my brethren."

"Gross!" I hollered, jumping off him. "You're a giant rat?" But when he hung his furry head, and his little ears twitched, I felt bad. "I mean, that's cool. My friend Sarah has a guinea pig—"

"I'm not a pig!"

We stared at each other for a moment, and I decided to make up for getting off on the wrong foot. Paw. Whatever. "Hope," I said, extending my hand toward his front leg.

"How nice," he said, gripping my hand with his webbed toes. "With a name like that, you always have hope, wherever you go."

"My dad always says that!" But when I told him that, he didn't look surprised. He only nuzzled his skittish self next to me and told me to jump back on.

"Is nightfall coming?" I said. He was so nervous he made me nervous. "The Fierce One—"

"First the treasure box, then the moonflower," he said, as we plodded deeper and deeper into the dark, mysterious forest.

TWENTY-EIGHT

S tory began her day with a lie.

"Yes," she said to Ivy's secretary after a fake cough, "tell her I'm coughing and throwing up. And have killer diarrhea . . . No! No, I don't need to talk to her," she said, before abruptly hanging up. But as soon as her hand released the phone receiver, she realized calling in to work was unnecessary. Unused to being a millionaire, Story had a hard time conceiving of being unemployed, but as she pondered a life of luxury, she decided she no longer needed to put up with Ivy's bullshit.

She picked the phone back up, hit redial, and had one more chat with Ivy's slave. "Hey, Laurie, it's Story again," she said. "On second thought, tell the Boss Lady I'm not throwing up—I'm throwing in the towel. And tell her I don't have a cough, and I don't have diarrhea. I have money. Lots of it. And I'm not coming to work again. Ever."

As silence set in on the other end, Story realized the moment didn't feel as glorious as she'd hoped—even to herself, she sounded like a spoiled brat. She lowered her voice. "Um, if Ivy dumps *Grief and Loss* on Carrie or Tony, tell them to call me and I'll give them a hand." She paused and tried something she usually avoided at work. "Hey, how'd the thing go . . . at the place . . . with the guy?" Laurie's boyfriend had just proposed to her, or something like that.

"Oh, Story, it was a dream," said Laurie. "I mean, I wasn't exactly surprised, but even though I thought it might happen, it was so magical, it seemed unexpected. I know that doesn't make any sense—"

"No, it doesn't—"

"He actually got down on his knees, as the sun was setting over the ocean, and from that moment on, I felt like it was all more than just a stupid story . . .

no offense, Story—"

"Oh, don't worr—"

"It was my *life*, you know, my new life starting right then and there."

Out of habit, Story almost made a gagging sound, her usual response to sugar-sweet tales of romance, but she stopped herself and said, "That's great, Laurie. I hope you live—"

"I know . . . happily ever after!"

After hanging up the phone again, she tried hard to focus on travel arrangements. With the map in front of her, she stared at the green blob with the word *Amazon* in the middle, spilling into surrounding countries, wondering if an anaconda could really swallow her whole, but then her mind wandered back to the terrace, and to the kiss. She relived his smell—aftershave, martini, hints of sawdust—and she couldn't stop smiling when she thought about him slipping her mother the egg.

"Okay, we'll need airplane tickets," she said out loud, "but where do we even fly into—Brazil, Ecuador, Columbia?" But now that she was rich, she found herself thinking about lavishing gifts on Hans. Maybe she'd build him a new workshop, equipped with all the latest woodworking chisel-things. Or maybe he'd like a new arsenal of magic gear. Top-of-the-line wands and rabbits. *Don't be weird. You hardly know him.* She thought about his strong arms around her, in the perfect squeeze.

"Okay, there'll be anacondas there. We'll need . . . machetes?" she said, realizing that going into the jungle without a safety net was not only going to be a pain in the ass, but also reckless. She was responsible for three other people, and contrary to what Claire Payne thought, there was no camera crew, no leader to protect them, and less than a day to find and hire either, and she'd still have to convince Martin Baxter to be their guide. And he'd already shown he had no problem saying no to Story. As she tried to think of possible solutions, the phone rang.

"Hello?" she said, and when she heard the sound of an electric saw in the background, she smiled.

The saw's screaming subsided. "Did you know that native Amazonians consider the kapok tree to be the spiritual leader of the forest?" said Hans.

"I did not," Story said, unconsciously twirling her hair.

"Yeah, so says the Internet. I needed to make sure I knew what it looked like before I tried to carve it."

"And . . ."

"It's *big*."

"Well, we'll see," Story said. Then she stammered, "About the tree, I mean. We'll see how big the tree is."

Hans chuckled. "Look, I don't want to sound bossy, especially before our second date, but I was thinking, we're gonna need more than a mythical, spiritual tree-leader to get us through the jungle without incident. Don't get me wrong, I'm up for the adventure. I'm ready to kick a jaguar's ass to protect you if I have to. But . . ." He stopped for a moment. "Does it have to be the *heart* of the jungle? Couldn't we just stay on the outskirts, peek in, maybe take some pictures?"

"The book says 'heart,'" she said, pausing, "so it has to be." Story had told Hans about the book, enough for him to know what the treasure box looked like, but he didn't realize yet how Cooper had hung on her every word.

"You know, I once got lost in Compton—middle of the night—with this woman." He sighed. "After two hours of her trying to read the map and yelling at me, I was happy to finally see a man with a gun."

"I promise not to stop in the jungle to ask for directions—"

"That's why we need a guide!" he laughed.

Exactly!

But as Story reveled in the fact that Hans was somehow reading her mind, Hans paused for a moment, and revealed something that came out like a secret. "Heartwood," he said softly.

"Heart wood?" said Story.

"You asked me earlier what I'm making the treasure box out of," he said in a matter-of-fact tone. "Except for the lid, where you said the tree and vines need to be carved, the box itself will be constructed from heartwood, the wood in the tree's center that's died and become resistant to decay."

"It's dead?" Story said into the phone, preferring the term *heartwood* to *deadwood*.

Story noticed Hans come to life when he said, "Well, funny you should ask. Some people believe heartwood is technically alive because it can still chemically react to decaying organisms."

Is he "some" people?

Story thought about this notion of something being part alive and part dead, and wondered if Hans thought about people in the same terms. Did he think of her as a solid oak beauty, or as disappointing plywood?

"So it's *kinda* dead?" she said, laughing.

But Hans didn't laugh back. Instead, he answered, "Yeah, I guess so," and Story suddenly felt as if they weren't talking about wood anymore. "Sapwood won't hold up . . . You want the box to last forever, right?" An uncomfortable silence arrived and then left. "I mean, the kid's experienced enough loss, I can at least make sure the damn box lasts."

Story was impressed that Hans had given Cooper that much thought. "Right."

Hans changed the subject. "You said it needs to be dark wood, so I think African Blackwood would work best. It's a beautiful hardwood," he said, enunciating clearly, because *heartwood* and *hardwood* might sound the same over the phone. "Slight grain, with a deep, dark, almost eggplant color."

Story, trying to keep up with him, spoke slowly. "So . . . heartwood from African Blackwood, except for the carved lid, for which you'll probably need a softwood."

"Yes." She could hear his smile.

Before she confused her hardwood and softwood, she said, "Hey, thanks for coming last night." She winced. "To the party—thanks for coming to the party."

"No problem."

"I know it was sort of weird—"

"Why are you doing this for him?" Hans interrupted. "He seems like a great kid . . . but why *you*?"

Story paused to gather her thoughts, but felt a sense of panic swell in her voice. "Because dads fix things," she said, "and when you don't have one . . ." She thought about father-daughter dances, about fathers showing daughters how to change tires so they could take care of themselves, and she thought about how fathers, even when their daughters become women, always think of them as their little girls. Or so she'd heard.

And then she thought about David Payne and how, if he could, he'd do anything to keep his promise to his only son. She thought about second chances, and what they mean to those who need them.

She thought of Cooper, for the rest of his life looking for a magic treasure box in every dark corner he encountered.

"But you barely know him, Story," said Hans, "and this could be a very dangerous trip, and if it doesn't work . . . Look, maybe I can help you find another way to make this happen. I could help you—"

"You never stop *fixing*, do you?" said Story. She knew her tone was angrier than she wanted it to be, but she felt as if she'd just solved a riddle. This is what she'd seen in his alert eyes, in the way his hands hovered, always on the verge of cradling every problem, the way he did magic tricks when he wanted people to smile, the way he looked at Story when she opened her own door.

Suddenly, she wanted to apologize, but she didn't know how. "I . . ."

And Hans, of course, rescued her. "It's fine, Story," he said, and Story knew that somewhere, on the other end of the phone line, inside the words he would not say, Hans was extending his hands in the form of a makeshift life raft.

Damn it, even his silence is comforting. "I know you're just trying to help, and you seem to be very good at it, at fixing things, I mean," she said, exasperated, finding herself, once again, alone in the middle of Failure Avenue. "But I'm not the one who needs to be saved here. Cooper needs . . ." A little embarrassed to be thinking of something as unrealistic as magic at such a real and tense moment, Story thought of herself as lost in *Once Upon A Moonflower*, searching for the treasure box that gave everyone what they needed. She tried a new approach. "Look, have you ever seen the look on a girl's face when she's fighting for something and a boy rushes in, sure he can make it all okay?"

Silence.

"Hans?" Story asked. She knew, without a doubt, that his frustration was showing in his hands, and she wished he were there in front of her.

Knowing he could not make it all okay, Hans did not attempt an answer.

"Well, if you had, I bet you'd know that we girls . . ." *God, this sounds like a retarded after-school special.* "Sometimes we don't want to be rescued or fixed. We just want . . ." *We just want to learn to fucking swim. And for you to like me the way I am—broken.* Story sighed into the phone receiver. *I'm drowning here.*

Story heard Hans let out a deep breath, and suddenly she hoped he was going to save the dismal conversation, but by the end of his exhale, she knew he'd let go. He'd loosened his grip on the Story rescue mission. But even as he distanced himself from her, his voice, soft and kind, washed over her. "Don't drink any standing water. And you'll need to get these special kinds of mosquito nets—"

"No, no, no, no." *I've screwed this up before I even got a second date. I am fucking unbelievable.* "I want you to come with—"

"No," he said in a stern voice, before adding, more softly, "I do, on occasion, follow directions, Story." And then Story thought she heard him mumble "Why am I here?" and as he uttered the words, they seemed familiar, as if he'd said them hundreds of times before. After a pause, he said, "But I can't *not* try to fix things. I can't *not* try to protect someone like . . ."

Like me? Story melted into her chair. *Shit!*

"Good luck, Story," he said, and then, as if Story might not have heard the sincerity, he added, "really. I hope you . . ."

I hope you . . . what? Find success? Dislodge your head from your ass? Get attacked by a jaguar and have to get rescued by natives who don't smell like hardware and bacon?

But he never said another word. The story ended with the dreaded ellipses. What kind of story had it been? Had it been a dream sequence that existed only in Story's mind? Had it been an adventure story that never got adventurous? Had it been a love story? *What can you say about a 25-year-old girl who died?* reverberated in Story's head. Love Story. *What a crock-of-shit story. When someone dies young, of course they're remembered as being perfect.*

When Story had a moment to realize the truth hiding in that thought, she instantly felt guilty for having said it. *When someone is gone long enough, do you eventually forget they ever existed?* Story imagined the magic treasure box hiding under leaves and roots in the heart of the Amazon. *If something has never been seen, does it mean it doesn't exist?*

She waited for more words from Hans, but they never came. Instead, she heard a cold dial tone. After saying a quiet, "Bye," she hung on to the last word he'd said—*you*—and heard the whisper of their words floating away in separate directions.

TWENTY-NINE

A squall of thoughts whipped around in Story's mind. *I've lost my boyfriend. I've lost my sherpa. I've lost . . . my magic treasure box! Damn it.* She knew she could muster up some kind of Plan B for the box, but she suddenly felt a horrible sadness come over her when she imagined Hans not being there when Cooper found the box. In that moment, his strong hands would not be there to hold hers, and somehow she knew that where Hans was concerned, there could be no Plan B. He was definitely Plan A.

But the task at hand would not wait for a mopey Story to get over her Plan A Man, so she tried to focus. She sat at her dining room table, surrounded by an ocean of green designed to make her feel alive. *I'm dead*, she thought. *This mission is dead. Totally stalled out. Totally screwed up. Totally failed.*

Resisting the urge to give up, she tried to start over. *Begin again*, she thought. *Think firsts.* She closed her eyes and tried to absorb any life force possibly coming from her green walls. *In the great green room, there was a telephone and a red balloon. Okay. Think. Talk it out. First problem . . .* "If Martin won't listen to me," Story said aloud, "who might he listen to?" She imagined Cooper floating through the jungle like Curious George, hanging on to one giant red balloon. "Duh! Cooper."

Okay, how can I get them in the same room? she thought. *I'm going to have to lie again. I need to know when his flight leaves, and I need to get him to Cooper's house.* She logged onto Arizona State's website, retrieving the information she'd need for her plan, and dialed Martin Baxter's number.

"Hello," he said, and he already sounded like he was in a hurry.

Story cleared her throat, threw her voice, and said, "Dr. Baxter? This is Harriet Johnson, in for Pauline at Merriam's office." Story was well-versed in pretending to be other people, so she sounded quite authentic as substitute secretary to Merriam Kane, head of the biology department and Martin's boss. "She wanted me to call you," Story said.

"Regarding . . ." he said.

"She needs you to meet with someone."

He sighed. "I'm leaving for an important expedition tomorrow, and I've still got so much to—"

"Yes, Ms. Kane knows, and she's terribly sorry to put you in a crunch this close to your trip, but she said it would mean the world to the department. And to her."

Martin sighed again. "Who is it? Who does she want me to meet with?"

Shit. I have no idea, thought Story.

"Oh, is it that Ph.D. candidate she had me call a while back?" said Martin.

"Yes!" Story said in her real voice. "Yes," she said, once again becoming Harriet, "that's right. She's having some trouble with her thesis."

"You mean *he*," Martin said with hesitation.

Story fumbled for more coffee. "Sorry, *he* is having some trouble with—"

"He's having trouble," said Martin, "because the dimwit can't tell the difference between an epiphyte and a neophyte . . . I told him to focus his research on cell death, but oh no, he was hell-bent on cell division, mitosis-loving bastard that he is. I mean, really! Have we not heard enough about identical daughter nuclei?!"

"I certainly have, sir," Story said via Harriet.

Martin's diatribe continued. "Chromosomal *pairings* . . . *double* helix, chemical *bonds*," he lamented. "No one wants to talk about the beauty of the *single* cell anymore, because they're so busy basking in their happy fucking couplings! And don't even get me started about overwrought photosynthesis. If I hear one more doctorate student defend chloroplasts, I swear to God . . ."

Letting out one more sigh, Martin said, more sadly, "It is a primal desire to see the perfect pairing—two things that truly belong together." A hint of hardened resignation enveloped his last declaration. "And all of this takes places under the perfect, goddamned setting sun, the source of all our strength and sustenance."

After a pause, alarming in its awkwardness, Story said, still in character, "Do you have a pen handy?"

"Sure," Martin said.

"Here's the *mitosis-loving bastard's* address," she said as equal parts Story and Harriet, giving him Claire Payne's home address.

And then Martin let out something that sounded like a chuckle. "When am I supposed—"

"That depends. When is your plane leaving?"

"Tomorrow. Eight in the morning."

"Well, you'll need to see him today, then. Three o'clock. I'll set it up. Thank you for doing this, Martin. Merriam thanks you."

After letting Claire Payne know she'd be coming by at three, Story called Angela Hahn, a travel agent friend of her mother's, to figure out which flight to take. "I'm confused," Angela said. "You don't know what city you want to fly into?"

Story snapped, "Just tell me which flight leaving the Phoenix Sky Harbor International Airport at 8 a.m. is headed toward South America." And then she mumbled, "Anywhere south, really."

"It's not that easy, Story. There are many connecting flights going to different places before they reach their final destination, and—"

"Look harder, Angela. Please?"

After some furious keyboard clicking, Angela said, "Okay. There's a Delta flight leaving at eight o'clock that picks up a connecting flight at LAX, switches to a TAM carrier in Lima, and arrives in Manaus, Amazonas, Brazil, at 8:12 p.m. their time—"

"That's it! Thank you, thank you! Book four tickets, Angela. Money's no problem—"

Angela laughed. "Story, money's not the problem here. You can't just up and go to Brazil with a day's notice."

"Why not? We all have passports—"

"Those passports need specific visa stickers for traveling to Brazil, and there's yellow fever to worry about, and what about lodging, and—"

"We'll figure out all those minor details later—"

"Minor details?" Angela laughed again.

"Just get us there, Angela, I'll figure everything else out." Story paused for a moment. "Could you take care of the little visa sticker thing?"

Angela let out a groan that said she would not.

"I'll make it worth your while," Story added. "*Really* worth your while."

And just as her mother had assured her, fairy godmothers don't carry wands, they carry checkbooks. "Okay," Angela said, "I know a guy, who knows a guy."

THIRTY

Finally, at the age of thirty, Story Easton was on the verge of greatness. By tomorrow, she would be standing in the heart of the Amazon rainforest, helping create a powerful, pivotal moment in Cooper Payne's life, fulfilling a promise made by the father who loved him.

But she still had to convince Martin Baxter to expand his travel party by three, and she still had to get someone to make a magic treasure box, and she still had to continue the *National Geographic* charade so Claire didn't get suspicious, all of this on top of wondering, every five minutes, what Hans's magic hands were touching—and was he thinking of her?

So what does a girl do when it's her against the world? She goes shopping, of course. On *The Best of Brazilian Travel Tips* website, Story had read what she needed for her travels, so at 10 a.m., when the mall opened, she headed out. She was so preoccupied with her big to-do list, she didn't even bother to comb her hair or change out of the ratty T-shirt and sweatpants she'd slept in. After all, she was going there to prepare for her trip, not to be photographed.

She was going to spend a lot of money, which was a first for her. So after arriving at the mall, enjoying the newfound luxury of buying things that weren't on sale (via her freshly-deposited trust fund), she purchased a big suitcase, complete with warranty and wheels, and began pulling it from store to store, throwing in necessities, like Gore-Tex walking shoes, and a safari hat with special mosquito netting.

At a nature store, she bought a fancy umbrella for Claire, a flashlight for Cooper, and a small hand-painted wooden egg for Hans, though she'd probably never give it to him. And because it felt like Christmas in October, she also picked up something for Martin—a pen with a wooden handle, carved into the shape of a curvy morning glory vine, and adorned with green leaves that looked like little hearts.

She treated herself at the food court's Mammoth Burger—home of the one-pound hamburger—wrapped up the half she couldn't eat, and stuffed it in the outside zipper of her suitcase. As she made her way through the mall, she walked past the bookstore, intrigued by what she saw propped up in the storefront window: *Once Upon A Moonflower* announced itself on a little white easel as she strolled by. Mini-mounds of fake grass, several cut-out trees, and one purple plastic fairy, which had fallen over, facedown in the grass, created a sad and hopeless synthetic forest. The book had been out for over a year, but the market offered nothing else like it, so the display had been maintained.

She entered the store rolling her giant, now heavy suitcase behind her. After accidentally crashing into a towering display of books, formerly stacked in a perfect stair-step pattern on the floor, she reached for Martin's book and knocked over a dozen different display books like a row of dominoes. She pulled her suitcase out of the other shoppers' way, pushed down the handle, and used the upright case as a makeshift seat. After placing her purse on the floor next to her, she sat down, opened the book, and tried to find where she'd left off.

A mousy store clerk with glasses and long, stringy hair approached her. "Can I *help* you?" she asked, clutching Stephen King's bloody *Carrie*, which needed to be re-shelved. The clerk stared at the wreckage, and also at Story's tattered outfit and half-eaten sandwich, peeking out of its pocket.

"No . . . thanks," Story said, not looking up, but flipping pages with each word she spoke, as if she were looking for the answer to an important riddle. "I . . . just . . . need . . . to . . . find . . . out . . . what . . . happens . . . to . . . the . . . fairy." She would soon be in the jungle with Cooper, and she'd need to know how the magic was supposed to unfold.

Though Story was too distracted to notice, she looked disheveled. So when the clerk softened her voice, winked, and whispered, "We're giving away free cookie samples in the back of the store, just past the *Story* area," Story didn't know, or care, why.

Focused only on the book, Story mumbled, "Invoking my name doesn't make me—"

"Pardon?" the clerk said. "That's our last copy, and it's not for sale, by the way."

"Shhhhh!" Flipping one page at a time, and skimming first through adventures with the sloth, then the snake, Story continued to try to find the last part that she'd read. "Where's the damn capybara . . ." she mumbled, still searching, until she found a spot close to where she'd left off. Story got more comfortable, repositioning herself on her suitcase, while the clerk lurked about, watching her every move.

With the capybara as my furry and dawdling (wicked-slow) taxicab, I rode for three hours, until he abruptly stopped next to a meandering river full of floating, colossal (gigantic) (big) lily pads.

"Don't dip your toes in the river," he said. "The caiman don't like it. Now the river moves fast, so you'll be able to reach the tree by—"

"You're leaving me? To float to my certain death?!"

His small, black eyes blinked once, and then he said, "All journeys require some solo effort. It was your wish. Don't you remember? 'I can do it myself!'" It was an annoyingly accurate impression of me. "'I'm not a baby anymore!'"

I swallowed. "But that was when my parents were hovering over me while I was doing my math homework." I folded my arms. "And wanting to walk to the mall by myself is not the same as—"

"When you get to the tree, it will still be light, so begin looking for it right away."

"For what? Looking for what?!"

My panic unsettled him. "The magic treasure box, of course," he said. "It will be hidden underneath leaves and roots, and on it you'll see an intricately carved kapok tree, the tree of life. Its lid will have a curvy, inviting handle made of several woody vines called lianas, interwoven in a braided arc. And shortly after you find the treasure box, you'll also find the moonflower." He paused and trembled, and fear enveloped (took over) his face. "Unless . . ."

"Unless that freaky fierce thing eats me! That's what you were thinking, weren't you?!" I said.

He seemed to search his mind for a comforting answer. After a moment, he shivered and squeaked out, "Yes."

"Who sends an unarmed eight year old into the jungle? Who's in charge around here? I wanna talk to the manager!" I yelled at him. "Who would that be?"

He hung his hairy head. "That'd be the Fierce One."

"*The one who wants to eat me? He's in charge?*" I nodded in angry defeat. "*Excellent.*"
"*Just figure out his riddles and you'll be fine.*"

I whimpered. *This was bad news. Riddles were my one weakness. They were Kryptonite to my otherwise impenetrable (impassable) intellect.* "*And what if I don't? Figure them out, that is?*"

Who knew a capybara could grimace?

"*Fine,*" *I sighed, resigned to doing enigmatic (unfathomable) (puzzling) battle with the beast.* "*How am I supposed to know when I get to this special tree?*"

"*You'll know.*" *His voice was soft but serious.* "*It is the most majestic tree of all, the tree of life—it is the keeper of the forest.*"

My face sobered. "*And if I do all this, if I do everything right, I get to go home. Right?*"

As soon as I said it, I knew, once again, I'd gotten ahead of myself.

"*First the treasure box, and then the moonflower,*" *he said, as he helped me aboard a lily pad so huge, even my imagination seemed surprised.*

"Ma'am?" the clerk said.

"Shhh," Story said, shooing her away like a fly. "She just jumped aboard a giant lily pad . . ." Story's right finger glided over the next page, forging furiously ahead to find where Hope discovered the treasure box. "Uh-oh," she said, her face twisting into a sincere expression of doom. "I think something really bad is going to happen."

"It is," the clerk said, directing Story's attention to a sign which read *No Loitering—Offenders Will Be Prosecuted.*

"You think I'm loitering?! This is a bookstore, is it not?" Story's tone became meaner and louder, as she thought about how much she still needed to get done today. "A place where one might find books, that one might want to *read*!" she said, still holding the book in her hand as if it were her own.

"Ma'am, please put the book down," the clerk said, backing away from Story as if she was armed.

Story tried to defuse the situation by lowering her voice, and the book. "Look, I'm sorry I yelled . . . and I'm sure you're sorry . . . for being such a bitch," said Story, "so why don't you just let me pay for the book, and I'll be on my way?"

In a bitter, definitive tone, the clerk said, "I told you. It's not for sale."

"What do you mean, it's not for sale?" Story said, walking toward the clerk and pointing to the price tag. "Nineteen-ninety-five. See, right there."

"It's a store copy," said the clerk.

"Well, you've got to have another!" Story said. "There's a display in the window!"

The clerk stood her ground and stared Story down. "We have the right to refuse service to anyone who we feel is—"

"Service? You call this service?" she said, shaking her finger in the clerk's face. "You . . . are a giant pain in my ass!" By now, the two of them stood at the center of the store in a face-off. Story, still clutching the book with her left hand, said, "Now, I'm going to go over by my bag, get my wallet, pay for this book, and leave."

As she turned to walk away, the clerk tried to grab the book. Story resisted at first, retaining the book in a death grip, but then the book slipped out of her grasp, and with no more resistance, the book's hard corner drove back into the clerk. With her face in her hands, the clerk dropped to the ground and screamed, "My nose!"

"Oh my God! I'm so sorry!" Story said, crouching down to help, while the clerk hid behind her own hands. "Here, let me see," Story said, trying to see the damage. When the clerk moved her hand, she revealed a snarling face smeared with blood.

And thanks to the other clerk who'd made the call, two prepubescent security officers with attitudes showed up just as the bloody clerk-victim, wearing a Sundance Books button that ironically read, *Hi, My Name Is Carrie*, yelled, "Get. Her. Away. From. Me!"

As one security guard, who looked barely eighteen, grabbed hold of Story and dragged her out of the store, the other one grabbed her suitcase. Story hollered, "My mother's a very important woman who will not be happy about this!" Her voice trailed behind in a blur of threats. "She's very rich and very mean! Beverly Easton—get to know that name!" And after remembering she was now rich, too, she yelled, "I could've spent a lot of money in this store!"

After escorting her to the mall security office, they told her she'd have to wait for the "local authorities," who were on their way. "The cops?!" Story shrieked, as they sat her down on a dirty couch in their office, where she imagined many a shoplifting teenager had sat. "Why are *they* coming?"

The taller one with a badge claiming he was "Rusty" read Story her shopping mall rap sheet. "Ma'am, you're charged with shoplifting, resisting arrest, assault—"

"With a deadly book? Are you kidding me?" She shook her head in defiance. "I was trying to pay for it! And I don't think I can technically be resisting arrest if you're not real police officers." After they scowled at her, she said, "No offense, but you don't need this mess. You need a babysitter."

"No offense, taken . . . *offender*," Rusty said, just as two police officers entered the office and put Story in handcuffs.

"Is this necessary?" she said, now bound and humiliated.

The stocky, olive-skinned officer, who looked a bit like Eric Estrada, put his hand on her wrist and said, "Just procedure, ma'am." He laughed, and added, "Don't have any more books on your person, do you?"

She rolled her eyes. "Yeah, I'm packin' a fully-loaded *Huck Finn* in my underwear."

The other officer threw a covert glance at her nice ass. For safety's sake.

After an embarrassing, extra-long frisking, a lengthy car ride, and a litany of stupid questions, Story found herself in front of a police station mug-shot camera, the last place she thought she'd end up on a simple shopping excursion. Treating it as if it was her driver's license, Story asked to see her final mug shot photo—an unusual request, but she figured it would be the only mug shot she'd ever have, and she wanted to look decent. Her half-smirk was the only cute thing about the picture. Hair—flat and lifeless. Lips—dry and cracked. And her outfit—so atrocious, it made the other criminals look fashion-forward.

In the middle of viewing her hideous picture, she heard her cell phone ring. It had been confiscated and stuck in a small bin of personal effects, which was stowed away on a shelf just a few feet away from the desk she sat behind. "That's my phone," she told Officer Sharpe, who was sitting in front of her, working on the incident report.

Dingaling.

"What?" he said, not looking up from the paperwork in front of him.

Dingaling.

"I need to get it. Don't I get one phone call? In the movies, the accused gets a phone call. I have rights, you know. I'm not sure you're following protocol, here, Officer Sharpe, and—"

Dingaling.

When he gave her the phone, she answered it with a loud, "Hello?!"

"Story, it's Angela. What are you up to?" Angela said.

"Oh, not much. What about you?" Story said, holding her phone with both cuffed hands.

"Well, the good news is I took care of the visas—"

"That's awesome! That's fan—"

"Wait. There's bad news."

"Okay," Story said, her bound hands now stuck together in prayer, while she used her neck and shoulder to clutch the phone.

"I'm so sorry I didn't see it when I first looked . . . It's so unfortunate . . . and actually quite surprising—"

"What?!"

Angela let out a defeated sigh. "The flight is full. I can't get you on it."

Story's stomach knotted up, putting her half-digested Mammoth Burger in an unforgiving chokehold. She looked around the police station, searching for a place to hide—any sort of metaphorical moonflower in which to curl up and smother herself to death would do—but with nothing of the sort in sight, she opted to steal a therapeutic phrase from a belligerent and feathered friend.

"Fuck it all!"

THIRTY-ONE

"**S**tory," Angela fired back, "you had to know this was an impossible situation. The passport itself has oodles of complications, not to mention how strict they're getting about immunizations, and . . ."

Story whispered to herself, "Whether I shall turn out to be the hero of my own life, or whether that station will be held by anybody else, these pages must show," then lifted her tiny phone up to her ear with her hands still fastened together by silver cuffs. "I need the passenger manifest for that flight, Angela," Story said, as if she was at the office asking someone for a pencil.

"You *what*?!" Angela said. "This trip is not going to happen for you, Story. With some more time, I'd be happy to—"

"Nope, no time. Need to be on that flight," Story said. She thought about the look on Cooper's face when she told him what he'd won, and she couldn't get it out of her head. "I need the passenger list, Angela."

Angela scoffed. "Sure. Okay. Totally reasonable request—illegal—but still, a really productive angle, especially since it can't possibly do you any good." Fully worked up by now, she said, snidely, "What? Are you gonna break into someone's house and steal their passports?"

Not a bad idea, Story thought, imagining herself sneaking through sliding glass doors and ransacking drawers, but she needed to take care of this before nighttime came. She'd have to devise another plan. "Just get me the passenger list, Angela."

"Do you have any idea how much trouble I could get into?"

"Get it, and I'll double what I gave you before."

"We're talking about losing my booking license, Story—"

"I'll triple it," said Story. "Last offer."

Slowly, Angela breathed a nervous sigh, and said, "Okay. I know a guy. Who knows an ex-con. Who works for an airline."

Officer Sharpe had heard from the bookstore owner that Story's mother was a multi-millionaire. After moving Story to a one-person holding cell with a small, lumpy cot, Sharpe, in hopes Beverly Easton's wealth might somehow benefit him, removed Story's handcuffs and let her keep her cell phone for more calls. Story dialed her mother, and after leaving five voicemail messages, came to the conclusion that by the time her workaholic mother found out she was in jail, she would've lost too much time. Story then tried Ivy, thinking she might help her if she agreed to come back to work for a while, maybe train a new writer. But after Story explained where she was, Ivy choked with laughter and reminded Story of her hideous infractions—arriving late every day, faking "monster" diarrhea, quitting a phenomenal job—and hung up on her.

But then a wave of humiliation started in Story's feet, traveled up to her gut, and settled hotly in her face when she realized there was one person left she could still call. But she couldn't really, could she? What she'd said to him came back to her in short, uncomfortable bursts. *You never stop fixing, do you? I'm not the one who needs saving.* Her face collapsed in her clammy hands. *We girls don't want to be saved or rescued.*

Maybe just today.

She dialed Hans's number. After barely a ring, Story heard his voice on the outgoing message. "If you need something fixed, you've reached the Fix-It-And-Forget-It Man, handyman extraordinaire. If you need a little magic in your life, you've reached Sleight of Hans, magician-for-hire." And then in true Hans fashion, he kept it short and sweet. "Talk to me."

Suddenly, Story Easton realized the composition of a perfect man: the rational dependability of someone who can fix anything, and the magical possibilities of a conjurer. *If you need magic in your life? Well, to be specific . . .*

The beep that followed was so abrupt, Story panicked.

"Shit. That was fast," she mumbled into the phone. "Uh, hey Hans. This is

Story." *Please don't erase this before you listen to the rest.* "How are you?" *I can't get your smile, your great ass, or your quiet charm out of my head.* "I'm, uh, in sort of a pickle." *Pickle?! Christ. I need your help. I need fixing. I need rescuing. I need saving. I need magic. I need everything I said I didn't.* "There was an incident . . ."—*brawl, misdemeanor, bloody mess*—". . . at Sundance Books in Park Ridge Mall because this bitch . . ." *I am not a violent stalker.* ". . . Anyway, oh, God, this sucks, I am such an ass . . . I'll just spit it out. I'm in—"

BEEP!

"No!" Story threw her cell phone down on the concrete cell floor, and then checked to see if she'd broken it. *Oh, God.* "Hello?" *Crap.* Dial tone.

Story dialed Hans's number a second time and felt a hint of vomit make its way up to her mouth. After hearing his message again, she stammered, "Sorry. Got cut off. I'm, um, sitting in a jail cell in Mesa . . . It's no big deal . . . I'm sure this will all work itself out . . . but I'm trying to make travel plans for . . . well, you know where . . ."

Suddenly, Story shook her head and said, "Forget it, forget what I said before. You . . . are . . . really lovely." *Ugh.* "And I wanted you to know . . ." *I don't deserve you rescuing me.* ". . . I can't think of anyone else I'd rather have trying to fix me." *Oh, God. Did that sound perverted? I did say "fix," right?* After a long pause, Story decided to quit while she was behind.

"Bye."

Story never would have guessed she could get real, quality sleep inside a jail cell, but as she waited, two hours turned into three, and when the long day's stress caught up with her, her head hit the pillow-less cot and she fell into a deep, strange slumber. Her dream took place in the Amazon rainforest, an imaginary Amazon based on pictures she'd seen. Story, clad in nothing but a deep purple cape, ran naked through the jungle, trying to get away from a twenty-foot tall castrated Santa with his fluffy innards hanging off him and trailing in the jungle breeze.

Suddenly, Santa morphed into a giant Easter Bunny with huge, exaggerated paws, and as Story hid behind a big tree, the maniacal bunny hurled big colored eggs at her head. When Story raised her black and white wand in an effort to combat her foe with magic, she discovered the wand was nothing but a stick with weak, blurry stars, incapable of anything supernatural.

Even in her dream, Story heard her mother's voice. *Magic is rubbish.* But before she had a chance to see how the story would end, she heard a faint key jingle-jangle outside her cell.

"Ma'am, you're free to go," an officer said as he swung the barred door open.

"Hello?" Story mumbled, and got to her feet, sleepy-eyed and disoriented. "What happened?" She rubbed her eyes, and smoothed back her hair. "Did my mother come?"

The tall officer wearing a badge that said *Hudson* shook his head, and when he said, "Nope," a surprising smile enveloped his face, contrasting with his stiff, unforgiving uniform. "This place is so . . . It's nice to have some fun once in a while," he said, almost apologetically. He reached into his front uniform pocket and removed its contents with his left hand.

In the center of his weathered, slightly unsteady hand sat a small wooden egg—ocean-blue and vibrant.

Story fixed her gaze on the egg, and stared at it so long, she imagined her green eyes filling up with azure seas. She was not crying, and there were no tears—there were never tears—but there was maybe gratitude, maybe regret, maybe love, and at the height of it, she envisioned other people, the kind capable of crying.

It is a fact that at any given point in time, an estimated three hundred thousand people, out of the planet's seven billion, are simultaneously crying somewhere in the world. Four percent cry out of fear, seven percent for sympathy, ten percent from anger, and the remaining sixty-nine percent? The majority of humans cry as a response to sadness or happiness, and as Story looked at the little blue egg, she realized that in life, the two emotions, supposedly opposite, are often inseparable.

Moments away from seeing Hans again, Story attempted to make herself presentable. "Did he post bail?" she said. "Did he bring a lawyer?"

As they walked down a small corridor toward the main office area, Officer Hudson gave her an incredulous look, which reminded Story who Hans was—a salt-of-the-earth guy who valued good old-fashioned common sense over money. "Nah," the officer said. "No lawyer. No bail. Just him. Somehow, he got the lady you beat up to drop the charges—"

"I did not beat her up. She is a fucking liar!" Story snapped in a loud, violent tone, sounding exactly like someone who should be imprisoned for assault.

The officer grabbed Story's arm, stopped in the middle of the hallway, and stared at her beautiful lips. "You talk to your mother with that mouth?"

Yes. Much worse, actually, but we're making progress in our relationship. "No," she said, and when he continued his stare, she added, "sir."

And then, as if nothing had happened, he let go of her arm and began walking and laughing at the same time. "Quite the magician, that guy," he said. "I ended up hiring him for the Oktoberfest block party I'm hosting tonight—damn clown I signed up cancelled this morning. But this guy's way better than a stupid clown. He made three different sets of handcuffs disappear."

Handcuffs? Story's face became flush, thinking about whether Hans had retained them for personal use.

"And it was such a slow day, he even fixed Pete's chair," Hudson said. "Didn't ask for a dime. Didn't say anything, actually. Helluva guy."

Story released her long hair from a disheveled, slept-on pony tail, and prepared to embrace her liberator. "Is he this way?" she asked, as they walked toward the main desk.

"No," the officer said, taking a bite of an apple he'd grabbed from the counter. "He left shortly after he got here."

A familiar sense of emptiness returned to Story, and as she stopped moving, she also tried to stop feeling. "Oh," she said. There was a long pause. "Did he say *anything?*"

"Not really," said the officer. "But . . ." And the officer began laughing again, this time more of an astonished laugh. "He left something for you. Normally, we don't allow this sorta thing, leaving items, you know, we just don't have the room, and there's liability—"

"Left what? What is it?" Story said, grabbing the officer's hand.

He looked down at his hand and glared until she released her grip.

"It's the damnedest thing," Hudson said. "Never seen anything like it. Quite the craftsman. He really is—"

"A helluva guy." Story nodded. *I know.*

The officer pointed to five other officers crouched down by the floor, near the personal effects cubbies attached to the far wall. They were looking at something, admiring something, and Story wondered what could so enthrall five middle-aged men. *It's too big to be a Playboy*, she thought. *Too small to be a TV. Too exciting to be a six-pack.* The officer led her back to them, and she noticed they were all completely silent. Maybe it was the way the saturated Phoenix sunlight poured through the large window nearby, or maybe it was something else, but golden, dazzling sunbeams weaved in and out of the five onlookers, bouncing off them as if the object they admired was the sun itself, lassoed from the sky for close inspection. The men's worn, whiskered faces were aglow with light and warmth, and they wore peaceful gazes—the kind you see on a child's face when he's witnessed something mystical.

As Story moved closer to the object, two of them got up and created a space for her. She inched her way in, but the view was still obstructed.

"What is it?" she said, unsure if she'd said it out loud.

And there it was. Like a piece of art on display at a museum, it sat proudly on the floor. With a handle made of carved vines, the majestic kapok tree came to life with each twist and turn, all of it freshly carved from deep, dark wood. African Blackwood. *Heartwood, not sapwood*, she remembered, feeling as if she could almost cry. Almost. But she knew Hans was right. Heart always trumps sap.

"It's a box," one of the officers said, looking at the beautiful and intricate lid, entwined with scores of creeping lianas vines and one giant kapok tree, "but don't get your hopes up. The story ends there. It's empty."

And when Story could finally see the beauty that lay before her, she closed her eyes for a moment, fixing the image into her mind for easy recall in future times of doubt. And then, as one rogue cloud cast a cool shadow over the box, Story called upon a host of make-believe notions—fairy godmothers, enchanted journeys, magic wands, *abracadabra*—to give her the strength she'd need to properly fill a magic treasure box.

THIRTY-TWO

A fter leaving the police station, the treasure box safely in her arms, Story took a cab to retrieve her car, and drove straight to Claire Payne's home, arriving with five seconds to spare, and just as Martin was pulling in. When he recognized Story behind him, he tried backing his car out of the driveway, but hers was blocking him.

"No, please. Just wait. Let me explain," Story said, hopping out of her car and knocking on his window.

In one swift, impatient maneuver, Martin shifted to park, rolled down his window, and mumbled, "I should've known a graduate student didn't live in a house this nice." When he got a look at Story's outfit, he said, "Glad to see you dressed up." He took a deep breath of the pseudo-country air laced with car exhaust. "Look, I get it. You're tenacious and you have a goal. I respect that, but—"

"His dad died," Story blurted out while leaning into the window. And when she had his attention, she continued, "Your book was the last book his dad ever read to him, and it's part of him now . . . your words are part of him." She stared into Martin Baxter's sad eyes. "Just introduce yourself, and maybe sign the book for him?"

Martin Baxter looked at his watch, then up at the oversized dollhouse with the inviting porch. "Ten minutes. And I'm not taking this kid on a goddamned vision quest in the jungle," he said, turning off the ignition.

"Got it," Story said, just happy to get him out of the car. While they walked up the sidewalk toward the wraparound porch, Story said, "By the way, I'm a botanist, too. And I work for *National Geographic*."

"Fine," he said, shaking his head.

When Claire Payne opened the door, she grinned, something she hadn't done a lot lately. A day away from the office, plus the prospect of making her son smile again, was enough to make her hostility disappear—so much so, she hadn't said the "F" word in three hours. "Hey, Story, we're pretty much packed, and . . ."

She stopped to stare at Martin. Her smile grew wider when she said, "Hello," and tucked her hair behind her ears as she did whenever she was nervous. "You must be the plant genius Story was telling us about."

Against his better judgment, Martin Baxter cracked a smile. "She's being inflammatory."

"No, really," Claire said, showing her enthusiasm. "I think it's fantastic we'll have such an expert with us on the trip."

"I'm actually not—"

"He's actually not . . . here to talk about the trip," Story said. "I have a surprise for you."

Claire beamed. "Another one? I don't know if I can take any more surprises," she said, still glancing at Martin with a curious eye. "Sorry, I don't know what I'm waiting for—come in, come in. I'll get us some drinks."

They walked through the entryway, past the collection of umbrellas, and after seating her guests and fetching their drinks, Claire sat down on the couch across from them. "Well . . ." she said, throwing her hands in the air.

"I know Martin from my work at the magazine," Story said, "but you know him, too. You just don't know you do."

After Claire gave her a confused look, Story said, "Claire, meet Martin Baxter."

Claire's smile left her face. She'd heard his name every night for the last year, and it wasn't that she didn't recognize it, but more that she didn't know how to react. After all, he'd been Claire's stiffest competition for months. She'd cursed him and his damn book so many times, she wondered if somehow he knew. "So, you're the one," she said, still staring, but now with a softer gaze.

After an awkward silence, Martin finally said, "Story tells me your son Cooper might like me to sign his book."

As Claire continued to stare, Cooper came bounding down the stairs and into the living room with *Once Upon A Moonflower* tucked under his left arm. "Story!" he yelled. He then added a casual "Hey," trying to sound cool instead of excited. "I was just trying to fit my book in my . . ." He trailed off, spotting Martin.

"Hey, Sport," Story said. "I have someone I think you'd like to meet."

"Okay," he said.

"Cooper," Story said, "this is Martin Baxter." She looked at Cooper in anticipation.

Without blinking, Cooper cocked his head to the side in a skeptical tilt. The moment dragged on until, finally, Cooper said, "What did Hope eat with her dad on Sunday mornings?"

"Cooper . . ." said Claire.

"No, it's all right," Martin said. He looked Cooper in the eye and let out a sigh of regret disguised as a mere breath. "They ate chocolate-chip pancakes. Together."

Something in the way Martin said *together* turned doubtful Cooper into a believer, but still Martin added, "And at her grandmother's she ate meatloaf." He smiled. "But she didn't like it very much."

And then a dreamy-eyed Claire joined in, taking in all of Martin, the man whose words she knew as if they were her own. "First the treasure box," she said softly, "then the moonflower."

"It's really you," said Cooper, sitting down between Martin and Story, the book on his lap. "You're Hope's dad."

Martin Baxter glanced down at the book's cover, which featured a two-dimensional version of the delicate blonde fairy he still saw in his dreams.

When Martin didn't answer, Cooper sat up straighter, and said again, "You're Hope's—"

"Yes, babe," Claire said, eyes on Martin. She recognized the look in Martin's eyes. It was a look she'd seen in her own eyes on the rare occasions when she looked in the mirror. To most, it would appear as mere sadness, but to someone linked with unimaginable loss, it's recognized as an unrelenting ache, present every second of every day, leaving only when their tired eyes . . . rest. It was then that Claire knew Hope had left Martin Baxter's life.

As Martin stared at the book cover, Claire said, "There's a Hope that lives in the story, in the forest." And she felt the tender twinge which she and Martin both shared flare up as she said, "And there was a real Hope."

"Real?" Cooper asked, confused by the notion of an unreal Hope.

Martin dismissed himself to the kitchen to dull the sharp reality. He pulled a small flask from his cargo pant pocket, poured bourbon into his iced tea, and drank it down. His throat was still warm from the burn when Claire entered the kitchen. "Those two are busy sharing their visions for the trip," she said, smiling anxiously. She joined him as he leaned on the center island. "I'm sorry about Cooper. He feels like he knows Hope, so . . ."

"He would've liked her," he said, taking another drink. "Everyone did."

Before she knew it, another apology came out of her mouth. "I'm so sorry about her."

"*Them*," he said, staring at his hands. "You're so sorry about *them*."

Even before the sound of the word had ceased to resonate, Martin's doubly tragic sorrow hit Claire in the gut. In an instant, she saw the solemn policeman at her door asking, "Are you Mrs. Payne?" and the sympathy cards with big, billowing flowers, abundant and full of life. She suddenly felt guilty for being paralyzed over just one loss, and she wondered how the hell this man got out of bed every day. The psychiatrist in her felt obligated to ask him where he was in the grieving process: denial, anger, acceptance? But the widow in her—the part that identified with the anguish of losing a lover, and who knew that on most days, the grieving stages were reduced to *sad*, *pissed*, and *fucking sad and pissed*—asked him a more realistic question.

"Need a Zanax?" Claire said, popping a little white pill in her mouth, careful not to use the word *want*, because that's the thing about grief—there's no energy left for want, only need.

"No. Thanks," Martin answered. He took out his flask again, reloaded his drink, and smiled. "Having a bad day?"

She looked at her watch, and laughed. "Let's see. Yeah, several . . . hundred bad days in a row. What are the odds?"

Martin nodded.

Claire fell deep in thought. "Haven't had a truly good day since . . ."

"June 20th, 2011," they said in unison, their voices trailing off as they realized yet another horrific fact they shared.

THIRTY-THREE

David Payne, Katherine Baxter, and Hope Baxter all died during the tenth hour on the twentieth day of the sixth month. It happened to be a Monday, the second day of the week, and although many other numbers are connected with the hour of their deaths—one phone call, two vehicles, four onlookers—it is the number three which is important. What sparked the tragic string of events was a three-minute conversation between Jake Harmon, a strung-out twenty-one year old, already high at ten in the morning, and his father Jim, driving his semi-truck down Portland's I-5.

Jake called his father, who, as always, was on the road. Perhaps the call was Jake's ill-fated attempt at being talked down from the proverbial ledge, or maybe it was to say goodbye, but either way, Jim Harmon sensed the desperation in his son's voice, and spoke into his cell phone, trying to sound fatherly. "Calm down, son" and "Don't do anything stupid" were the last things he said before he heard a gunshot. Startled by the fact that his only son had either shot himself or someone else, Jim Harmon looked down at his phone in disbelief—and then, trying to right his now swerving twenty-ton truck, he drove, head on, into Katherine Baxter's Subaru. The massive force of the collision collapsed the car in one split-second, reducing it to a compressed accordion, melding it onto the truck's front grill as a permanent fixture, and crushing and killing Katherine and Hope Baxter on impact.

The girls had been on their way to Portland's annual Rose Festival to see, as advertised, three thousand roses, of every variety and color, thriving in the city's shady, moist climate. Katherine, not enamored of flowers, loved how her husband and daughter took delight in them, and facilitated their enjoyment of them whenever she could. Three seconds before the accident, Katherine Baxter, out of nowhere, was struck by the beauty of her lucky, charmed life—a husband she adored and a daughter she lived for—and by chance felt compelled to tell

Hope, who was leaning against her window, soaking up hints of sun, how she felt. "I love you," she said, and then it all ended.

Three minutes.

Three thousand roses.

Three seconds.

Three words.

Three people—ceasing to be.

And three weeks later, after Martin Baxter and Claire Payne had finally realized it was not just a horrific nightmare, but a real-life horror, Martin watched the Portland roses wilt, and Claire found herself enveloped by hundreds of post-funeral roses, all dying.

But neither Claire nor Martin knew the particulars which connected them, because life doesn't always provide them. It simply waits until those inevitably linked manage to find each other.

After saying *June 20th, 2011* aloud, they chose not to discuss it, but rather leave it to coincidence, and as they stood together in Claire's kitchen, bonded by one fateful day, Claire put her hand on top of Martin's, only for a second, to feel how someone else's pain felt. She decided it felt a lot like hers.

When Martin looked up at her, she removed her hand and focused her attention out the kitchen window, to the backyard, at five paloverde saplings. She and David had planted them two weeks before he died. In her grief-stricken state, she'd neglected them, and now three of them were weak, brown, and on the brink of death.

"*Cercidium floridum,*" Martin said under his breath as he looked out at the five saplings. "Two of them are going to make it—if you take care of them. They'll bloom soon. Little yellow flowers."

Martin studied Claire's glistening skin and thought about how all women look different in different light. Claire's skin became almost translucent, with a trace of shimmer, in direct sunlight. Fighting the allure, he broke his gaze, and directed his attention back to the trees outside. The hardiest trees, the two on the end that showed the most hope for survival, stood together.

He used his eyes to direct Claire's attention to the trees, which reached for the sun. *They might make it*, Martin thought, *if they let the sun do its job.* It was, simply, the nature of things.

THIRTY-FOUR

Claire and Martin left the kitchen together and rejoined Cooper and Story in the living room. Cooper looked at Martin and held up the book "Would you sign it?" he asked, as Story handed Martin the pen she'd bought for him at the mall.

When he noticed the wooden morning glories adorning the pen, he let his fingers glide over the petals and the heart-shaped leaves, and for the first time in a long time, the urge to smile felt stronger than the urge to cry. "Sure," he said, opening the book's cover and signing the inside. *For Cooper . . .* he wrote. And then, he asked Cooper a question he often asked when he was signing books: "What do you want to be when you grow up, Cooper? What do you see in your dreams?"

Cooper looked up at Martin with wide-open eyes. "My dad said as soon as I found the magic treasure box," he said, letting out a slightly embarrassed laugh, "we'd run around with our grown-up flashlight, and lead everyone out of the jungle." He paused for a moment, then added, "And *then* he said I would be a Rainforest Superhero."

Cooper added one more thing, in a matter-of-fact tone, as if he were asking for a second glass of milk. "But I think I want to be a regular hero. Like him."

Story bit her lip to keep her cool, and Martin Baxter concentrated on finishing the inscription. *To Cooper . . . A super kid and Superhero any dad would be proud of. – Martin Baxter.*

Cooper's face lit up when he read it. When Claire looked at Martin, her question came out more like a plea. "So," she said, "will you be coming with us to the—"

"Definitely," Martin said, walking toward Claire. When he was close enough to look into her eyes and see his own reflection, he said, "We're going to find the treasure box *and* the moonflower."

"And he'll point out all of the plants he's researched for *National Geographic*," said Story. "It's all part of the prize."

As Cooper, excited, tore up the stairs to finish packing, Claire stared into Martin's eyes and said, "Thank you. From both of—"

"It's gonna be a great trip," he interrupted, before Claire could mention her husband.

On the way out to their cars, halfway down the porch stairs, Story smirked. "So I guess you changed your mind about taking the kid on a *goddamned vision quest* in the jungle."

Martin smiled. "Guess I did." He turned to her. "How the hell did you get everyone on my flight?"

I didn't . . . yet, she thought. *But I will.* "I work best under pressure," Story said as she walked across the gravel driveway.

When he reached his car, Martin sighed. "We're gonna need a box, you know—"

"Yeah," Story said proudly, thinking of Hans's masterpiece. "Kapok tree and all."

Martin gave her a look bordering on respect. "So, you read it."

"Pretty much," Story said. "I ran into some trouble at the bookstore, so I still don't know how it ends."

With his hand resting tentatively on his door handle, he said to her, "Every *good* story has more than one possible ending."

Story nodded, feeling particularly *good*, and walked to her car, thinking about what was left of the day. In her mind, she raised a glass and made a toast.

To good stories and happy endings.

THIRTY-FIVE

There is an urban legend involving, of all things, a simple dollar bill. People all over the countryside like to tell the story because it reminds them that everyone and everything, even a worn and wrinkled dollar, has a destiny, and that the millions of souls roaming the planet are undeniably connected.

The story goes like this: A man meets a beautiful woman and, wanting to impress her when it's time to say goodbye, takes a dollar bill from his pocket and makes a declaration. "If we are meant to be together," he says, "this dollar bill, this very dollar bill, will find its way back to you." Smiling, the woman asks how she will know it is the *very* dollar bill, so the man tells her he'll mark it with something indelible. And when the woman gives the man a desirous, yet skeptical look, inquiring, "How long will I have to wait?" and "Where do you suppose I will come in contact with it again?", he shakes his head. On the top edge of the bill he writes in red ink, *Live for the journey, not the destination*, shows it to her, adds the date when she coyly lowers her head, then holds it in the air and lets it float out of his hand. He kisses her and walks away before the bill hits the floor.

A month passes. Then a year, two years, five years. Long after the woman, now focused on her own journey, has forgotten about it, she receives the dollar bill back as change after buying a newspaper on a street corner, and as she observes the familiar red lettering from so long ago, she realizes she has never really forgotten about it, only tucked it deep inside, where secret dreams reside. Minutes later, with the dollar bill still in her pocket, the shocked woman sees the man from her past, older, but definitely the same man. What she doesn't know is that this hopelessly romantic man, to increase his unrealistic odds, had written the same red-lettered phrase on every dollar bill that had passed through his hands for the last seven years. Finally, one had come back to her. But what he didn't know was that the dollar bill in her pocket was the very one he'd written on seven years ago, because some paths are meant to cross.

What the dreamy reunited couple didn't know was that the scores of inspired, red-lettered bills with their message of living for the journey had affected hundreds of other people. After a young woman saw the message on her dollar bill, she viewed it as a striking revelation and left her bitter marriage to open a much sweeter pastry shop. After a workaholic father saw the message on his dollar bill, he took the advice to heart and gave up working twelve-hour days to take his son on a year-long sailing trip instead. Every recipient received the message at just the right time in their life's journey, and found the strength to let go of the past and alter the future.

When a young Hans Turner first heard this story from his idealistic mother, he secretly cherished it, and just like his mother and young Greta, he believed in the warm safety net of fate. But after losing Greta, when fate had its way with Hans and his once-charmed life, he no longer found the story enchanting. In fact, when he heard the same story years later in college from an overly optimistic, pony-tailed blonde, he was unimpressed. "The man should've just gotten the woman's damn phone number in the first place," Hans scoffed. "Would've saved him a lot of red ink."

Now, as Hans sat at his kitchen table, holding a greenback he would use in his magic gig in an hour, he thought of the red-lettered dollar bill story. He thought about his sister. He thought about people who exit our lives when we least expect it. He thought about people who suddenly enter our lives, changing the way we look at the world forever. And then he thought about Story, and his hands ached. *Did she get the treasure box?* he wondered. *Does it look like the one described in the book? Has she assaulted anyone else in the last two hours?*

And then, as an act of faith, or perhaps as a tribute to Greta, the princess who danced in his memory and hovered in his future, but mostly for Story, who made him want to experiment with happily-ever-afters, Hans Turner found a red felt-tip marker and inscribed on the bill a message he thought held some truth, but one he knew would be unread and therefore insignificant.

Hans packed up his magic gear and headed for Officer Hudson's annual Oktoberfest party. This was a big gathering, so in his head, Hans planned out a few extra tricks he could perform in whatever location Officer Hudson and his wife set aside for him. Hans drove east on the interstate, and let out a deep sigh when he recalled what Officer Hudson had told him when he called with directions. "We won't put you by the pool. We want to keep the guests out front," he'd said.

Of course there was a pool. It was blazing hot in Phoenix. Lots of people had pools. But it was ironic. Hans had left watery Florida to get away from its many bodies of water—ocean water, lake water, raging river water—and he'd moved west to the driest place on the map, hoping to leave his memories of water behind.

After checking in his side mirror to change lanes, he caught a glimpse of the simple, black-lettered sign on his truck—*Fix-It-And-Forget-It Man*—and for the first time since he'd purchased it, Hans found it laughable. In a flash of courage brought on by the bold Phoenix sun streaming through his truck window, he knew it was, in fact, a lie. Half of it, anyway. The *Fix It* part was accurate, but the *Forget It* part was a crock of shit and he knew it. He knew right then, on that October afternoon, that he could fix, but he could not forget, no matter how hard he tried. Every day, without acknowledging it, he drowned himself in deep-water memories of a vibrant river princess, and each time his guilt surfaced, he attempted to rescue anything—anyone—in his path.

When he reached Hudson's house, Hans realized he'd performed in this neighborhood before. He recognized the street, Sunset Drive, and wondered what it would be like to inhabit a street named after a sunset—an event in nature that implied an *ending*—and every morning look at a street sign that contradicted the dawn.

After Hans covered his *Fix-It-And-Forget-It* sign with his *Sleight of Hans* sign, he collected his shiny gray toolbox and approached the house. He followed the sidewalk, which meandered through a crowd of people—dozens of kids, some with hula-hoops, some kicking soccer balls, and several adults mingling by a large buffet table overflowing with bratwurst and potato salad. Hanging from the table was a sign that read "Welcome to the Hudsons' Annual Oktoberfest Block Party." Officer Hudson wiped his hands and came from behind the table to greet Hans.

"Hey, thanks for doing this. The kids are gonna flip," he said, giving Hans a strong, authoritative handshake. After observing Hans's retro tux and unconventional magic trick carrier, he smiled. "Way cooler than a clown."

The two of them walked to an empty table in the front yard, which would be Hans's makeshift stage and designated performance area, and after some brief setup, Hans began his quiet but spectacular show. At first, nobody paid attention, but within a few minutes, an audience gathered, one by one, to watch him pull flower bouquets out of nowhere and create little blue eggs from nothing. Soon, the majority of the guests stood, mesmerized, in front of Hans, and watched him silently work his magic amidst the din of laughter and party music coming from two large speakers.

Hans's hands, as usual, were his voice; each fluid movement acted as a sentence, a thought, some utterance that needed no sound, only feeling. Pulling a card or holding a small blue egg was simply a series of hanging on and letting go, and on the stage, at least, he was good at doing both. He found comfort in long, drawn-out dramatic moments—his strong grip was the key to making magic. A subtle repositioning of a finger, or a delicate change of his hand position, spoke volumes, and at least one person was listening. Really listening.

As Hans held up the dollar, displaying its authenticity and its special red markings before he attempted to make it disappear, a sweet voice hollered, "Dollar fuck!" Not everyone heard the comment over the other party noises, but Hans did. And he knew it was not a solicitation for an inexpensive sexual act, but an uncontrollable blurt from an old friend who, accompanied by her parents, had walked five blocks to the annual block party. Sarah Hartsinger stood three rows back in the gathered crowd, and when her sorry eyes met Hans's, she and Hans exchanged smiles.

But before the smile faded, she cried, accidentally, "It's fake! It's all f-f-fake!" She looked sorry, and embarrassed, as the word hung in the festive air.

The crowd gasped, but when they returned their focus to Hans, he looked back at Sarah, shook his head, and then flashed a mysterious grin, at her and at the rest of the audience.

With the dollar bill clutched tightly, Hans's hands danced, exploding like a shimmering firework with a blue-sky backdrop. And just like that—*poof!*—the dollar bill disappeared into the warm Arizona air.

That is, until Hans mimed a request for the audience members to check their pockets. A yardful of hands checked work pants pockets, skirt pockets, jacket pockets. But then one lucky recipient reached into her pocket and pulled out the dollar bill—the same one, with the red-letter message. The crowd went silent when they saw what had happened. Jaws dropped. A low murmur swept through the yard as the music was silenced. With all eyes on Sarah Hartsinger, nerves revolted and her subconscious took her hostage.

"Magic . . . bitch dollar!" she blurted, looking at the dollar bill, adorned with a red-letter message. Then, in a series of detonations, she blew. "October . . . fuck . . . fest!" Sarah Hartsinger mouthed *sorry* and walked slowly toward the Hudsons' front door.

Hans propped up a sign indicating a brief show intermission, and although the party was still in full force—kids continued to run about, the music resumed—Hans felt consumed by Sarah's personal pain, and suddenly felt stupid about the message he'd written on the dollar bill. He rubbed the dull ache from his hands, thinking about how Sarah was twelve years old, the age when you don't want to be told what to do, and the age when the word *journey* is as intangible as the sun.

Then a sense of immediacy overcame Hans, and he began walking toward the Hudsons' house, retracing Sarah's steps as if she'd become lost in some metaphorical woods, and would need help finding the right path. The party noises faded away as Hans looked first in the kitchen, then the family room. Finally, after checking in a dining area, he walked past glass French doors and caught a glimpse of something in the backyard.

Through peripheral vision, Hans sensed an unnatural presence—a vast stretch of shimmering turquoise so blue the azure sky paled in comparison. And while Hans's body was still in motion, before he had a chance to acknowledge his aversion to water, he saw her. Perched on the pool's unforgiving edge, Sarah Hartsinger leaned forward, extending her right arm toward something floating inches out of her reach.

Before Hans could say a word, Sarah reached too far, and her bright blue T-shirt disappeared into the too-blue water.

"Sarah!" Hans ran toward the pool with his arm outstretched, and his hand, now throbbing, was open wide, ready for Sarah to grasp it. But as Hans reached the pool's edge, he watched in amazement and horror as Sarah sank in slow motion like a lifeless doll thrown overboard, falling through deep ocean waters. *She fell into the deep end. Of course.* Near them was a jumping rock, the aesthetic answer to an ugly diving board, and by the deep, saturated blueness of the pool, Hans assessed it was the extra deep kind, safe for diving.

She had gasped a couple of times, trying to keep her head above water, but there had been no flailing, no thrashing about, as one might expect from someone who was drowning. Most people would expect that. Most people had no experience with this type of thing. But Hans was not most people; ever since the battle lost with the Crystal River, he'd avoided all water and the dirty word, in all its forms, that usually accompanied it. *Like a drowned rat. Drown your sorrows. Drowning in regret.*

Instinct told Hans that if he offered his hand, she would somehow make her way to the surface, and he'd help her to the safety of the poolside concrete. But he soon realized that was not going to happen. What he didn't know was that Sarah Hartsinger couldn't swim. She couldn't float on her back. She couldn't even tread water. Having been banned from swim lessons after an episode of repetitive, slightly unintelligible, yet still profane, commentary at the age of four, she was the only twelve year old on the block who skipped pool parties and refused to frequent the nearby water park.

"Hang on, Sarah!" Hans hollered, not sure if she could hear him. He dove into the pool and swam down to where she floated, her shiny brown hair waving in the water like silky seaweed. She was still sinking, inch by inch, but now she made slight movements with her arms, and looked up toward the surface where the sun tried to break through. Sarah had held her breath—she'd managed that much—and now looked like a puffer fish, cheeks bursting, eyes bulging a bit.

Hans grabbed her and held her tight, and as they traveled up, up, up toward the sun, he looked at Sarah and saw something in her eyes that he'd seen before— not in *her* eyes, but in another's. It's difficult to describe what peace looks like. For a moment, time ceased to be, and Hans heard voices. One was his own.

I'm sorry.

I know.

My hand . . . I tried to hold out—

But you never let go. I did. It's okay.

Okay?

To let go.

Okay.
This is why you were there.
This?
This.

As they approached the surface, Hans looked at a tranquil Sarah, who looked back at him. And then he knew—he had been there so that the last face she saw before she floated out of his life forever . . . was *his*. When he remembered her eyes, he saw not fear, but hope, and realized she wasn't in distress. *None of them was.*

And then time resumed. The sun broke free from the clouds, the throbbing in Hans's hands stopped for a moment, and Hans and Sarah emerged through the water's surface together, strong and buoyant. When sunbeams hit Hans's skin, they seemed to come from a completely different orb than had lit his world for the past thirty-two years.

Hans loosened his grip on Sarah as they made their way toward the pool's edge, allowing her to move her own arms a little. And as the finale of his best trick ever, he gently placed Sarah on the concrete patio. Still catching her breath, Sarah gasped, "I . . . take . . . it . . . back. You're actually . . . a really good . . . magician."

Hans laughed as he collapsed onto the concrete.

"No . . . really." She concentrated on breathing in and out, and when she felt her voice might betray her, she remembered the beautiful silence under the water. "That's why . . . I fell . . . in the pool—I was reaching . . . for that."

Hans turned his head as Sarah pointed to what she had accidentally let out of her hands—a saturated dollar bill, perfectly flat, floating on the surface of the water. It bobbed a little when insignificant ripples traveled beneath it, but it remained in one spot, anchored like a small green island in a sea of blue. From where they stood, they could faintly see the series of red letters beginning to bleed into the water, but while *destination* had all but disappeared, *journey*, the darker of the two words, remained.

Hans searched for his own words, but it was Sarah, getting to her feet, who spoke in a clear, strong voice, "If magic is real . . ." She let out one big sigh.

By now, the dollar, having drifted to the pool's edge, bumped into the tiled side in sync with the gentle lapping of undulating water. Sarah leaned over and picked it up, careful not to rip it, and held it flat in her hand. She felt the sun drying her shirt.

Offering her hand to Hans, Sarah looked forward at the pebbled path of stepping-stones leading them away from the water. Soon, the two of them, drenched in chlorinated water, re-entered the party as new guests.

After some simplified explanations of what had happened, Hans finished his magic show wearing a pair of Officer Hudson's plaid golf pants and an old police academy T-shirt. When it came time to say goodbye, Sarah handed Hans the dollar bill, now dry and without its message.

"Keep it," Hans said. "Make a new message."

And in her head, Sarah formed many messages, all clear and unfaltering.

But as Hans breathed in the happy moment, it tasted bittersweet. And then like a good plot twist, his hands began to ache again. Minutes earlier, Hans had discovered the answer to the question he'd asked his whole life, only to replace it with another question. If he was finally able to let go of his past, why did he feel as if something was missing from his future?

At last, he knew why he was here. But he could not help wondering how he got there, and he could not stop thinking about who had brought him. He retraced the last leg of his journey. The Paynes' broken door, a police station, an unexpected magic gig and reunion with Sarah—all linked together by one beautiful stranger who somehow made him want to stop saving everyone else and save himself.

And then there was the treasure box, and the tiny wooden machete: real art crafted for a real muse.

Hans looked as if he'd just figured out a riddle and wanted to say something, so with a teasing smile, Sarah asked, "Are you gonna tell me a story?"

Suddenly the idea of a story, in-progress and able to be revised, made his hands stop throbbing for a moment. And then he recalled something his mother, the first storyteller he ever heard, used to say. *Stories comfort the afflicted and afflict the comfortable.* "Once upon a time," Hans said for the first time in a long time, "there was a great story."

A knowing smile settled into Sarah's face. "What's her name?"

"You wouldn't believe me if I told you."

"Don't make me say something inappropriate."

They both smiled, but neither could possibly say goodbye, so instead, Sarah sang an angelic, happy tune while Hans left her and drove away, down Sunset Drive. He did not think about the end that it implied, but instead about the sunrise.

This time, though, even hopes of the next day's sunrise left him feeling empty. What good, after all, was a sunrise, when it was viewed by one man, from one window, in one quiet house? Hans knew it didn't feel right to give up on the sun. And he knew, no matter what, it would still be there tomorrow. But most of all, he knew if he could share its story with a beautiful stranger, his journey would be complete.

THIRTY-SIX

"So this is it?" Story asked, standing in the middle of Angela's travel agency office at the end of an extra-long work day. She took the passenger list from her. "Sharon Young . . . Peter Ramirez . . . Teddy Bell . . ." Story said, moving closer to Angela and gliding her finger over each name.

Angela sat at her desk, eyebrows raised and hand outstretched. "Aren't you forgetting something?"

"Right. Sorry." Story handed her a brown envelope bulging with green goodness. "I put in a little extra for your efforts."

Angela's eyes widened when she felt the weight of it in her hands. "Nice doin' business with you, Story," she said with a smile.

In the parking lot in front of the travel agency, Story sat in her car, studying the list, looking for a party of four that were destined for Manaus. *Luke Ross. Rachel Ross. Kaleb Ross. Hannah Ross.* "Bingo!" she said out loud when she saw their address: 1349 24th Street, Scottsdale. She was familiar with the area, having *visited* a nearby home a few weeks back.

There was no time to spare. If Story didn't get four plane tickets, her plan would be obliterated and Cooper's birthday would be one major event away from a fairy tale ending. After completing a twenty-minute drive in ten minutes, Story's Volvo screeched to a stop in front of the Ross residence. She dashed up the walk, and was greeted by a large American flag hanging from a porch beam, swaying in the breeze. The man of the house, Luke Ross, answered the door wearing a baseball cap, jeans, a little silver cross, and a carefree smile that men in their late thirties wear only when they're on vacation, or on their way.

"Hi," he said. "Can I help you?"

Yes, you can. You have to. "I need to talk to you and your wife," she said, nearly out of breath, "about your trip to Brazil." Despite her best efforts, Story looked desperate, because she was. "It's really important," she said with a grimace, realizing how crazy she sounded.

"Um, okay . . ." he said. "Is there something wrong? Are you from the travel agency?"

Story was tempted to lie. After all, she was getting good at it, and perhaps always was. But she went for truth instead. "I need to get me and three of my friends on your flight to Brazil tomorrow, and you and your family are taking our seats, so we're gonna have to come to some sort of agreement."

Luke stammered, his smile waning, as he cowered in his own doorway. "We're already packed . . . and the kids have been studying Brazilian culture."

Of course they have. "Failure's not an option, Luke." Story stared him down, standing tall and undaunted.

Luke Ross, confused and unnerved, hollered toward the backyard at the real man of the house. "Honey . . . could ya come here for a minute?" he said. His wife yelled back that she was busy, so Luke motioned for Story to follow him. The two of them walked through the living room and a small kitchen to the back patio, where the pants-wearing Rachel Ross was hunched over a fire pit, shoveling out ashes.

"I'd already showered," an embarrassed Luke said to explain why his wife, instead of him, was engaged in dirty work. "Honey, this is . . ." Luke said to his wife, and looked to Story for clarification.

"Story Easton," Story said, extending her hand to the dirty stranger.

"Oh, I don't want to get you all messy," Rachel said as she stood up, wearing smeared ashes on her face and hands. A little silver cross, just like Luke's, hung proudly from her neck. She mumbled, "Just finishing up some chores around here before our big . . . I'm sorry, I didn't catch who you were."

"There's some sort of problem with the trip," Luke said from five paces away, sneaking back into the house in case it got ugly.

"Problem?" Rachel said, guarded and stern, taking a small step toward Story.

Ugh! Story glanced down at her watch and stared at the second hand, ticking away toward failure. She needed a new angle, so she looked out into their yard at a slice of Americana. With a blue-sky backdrop, the two Ross children, wearing Levis and T-shirts, jumped up and down on a trampoline. "Ah, they must be Kaleb and Hannah," said Story. "They're darling."

Rachel Ross was not impressed. "Who are you, exactly?"

"Think of me as one giant checkbook," Story said, arms folded, "here to motivate you to reschedule your trip."

The two women moved closer to each other, beginning what looked like a standoff in the center of the Ross family patio. "Look, I'm sorry you have some sort of dilemma," Rachel said, "but if you knew us, you'd know we can't be bought. We value lots of things—the Lord's grace, time spent together, education." She pointed to the white metal patio table beneath a giant stack of Socra-Tots® books—the *Right At Home* series, designed for families who home-school.

"That's a great series," Story said, looking at the stack of Socra-Tots® merchandise in a positive way for once. It was, after all, funding her trip, and funding her life. "You know, they have a whole geography collection that focuses on—"

"Yes, we have it!" Rachel said, suddenly feeling friendlier as she walked over to the stack and pulled out *Brazil: Can You Spell Rio De Janeiro?* "That's why we're going on this trip. The kids and I were studying Brazil, and by using some appropriate question-asking strategies, I learned that the kids really wanted to go."

My mother, the genius. Just put it in the form of a question, and they will buy it. Story laughed out loud, thinking of what a kid would say yes to. *Should we eat Twinkies for breakfast? Should we put the cat in the microwave? Should we visit Brazil?*

"Are you familiar with the Socratic Method?" Rachel asked, her face covered with ash and condescension as she invited Story to join her at the patio table.

Story sat down in the chair next to her, and just for fun, answered, "Are you?"

"Yes, and we can't wait to apply it to our travels—"

"Right. About that. How about if I give you a whole lot of money to go to Brazil on a different flight?"

"I thought I made myself clear, my dear. We can't be bou—"

"Have you heard about the horrible kidnapping problem in South America?" Story said, scowling. "Literally, *kid*-napping, and they *love* the little blonde ones." She stared at the very blonde Hannah and Kaleb, still jumping on the trampoline.

Rachel remained unfazed. "We've studied how to avoid being a target for that kind of thing," she said with a scrunched-up nose. "Besides, most of the time we'll be with other people of our kind, spreading The Word. And God watches over us."

Story, now feeling like the pagan whom God would not protect, began to panic. *Okay. Start with a question. Always start with a question.* "How long have you lived in Scottsdale?"

"Forever," she said, smiling, taking in her perfect children, her perfect rose bushes, and her Norman Rockwell backyard scene.

"Then you must be familiar with what an actual phoenix is," Story said, tapping her fingers on the table now, impatient. "Did you know that according to the Greek myth, only one phoenix can exist at any given time?"

"And it's always male," Luke Ross quietly interjected through the open kitchen window that overlooked the patio, but Rachel dismissed him with an audible scoff.

Story continued. "Only one true phoenix can be on that flight tomorrow morning. Only one person at a time can experience rebirth, and rise out of the ashes." Story stared at ash-covered Rachel, and said, "You've already risen. All of you . . . are already born again."

Rachel nodded and whispered in a heavenly tone, "You're right."

"But there is a person," said Story, trying to muster a little faith, "a child, who needs to be on that flight, who needs more than anything to be reborn, to reconnect with a more innocent time."

Rachel continued her nodding, her eyes growing misty. "Yes, every one of God's children deserves the chance to reconnect."

Sure she'd made a breakthrough, Story said, "I'm so glad you under—"

"I hear your cry, my sweet child. *You* will be reborn!" Rachel announced, as she took Story's head in her hands, smudging her with ash. "In the name of the Father, Son, and Holy Ghost," Rachel said, using ash from her index finger to wipe the shape of a cross on Story's forehead.

Expecting some sort of ceremony to follow, Story closed her eyes and said, "So, what do I have to do?" *I need a miracle. I need magic. I need you, fairy godmother, if you exist, to lift your wand for me just this once and cut me some damn slack.*

Rachel smiled. "Nothing, my dear. You've already done it . . . You let the

Lord into your heart. You are reborn."

I did? I am? "That's it?" Story said with raised eyebrows, glancing at her watch and thinking of Cooper, his unexpected green umbrella, and the magic treasure that would save him.

"And you'll have to complete your mission, of course," Rachel said, as if that were implied.

For a moment, Story put her mocking aside, and wondered if God was actually there. How else could she know about Cooper's mission?

Rachel raised her own skeptical brows. "You *are* here about the Brazil mission, right? Pastor Reynolds sent you, right?"

"Yes?" Story said, trying to sound confident. And saved.

A dubious Rachel Ross cocked an eyebrow and applied her holy sixth sense. "You're not!" she gasped, as she got up from the table and raised a finger in Story's face. "What do you want from us?"

"Your seats," Story said with resolve, as she reached into her purse, took out her checkbook, and made out a check to Rachel Ross. "I'm offering this," she said, handing Rachel the check, "plus every single product Socra-Tots® has to offer."

When Rachel saw the amount on the check, she made the sign of the cross over her head and heart as she whispered, "Grace be to God. You must be an angel!" She shut her eyes and wobbled for a moment, as if she was going to faint, but then regained her footing and sounded as calm as a miracle. "And you'll include the new *The Sun and You* outer space series?" she asked, opening one eye just enough to see Story's face.

Story nodded, summoning celestial stars in her eyes, and thinking of millions of different people under one uniting sun.

Mumbling, Rachel said, "It's just that we don't normally . . . I mean, in the past . . ."

"The past is a foreign country; they do things differently there," Story whispered.

Rachel looked in Story's eyes. "I guess God would want me to. For the kids," she said, dreaming of salvation and the American Dream.

"Yes, for the kids," Story said, waiting for the word.

"Okay," Rachel said.

And the word was good.

Already behind schedule, Story left the Ross household, allowing the extra-bright sun to warm her. Its rays shot down to earth, speaking to her with strength and authority while she ran down the sidewalk holding four plane tickets tightly in her hands. The official trip was not yet underway, but she was sure someone, something, had deemed it charmed. She alone could not have done the job—she never had before. So to show her gratitude, Story stopped running for a moment, looked up, and whispered "Thank you" to the fairy godmother in the sky.

THIRTY-SEVEN

It was the night before Cooper's big journey to the Amazon and, too excited to entertain sleep, he found himself in his dad's office.

"Hey," Cooper said to Sonny, who didn't respond, but sat perched in silence on his little yellow trapeze.

Cooper stared at the blank wall before him—a wall made bare when his mother took down three photos that made her cry. But Cooper remembered them. Frozen in his mind, they still hung in their happy, walnut-framed trio. The one on the left had been a black-and-white of his parents on their wedding day—not one of those posed, hand-touching-hand shots, but one taken when they didn't know anyone was looking. Those are usually the best kind. He remembered his mom's face in that picture. She was all bright and shimmering, looking sort of surprised, even astounded, at her own happiness. But Cooper remembered his dad flashing this one special smile he always saved for his mom. Cooper had seen his dad give his mom this smile when they didn't think he was watching. But he was.

The photo on the right, another black-and-white, had been a family shot of the three of them in front of a giant pyramid in Egypt. Cooper remembered his dad asking a stranger to take the camera. In a funny accent, the stranger had kept repeating that they were a beautiful family, and he kept backing up, trying to get the whole pyramid in the shot. But Cooper remembered his dad laughing, telling the stranger not to worry about getting the *massive wonder that we traveled around the world to see* in the shot. *Just get us*, he'd said. *Just get us. Thanks.*

The biggest of the three, a color photo that had been in the middle, was the one Cooper remembered in the most detail. It was one of those stick-out-your-arm self-portraits that his dad had taken of the two of them. The photo wasn't taken in Egypt, or at Disneyland, or at a World Series game, but on the couch in their living room. Cooper wore his gray and white baseball uniform and red cap, muddied from a good game, and his dad wore the soft navy button-down sweater his mom said he looked handsome in. Neither Cooper nor his dad looked straight at the camera, but more at each other, because his dad had been talking about Cooper catching his first fly ball. Cooper used to look at this photo for long stretches at a time, even before *it* all happened, and after staring at it long enough, his dad became animated.

But he wasn't animated now, and as Cooper stared at the picture in his mind, one second turning into several minutes, a horrible ache settled in his belly. At that moment, Cooper Payne realized that his dad would not be joining him on this trip, or any trip. Ever.

And even then, fully understanding for the first time that magic was for naïve little boys, he looked again at Sonny. "Hey."

Silence.

Needing some warmth and maybe even a little light, Cooper thought of Hope. He looked at the blank wall before him, and imagined her floating near the ceiling where the sky would be if they were in the rainforest. Hope knew to follow the sun. *That must be where people go when they leave*, he thought. *That must be what they need.* He imagined Hope dancing on the forest floor, and then flying through the air, and he even imagined creating her out of paper, right then and there, and adding her to the wall—but that would be silly. If she was made of something real, she would eventually break down, rip, disintegrate. If she stayed in his imagination, no one could ever take that away.

But was that true of the treasure box, too? *What if the real magic treasure box isn't magical at all? If it isn't magical, then it can't give people what they really need.* At that moment, he hated Martin Baxter. He hated him for making him believe in the unbelievable.

In his mind, he heard his dad making the case for magic, for having faith that things always work out, but Cooper felt as if everything he'd ever believed in might have been a lie. All of it. And in the darkest, most faithless corners of himself, he dared to wonder if he'd even imagined his dad, larger than life, flying through his dreams. Cooper stood alone, looking at his own olive skin, running his fingers through his dark, coarse hair, all of it evidence of his undeniable connection to the ghost of a hero he longed to see one last time.

Go toward the sun, he imagined Hope saying, but the sun had long set, and there was only night.

"Coop?" Claire said, entering the room to see Cooper standing alone, looking at the blank wall.

"Hey, Mom," he said, in a voice that fell somewhere between a boy and a man.

She joined him, and the two of them were now fixed on the wall before them, turning their backs on David's desk.

"I can't ever remember telling him," Cooper said.

"Tell who . . . what?" Claire said.

He hesitated. "I don't think I told Dad I loved him."

Unable to look in Cooper's eyes, Claire stared straight ahead, looking at nothing and everything. "Sure you did, Coop, lots of times," she said.

"When?" Cooper asked, focusing his gaze on a sun that wasn't there.

Claire fumbled her way through tired, painful memories. "At night, Coop, you used to tell him before you went to bed."

"No!" he said, sounding adamant and much older. "The last time he . . ." And then he said, "All I said was *goodnight*." And then the boy came back. "If I could talk to him just one more time, not even for very long, just enough for him to maybe tell me stuff, and I could make sure he knew . . ." He paused for a moment, starting to cry.

Claire turned to him, looking deep into familiar brown eyes, and whispered, "He knew, Coop. He knew." And then, without her permission, Claire's left eye released one giant teardrop, slowly turning end over end until it finally landed on the floor with a gentle splash.

In Cooper's imagination, though, it wasn't a teardrop, but a rain-fresh droplet from one of the Amazon's many waterfalls, and he wanted to bathe in it while he waited for Hope to come and tell him how to stop looking backwards.

"Do you like him?" Cooper abruptly asked his mother, who had walked over to Sonny's cage.

"Who?" she said.

But Cooper could tell she knew. The room was starting to get crowded. "Martin," he said.

Claire broke eye contact with Sonny, and said, "Yes. I like him."

After a long silence, Cooper spoke. "He probably doesn't even like baseball."

There was nothing she could say after that, and Cooper knew it. He suddenly felt sorry for his mom, who was now looking to a small green bird for guidance, and he added an eight year old's version of a peace offering. "Whatever," he said.

The silence returned. Neither Cooper nor Claire knew how they were going to exit that room. Cooper finally said, "There's just one sun, right?" He needed to make sure he hadn't missed something in science class. He needed to make sure the same sun that hung in his Arizona sky also hung over the Amazon.

"Just one," a smiling Claire confirmed as she forced her way out of the room.

"Okay," Cooper whispered as she walked away, but he suddenly knew that not even one uniting sun could bring together two people that far apart. His dad wouldn't be there, and no stupid book or wishful thinking could create magic when it didn't exist.

He stared once again at the bare wall, with no trace of the sun, no glimmer of Hope, no physical proof that his dad even knew he was there.

Magic was officially dead. The signs were everywhere.

Cooper turned to leave, and as he put one foot in front of the other, he felt older with each step. One. *Goodbye birthday dream.* Two. *Goodbye magic.* Three. *Goodbye da—*

"Miss you," Sonny suddenly squawked.

Cooper froze, unable to believe his own ears. But the words were there. They resonated longer than usual, and they seemed somehow clearer. Cooper turned back to look at Sonny, and then, without any real logical thought, more like a compulsion, he went to the closet and took out a box.

He had a lot of work to do.

And with Sonny watching from afar, he knew what he wanted to do. He wanted to give his dad a preview of what lay ahead.

Tomorrow we're gonna find It.

Together.

THIRTY-EIGHT

"It's beautiful," was all Story could say when she called to thank Hans for the treasure box. She now had an official, full-blown relationship with Hans's answering machine, and she thought maybe, if she kept her distance and kept her big mouth shut, she and her machine-boyfriend might just make it. Even Story, failure extraordinaire, thought she could effectively date an answering machine. Thirty-second conversations and random blinking didn't sound all that different from other dates she'd had.

But dating Hans was another thing entirely, and Story knew it was unlikely she'd ever get the chance. *He's probably fixing some pretty, soft-spoken girl right now as I leave this dumbass message*, she thought. *He's probably laughing at the very idea of having temporarily fallen for me—a potty-mouthed criminal of a girl trying to find redemption in the Amazon jungle.*

"Thank you. It's beautiful," she repeated into the phone. "I . . . don't know what to say." She laughed at the notion of being speechless. "I know. Shocker." She thought about saying all sorts of things—how talented and wonderful he was, how stupid she was, how sorry she was—but as a tribute to Hans, she kept it brief and honest. "Miss you."

After hanging up, she finished packing, and put last-minute touches on her big plans for the next day's adventure. She placed the treasure box near the bed where she could see it, and as she let her hand slide over the tiny grooves in the carved tree on top, it felt bittersweet to Story: It would be the last thing she touched before sleep.

Nervousness settled in her stomach as she thought about what was at stake. It was the eve of a big battle, and she needed to win this one—not just for her, but for all of them. She wanted Claire and Cooper to find something worth believing in. She wanted Martin to find the man he used to be. And for herself? Just once, she wanted to taste success.

Exhausted, Story took off her clothes and, too tired to put on pajamas, collapsed into bed. As soon as her head hit the pillow, she fell into a deep sleep and soon, she slipped into a dream—something about questions and Ivy and failing ballroom dancing. A little bell dinged.

Ding.

Ding.

Ding.

It took Story three real *dings* to realize it was her doorbell. After looking at the clock, which read 11:22 p.m., she sprang out of bed and instinctively grabbed her robe. Still half-asleep, a groggy Story pondered who could be at her door. *Maybe Mom paid someone to befriend me again*, she thought. *Maybe Ivy's tendrils have grown so long they've come to strangle me. But why would they ring the doorbell?* Or worse. *Maybe the police realized I was, indeed, a danger to society and they're here to arrest me. Again.*

But when she opened the door, she saw the ultimate door prize: a Greek god bathed in moonlight. Was he really standing there? She rubbed her eyes to make sure. Yes. He had followed the small path that led to her door, and he was standing there, silent and strong. Why was he wearing jeans and a white T-shirt? Shouldn't he be wrapped in a sheet or something? And in her fog, Story then thought it might be Prince Charming. *Where'd he park his horse?*

If I am out of my mind, it's all right with me, thought Moses Herzog.

But as soon as the cool night air touched her skin, Story fully awoke and realized who stood before her. They stared at each other for several long seconds before Story broke the silence. "Did you get my message? I . . . I'm such a jackass." She closed her eyes for a moment. "Tomorrow is . . ." She paused to gather the strength required for guarded honesty, but abandoned it. *Who am I kidding? Tomorrow changes other people, but not me, not completely. But I can be better than I am today.*

She could tell that for Hans, tomorrow was just another day in the rainforest. He was more concerned with the right now. Without saying a word, he took her hand and placed something in it, and the feather-light feel of it made her stomach flutter. When she looked down at her hand, she saw a tiny wooden machete carved with precision. Perfect for cutting one's way through a dense forest. Perfect for finding magic.

She grasped the small machete firmly between her thumb and index finger, then held it up in the night sky and let moonlight flood around its shape, revealing the exact lines Hans had carved. *This story just got really interesting. Breathe. Okay. Don't ruin this. Just appreciate the fact that you've received a really beautiful tool from a really handsome handyman who happens to think you deserve it. If this were some cheesy romantic comedy, Hans would say he made it with love, and I would say I know, looking super hot in my super-hot . . .* She looked down. *Terry cloth robe? F-word.*

But he *did* make it with love. That was evident—not from the fine craftsmanship, which clearly existed in the piece of carved art that lay before her, but from the look in his eyes. When Story got the nerve to look deep into them, he stepped toward her, took her in his arms, and kissed her with a sense of urgency that made Story tense up for a moment. But when she breathed in his smell, she let herself melt into him. Hans showed no signs of ending the kiss, and as Story felt her body pulse with heat, she wondered if he could feel her heart pounding. She tried to slow down her heartbeat, tried not to give away how he made her body do things without her consent, but she knew she could not control her heart.

There was a slight hesitation on Hans's part, as if he didn't want to enter through Story's door without her approval, and once again, they found themselves standing on a threshold, blessed by the moon.

Story knew that men as attractive as Hans didn't have to try that hard to bed a woman, but what she didn't know was that of all his past sexual encounters, this was the first time his hands felt this secure. Still, she sensed he was taking a risk, and that this risk was somehow part of his journey—this she understood firsthand. To show her gratitude, she instinctively took his hands in hers. After inspecting them for the magic she suspected they held, she discovered they weren't magic at all, but mere tools to carry out the tasks of a magic man.

Overwhelmed that she was the one he wanted to be with, a fleeting thought— more a feeling—swept through her. She was getting something right. She was getting *this* right.

And nothing else before this had ever really been okay.

She switched her focus from herself to the man in front of her. Vulnerable, she placed his hands around the small of her back, then draped her hands around his neck, and waited.

Right then, Hans, the man, knew that Story, the woman, understood the difference between being saved and being lifted up. Suddenly, so did he.

And so Hans Turner lifted Story Easton across the threshold of what used to be, and into the story that was meant to be.

As soon as they were in the house, Hans kicked the door shut behind him, and in one swift movement, lifted Story up onto the entryway table and placed her between three short story anthologies and a short stack of paperbacks from the Phoenix Public Library. The sound of the slamming door lingered in the air as Hans secured Story's position, then stopped, looking at his hands as if he'd never seen them before. He turned them over, back over again, and then let out a small breath of surprise, as if they'd been cured of some painful disease. He glanced over at the door, and when he looked back at Story, she noticed a new calmness in his eyes. With this new hope settled deep inside him, he greeted Story, for the first time, without the fear of losing her.

From that moment on, the touch of his hands escalated to an unearthly status. As he gently explored her face with his new hands, she felt jealous of what she imagined was in his bag of magic tricks—tiny eggs, rainbow scarves, silver coins—all of them getting touched, over and over and over again, by those hands.

When he began to kiss her neck, she held her breath for a moment, for fear she'd let out some sort of primal groan. A wave now undulated somewhere deep in her belly, fluttering inside her as if she was teetering at the apex of a roller-coaster, preparing for a downward spiral.

Hans removed his hands from her face and slipped them underneath her white terry cloth robe. As moonlight flooded through a small window in the front door, Hans saw hints of Story's lacy black bra lying against her skin, now warm and pink. As she watched Hans react, Story was grateful for having on matching bra and panties, a rare and lucky event. *Thank you*, she said to the gods of undergarment planning, *for not letting me do my laundry for two weeks.*

As if he were opening an extraordinary present he never expected to receive, Hans peeled the robe away from her shoulders and let it fall to the floor. Story trembled a bit when he put his hands on her waist and pulled her closer to him. But for her, it still wasn't close enough. He was really there, in the flesh, and she wanted no distance between them. She wrapped her bare legs around his waist, drawing him even closer, and she heard him let out a soft moan as one of his hands slid over her hips and eventually made its way to her inner thigh. He'd had to push her away from him a bit in order to complete his magic trick, but Story felt more than compensated.

The logistics of what happened next eluded Story. As he kissed a tender part of her neck she never knew existed, Hans took his time to thoroughly explore all of her with a gentle and steady hand, and Story realized she had not been at the rollercoaster's apex earlier, because she was there now. Teetering. And then she fell.

Sweet.

Sweet.

Success.

After a giant whimper, Story had no choice but to whisper, breathless, "Thank you," and then she added a faint, "God . . ." unsure if she should continue to speak out loud. *He should insure those hands. I'll pay the premium.*

Hans smiled at her, *You're welcome* in his eyes. Then Story led Hans down a hallway lined with bookshelves teeming with first lines, and finally, to her bedroom, where the real treasure lay, and then thanked him in her own special way.

For some things, there are no words, so for a while, as the two of them lay entangled in the moon's strong light, they said nothing. But finally, Story rested her head on Hans's chest and let out a little laugh. "So . . . since I really, really, really like you, that makes me *not* a slut for having sex with you on a second date. Right?"

He gently kissed the top of her head. "We're counting this as a date?" he laughed, and Story play-slapped him. He sighed and brushed a piece of shiny auburn hair away from her eye. "I've always wanted to date a slut."

Story laughed with him, partly because she knew if she spoke too much, she'd ruin everything, and partly because he'd already proven his affection. He'd carved it into a masterpiece that sat on the floor just two feet away from them, waiting to be opened.

"I *have* met your mother, you know," he said. "So I'm pretty sure that absolves you from sluthood." And while he caressed her bare shoulder, Story enjoyed watching his magic hands move up-close.

"Come with me," Story blurted. Hans smiled, and it made Story blush. "No, seriously. I still have your ticket . . . and it was never going to be the same without you . . . and even if you get sick of me, you can just think of it as a vacation, and—"

"Okay."

Story watched both of their chests move up and down for several breaths before she could speak. "Okay?"

"Okay," he said again, now laughing. Then he said, "But I'm not saving your cute ass from jungle predators. You're on your own," which Story knew was bullshit.

"Okay." Story got giddy when she thought about the two of them romping around the jungle on their third date. "Okay," she said, turning her head so he didn't see her wide, pleased smile. She knew she should probably quit talking, but something in her wanted to explain to him why the trip was so important. She proceeded with trepidation. "If I pull this off," she sighed, "if I don't screw this up, people's lives might actually . . ."

For once, Hans spoke for her. "Change?" With some hesitation, he said, "Are you sure you need a jungle for that to happen?"

Yes, I need the jungle to pull this off. What kind of question is that? she thought. *I'm in charge of this rescue mission.* The universe must have been watching out for her, though, because before speaking, she paused long enough to see the truth. Hans actually thought she could change her life as surely as she could change Cooper's—as surely as she'd changed his—and damn it if she wasn't starting to believe it. She thought about all of the homes she'd broken into, seeking someone else's identity, and realized she'd taken the easy way out. Anyone can pretend to be someone who makes things better, but it's another thing to really do it. Story had resolved to help someone else, and for both their sakes, she had to succeed.

She took a deep breath. "Maybe I don't need the jungle for it to happen, but Cooper does."

Satisfied with her answer, Hans responded in a resolved, confident tone, "Then to the jungle we'll go."

"Okay," she said.

Hans snuggled up next to her. "Okay." And then, as if he'd forgotten to mention an important contractual clause, he said, "But first, you have to make three secret wishes." When Story raised her eyebrows, he smiled, slightly embarrassed. "Just humor me. It's a thing my mom used to make us do before we went on trips."

Us? thought Story. But satisfied with the reason, Story said, "Why three?"

"Why three?!" he teased, pulling Story on top of him. "Because there is power in the number three." Story straddled his body and returned the smile. He pulled her closer and kissed her three times: once on her forehead, once on her cheek, and once on her plump, pouty lips. "Think about it. There's the Three Musketeers," he said with a kiss. "The Three Kings," with another kiss. "The Three Wise Men," with a third kiss. "And think of fairy tales—the Three Little Pigs, the Three Bears—two things are just a coincidence, but three things make . . . magic." When he said *magic*, he couldn't help but laugh, and wave his hands over her face as if she was his act's finale.

Story accepted it. After all, stories did work in threes. *Beginning, middle, end.* And people worked in threes. *Birth, life, death.*

"Okay," Story said, closing her eyes. "I made my wishes. Your turn."

Hans stared deep into her. "Done."

When he let the back of his hand glide over her chest, she held back a giggle. "We have an early start tomorrow. We should probably get some sleep."

Hans smiled and touched her with both hands now. "Probably."

Outside, the Phoenix skyline twinkled, and the stars competed with the moon to see which could shine brighter. Inside, where light from both found its way into their bed, Hans and Story tried, unsuccessfully, to sleep.

THIRTY-NINE

Martin Baxter sat on a bed of pink, accompanied by a yellow cartoon sun, and stared at the understory painted on the wall in front of him. He sipped his whiskey and Coke, and let the magnitude of tomorrow's trip swirl inside him along with the alcohol. He relocated his gaze from the bustling understory to the canopy, the upper limit that acted as a threshold between the forest and the sky. *Everybody loves the canopy.* To the lesser-trained eye, the canopy had allure and mystery. Those unfamiliar with what it takes to create life, and sustain it, viewed the canopy, the layer closest to the sun, as a final destination—but the real work was actually done closer to the ground.

The house was quiet, something he'd tried to get used to, but never had. He picked up *Once Upon A Moonflower*, sitting on the bedside table, and forced himself to open it. He recalled another time he'd tried to read it, a year before, in a dark lecture hall full of students. After he'd delivered a lecture about shade-loving plants of the Amazon, a student in the front row asked Martin to read from his latest book. He tried to get out of it, but the girl held it up in the air and challenged him. He could never resist the call to adventure, so he began reading his book by podium light. The only words he got to read before he was interrupted were *For Hope, the project I'm most proud of.* As soon as he'd said it, two police officers casting mean shadows on the lecture hall wall uttered words that still haunted him. *I'm sorry. Horrible accident. So sorry.*

A year later, he still had trouble opening the cover, but something inside him, not the scientist but the man, told him he needed to. When he turned the page and saw *For Hope, the project I'm most proud of,* he nodded, knowing, without thinking, that he hadn't changed his mind about that. He touched the words on the page, remembering the girl who had inspired them.

"I'm coming!" Martin said, laughing. "For the fifth time, I'm coming."

"Dad, come on, it's time to finish it. I feel it!" Hope hollered. When Martin arrived, he found Hope sitting at a little white desk in her room, holding a yellow spiral notebook opened to the last page, its empty lines begging for words.

He pulled up a chair, looked at Hope, and said, "If you think it's time, then it's time." He touched her little nose with a playful, gentle poke, and said, "So, how does this story end? We have to find a way to get her out of the forest and back home."

Hope sank a little in her chair and let out a sigh. "Yes, I *suppose* so."

Martin handed her a pencil. "What? What did *you* have in mind?"

"She doesn't want to leave the forest," said Hope. "It's her new home now. She wants to stay there . . . for affinity." She paused, embarrassed she hadn't gotten it quite right. "She wants to stay there for infinity. For . . . forever," she said, giving her pencil a nervous twirl and glancing up to see her dad's reaction.

"Hmmm," Martin said, smoothing down his salt-and-pepper hair. He ached a little at the thought, but said, "Makes sense, actually, that she would want to stay." Martin recalled his own visits to the Amazon. "The rainforest has a strong allure. And it has a way of changing people—giving them what they need."

Hope smiled and handed Martin the pencil. "Here. Surprise me. Astonish me! But let her stay, Dad. Let her be a-lured. Let her end up where she belongs." A dreamy stare came over her, and she said, "Or somewhere even better."

Martin smiled. "I can't do it on my own," he said.

"Don't patronize me, Daddy," she said, laughing. There was a sweet sincerity in her voice. "Why would you need me?" she asked, as serious as a silly girl could be. "You can do anything."

He smiled at Hope. "You wrote the first line, so you should write the last line, too."

With the floor-to-ceiling rainforest still in full view, Martin clutched the book like a toddler latching onto his blanket—not sure why he needed it, but bound to it nonetheless. He felt torn. Still sipping his drink, he realized for the first time since his world came crashing down around him that he was at a crossroads, and it seemed he had two choices. Should he look to his beloved rainforest for guidance, or should he look to the book that he and Hope created together?

Right then, the lights flickered, Martin's drink slipped almost out of his grip, and as he tried to recover it, he dropped the book. Its binding hit the carpet, and the book fell open on page thirty-one, the next to last page. One rectangular ice cube, light amber from the whiskey, sloshed over the side of the glass, plunged toward the floor, and landed on the page. When Martin went to retrieve the ice cube, his eyes became fixed on it, fixed on the words that could be seen through the clear piece of ice. The letters were slightly blurry, but they were bigger than the others on the page.

They were his words, but they were so unfamiliar, they seemed like strangers. So Martin read them. And read them. Then read them again, until he remembered the man who wrote them, and remembered what they meant.

Then, in a series of motions his body seemed to perform on its own, he retrieved a can of white paint and a paintbrush from the basement closet and returned to the room. He tackled the high-up emergents and the canopy first, and then swiped his brush, dripping with white paint, over each part of the understory, except for one. White brush strokes replaced the colorful swirling lines used to create the bustling life present in the trees, and when it was all gone, all erased, Martin looked at the darkest part of the mural. Deep greens, dark browns, and black shadows spilled onto the wall to make up the forest floor, where all life began. He knew it had to be done, so he dipped in the can, soaking the brush with as much white paint as it would hold.

He returned to the part he'd left still alive in the understory—the moon-flower bud—and was unsure if he could muster up the strength to erase it. He thought of Cooper, wanting to find the treasure box with his dad—his hero. At first, he thought of this word applying only to Cooper's dad, but then a strange feeling came over him as he recalled his only daughter's own words.

You can do anything.

Martin took a drink, trying to push the question out of his mind, but it wouldn't leave. Had he been Hope's hero? While he took another drink, waiting for an answer to come, the lights suddenly flickered one last time, and then went out. For good.

Everything was black except for some moonlight coming through an open side window, so Martin crawled over to the top bureau drawer and felt around for the flashlight he'd put there when first moving in. He turned it on, bathing in the light for a minute, remembering a little girl who loved the sun. And him.

Then he thought about what Cooper had said. *We'd run around with our flash-lights, and lead everyone out of the jungle. And then we would be Rainforest Superheroes.* But that was too much to deal with, and Martin turned off the flashlight, hiding in the dark, afraid he could not fulfill any of their expectations.

So Martin sat. And sat. Without light. Without direction. Without a way out of his forest-hell. He sat for a very long time until, suddenly, he remembered. *I will be the fabulous fairy that sleeps deep inside the moonflower bud!* The words were clear and strong. *And you will release me.*

Of course he would. He could do anything.

And then he knew what he needed to do. Heroes do what they promise. Heroes press on through the dark. Heroes move on.

Hope would expect nothing less.

By flashlight, Martin Baxter walked over to the understory on the wall, took the edge of the brush, and changed the tightly closed bud into an ethereal moon-flower, in full bloom. This, of course, was something he'd never seen, so he called upon his imagination to help him with proportion, vibrancy, translucence. And when he completed the thing he'd seen in his dreams, the same thing his mother had seen in hers, he let her go.

When it was done, a rare night breeze announced itself near the open window. At first it was just a wisp of a thing, but then it gained momentum, and soon it was a full-fledged gust, delivering an unidentifiable sweet smell to the shadowy room.

She could make you fall in love with the wind.

When it died down, Martin painted over the moonflower, careful to preserve the image in his memory, because nothing is ever as beautiful in real life as it is in a dream. He looked at the new white wall and imagined what he'd left behind. But he did let one thing stay. Peeking out from a small patch of blue sky was a radiant yellow-orange sun. This would shine as long as he wanted.

As he shined the light on the spot where the moonflower used to be, he remembered seven little words that reminded him who he was. *I love you more than the moonflower.*

About that, there was no question.

With flashlight in hand, he walked over to the book, still on the floor, the last page wet with melted ice-cube water. The water had washed over the fifteen words, and although they now blended in with the others on the page, they were cleansed with new meaning. *Life is a series of knowing when to let go, and when to hang on.*

For the first time, he read, really *read*, his own words, and in doing so remembered someone else's. On his mother's deathbed, she'd said something that hadn't made sense to Martin until that very moment. After promising that, for her, he would find the moonflower, she looked up at him and said, with a slow wink, "Ah, hell, it's just a flower, Martin." She then gave him a knowing look, and delivered one last sentence which, until now, had been a bit of a riddle. "Besides," she said, trying to mask her weakness, "the moonflower doesn't really live in the Amazon." And then, later that same day, that woman, who had made sixteen Amazon journeys to find the elusive moonflower, died.

Martin put his drink down and focused on things lost, things found, and things that are both—things carried deep inside. He then gave his attention to the book's final words, which he remembered were not final—two small but important words lying among an ocean of white space on the next page. They signified closure, something Martin was trying to embrace, so he concentrated on doing just that, and decided to turn the page.

FRIDAY

Floating down the jungle's river on my own personal lily pad reminded me of riding on an inner tube through the tame, man-made river at Wacky Waters, a water park back home. Except for the piranha. And the caiman. And the fierce and deadly creature awaiting me at the other end.

When I finally saw the kapok tree, the sun was beginning to set, and one lonely beam of light bathed the large tree in its warmth. I tried to play it cool, but it was a sight to behold. It stretched well beyond all the other trees, reaching so high, I truly couldn't see where its top branches met the sky. And the base of it was so big, it was unhuggable. Well, maybe a giant could embrace it. Or Plastic Man.

Either way, it was magnificent, and as I hopped off my lily pad and crept up the riverbank, I was drawn toward the tree's proud presence. I walked around the tree several times, and when I didn't see the treasure box, I ventured forth, scouring the forest floor for magic. But there was nothing but forest things: leaves, dirt, leaf-cutter ants.

"Magic treasure box," I sneered. "Lunatics—that's what all these animals are," I said to no one as I looked above me, waiting for a mischievous monkey or a brazen bird to swoop down and continue more of their conspired, misguided plot against me. But right as I was about to curse the entire jungle for sending me on this wild scavenger hunt for nonexistent magic, I tripped over something. When I landed, I looked back at what I'd stumbled over: a large, intertwined buttress root, and a strange-looking box.

I crouched down near the box, moving my hands across all four sides, and then the lid, letting the pads of my fingers sink into the smooth carved grooves of a miniature kapok tree, a smaller version of the one that towered above me. A shiver raced through me as I thought about opening the box. What treasure did the forest have in store for me? "The treasure box has what you need," the sloth had said, but what did I need? Five servings of fruits and vegetables a day, says my teacher, but that wouldn't be very magical. And my parents once told me I needed a reality check, but reality didn't seem to be a very good companion for magic either.

I had my thumb on the tiny brass clasp fastening the lid to the lower half, and was just about ready to reveal my personalized treasure, when I heard a low growl coming from a nearby bush. When I looked toward the noise, it dissipated (scattered) (weakened) and re-emerged in another bush ten feet away. Whatever it was, it was everywhere.

And then it was suddenly in front of me, pacing and purring in-between words. "Bravo, you made it," said the sleek and spotted cat as he flipped on his back and began licking his ominous (threatening) (scary) clawed paws.

Not good. Not good at all.

"Now, if you can answer three riddles, I will look elsewhere for dinner. If not . . ." And with that, he winked, then smiled, displaying his impressive teeth.

The Fierce One would not be getting a Valentine from me. "Wait!" I begged, now clutching the treasure box close to my heart, "How about random trivia. That's really more of a strength for me—"

"Number one," he purred, the buzzing vibration settling in my frightened belly, "what's white and black and red all over?"

I thought maybe he should change his name from Fierce One to Lame One. "A newspaper. Challenge me, already," I said, trying to hide my fear.

"Wrong!" he yelled, and I imagined his teeth ripping me to shreds. "An embarrassed skunk!" But then his anger quickly evolved into playful banter. "Oh, I'm just kidding. I'll accept either answer." His tail confidently flopped against the forest floor as he continued. "Number two. What goes around the house and in the house but never touches the house?"

Let me give you some advice: If your life ever depends on an answer to a riddle, run! "Um," I said, stalling as nightfall crept in. "The sun!" I exclaimed.

Looking hungrier, he hummed, "Hmmm, not bad, but there is one more riddle. Number three. When one does not know what it is, then it is something. But when one knows what it is, then it is nothing. What is it?"

Sensing my impending failure, he rolled over, got back on his feet, and prowled toward me, his tail now whipping the ground. This was it. I was definitely dinner. Stupid riddles. "Is my getting eaten supposed to teach me a lesson?" I protested. "Why couldn't I just get grounded? Or get more chores or something?"

Then he narrowed his golden eyes and lifted a paw, saying, "You." Then he lifted another paw. "Universe," he said in a mocking tone. He rotated the universe around the *paw, my stand-in. "Lessons are not for one, but for many."*

More riddles. Have I mentioned I hate cats?

He crept closer, until finally I felt his whiskers tickle my cheek, and as he licked his teeth, he gave me one consolation prize: an answer instead of a question. "When one does not know what it is," he said, "it is a riddle."

FORTY

On the morning of her day of battle, the day she'd take on the Amazon to hunt for its magic, Story awoke next to Hans—in complete blackness. Luckily, Story had used a battery-powered alarm clock as a backup, because the blackout from the night before was still going on. They needed to be at Claire and Cooper's by 6 a.m. to make their flight, so they grabbed two flashlights, packed the car, and hurried out the door into the cool dark morning with the treasure box hiding in the trunk.

Story tried not to let it show, but as she drove down the Interstate, not one streetlight aglow, the corners of her mouth began to curl. She fought back her smile, because if Hans saw it, he might ask why she was smiling. And then she would have to try to explain how good it felt to have him next to her, how good it felt to be on her way to changing the course of a little boy's life, and how good it felt to be successful.

When they arrived at the Payne house and pulled into the driveway, their headlights the only illumination, they could see shadows of people moving on the other side of the living room window. As the two silhouettes, carrying handheld lights, bustled around inside, excitement swelled in Story. She envisioned them both basking in a warm, bright light emanating from their future.

There was a moment of silence as Hans and Story sat in the car, listening to the quiet ticking of the motor. "Ready?" Hans said, smiling and placing his hand on her thigh.

She nodded, turned the engine off, and exited the car, gripping the heavy, silver flashlight. With the usual city sounds quieted, she could actually hear crickets chirping, and she imagined them cheering her on. She stepped over a row of large rocks lining the sidewalk, and she stepped into her new life. *Story Easton's Life,*

Part Deux: Bigger, Better, and Less Fucked Up. She vowed never to look back, and focused instead on the three front steps leading to the Paynes' front porch.

But then she heard her cell phone ring. She'd left it sitting on her car console, and the ominous sound made her stomach clench, knotting up with each piercing ring. *Who would be calling me at 6:15 in the morning?*

"Mom?" she said, breathless from running back to the car. She hadn't talked to her mother since she'd left those messages from inside a jail cell.

"Story? It's Angela."

It took Story a moment for Angela's name to register. "Angela? We're on our way to the—"

"I know. I wanted to let you know . . . I wanted to see if . . ." Her tone made Story nervous. "You were so generous, what you paid me, I mean, and I don't want you to get all the way there and—"

This is not happening. "And what? What is it, Angela?"

"Just tell me you decided to get the shots."

This is not happening. "No, no, no, no, this is not happening."

Buck did not read the newspapers, or he would have known that trouble was brewing.

Angela sighed, and mid-breath, she said, "I was up early making some last minute arrangements for some other travelers, and as I was surfing around a few websites, I saw . . . Apparently, there's been a surge in Yellow Fever cases, and a couple of months ago, they started requiring proof of—"

"Okay," Story said. "Money's no object, Angela. We have to get someone over here to give us whatever stupid shots we need," she said, sounding a little crazed as her voice drifted off, "or maybe they could meet us at the airport."

Angela let out a sorry, but shocked, laugh. "Story. The shots are given over a three-day period. You can't just—"

"*Can't* is no longer part of my vocabulary!" Story exploded. Hans, aware that something was terribly wrong, tried to approach Story, but she swatted him away with her flashlight.

"I know you're on some sort of deadline, but you'll have to reschedule. You can still get there in a few days—"

"You don't understand! It has to be today!" Story hit herself in the forehead with her phone for a second, and then began to retreat to familiar territory. Her voice softened. "Oh my God. It's true."

"Story?" Angela matched Story's now quiet voice.

This is the saddest story I have ever heard.

"No one should ever count on me." By now, the shadows inside the house appeared on the front steps in the form of two real people Story had grown to love. Their small yellowed lights glowed strong, and the beauty of the two of them standing side by side was too much to bear. She averted her gaze and conjured up the scene she'd carried inside her since accepting her calling. *Happy Birthday, Cooper. You did it. You found the treasure.*

Story figured this would be the time when most people would cry. She waited for tears, or even one tear, to emerge, but no tears came. *Of course.*

"Story?" Cooper called from the dark morning air. He wore a light blue button-down shirt, dressy compared to his usual T-shirts. "Where are the camera guys?" he said, patting his chest. "Mom said this would look good on film. What'dya think?"

Forcing a smile, Story thought about the local Brazilians she'd hired to be fake cameramen, and all of the other details she'd arranged to maintain her fake documentary. "You look great, Coop. Happy birthday."

He didn't answer, but shook his head. "Nope. Not yet." And Story knew, for Cooper, only one thing would make his birthday official.

By now, Hans had approached Story's side, and the two of them looked at Claire, deflated, standing on her porch. "What's wrong?" was what she asked, but it was a rhetorical question. It didn't matter that Story had been weaving a lie, and it didn't matter that her fake cameramen would wait all afternoon at the Manaus airport, thinking they'd gotten the time wrong. All that mattered to Claire was that her son was about to be heartbroken. She instinctively put her arm around Cooper.

Story could not utter a sound. Breathing was enough of a difficulty, so Hans spoke for her. "There's been some sort of . . . complication," he said.

Before anyone could explain, Cooper took one last look at Story, then turned around and walked through the entryway and up the stairs. Claire followed close behind.

Why is he not yelling? Or running? With her feet planted firmly on the sidewalk, Story was stuck, frozen with shame. She knew she needed to talk to him, apologize, something, but at that moment, Story felt an overwhelming need to be near the treasure box. She knew it was just a box made of wood—four sides, a top and bottom—but she let her mind drift to a place of hope. *When I hold it near me, this mess will be erased*, she thought. *When I hold it near me, Cooper's dream will survive.*

With Hans trailing behind her, she went to her trunk and lifted it into her arms.

"Story . . ." Hans said, but she walked into the Paynes' house alone, carrying the box that was never supposed to be there. Not knowing what to do next, she stopped right inside the door, with just enough time for reality to set in. There would be no rainforest, so there would be no treasure, and there would be no magic. And contrary to what Cooper thought, he would, indeed, turn nine. Without the treasure box. Without magic. Without his father.

Story heard Claire, upstairs, banging on Cooper's door, and she knew she should go upstairs and talk to him, but even though it didn't matter anymore, Story was not ready for him to see the treasure box—she would put it in the coat closet until she could take her time, and explain in her own way. But suddenly, Cooper came bounding down the stairs, flashlight in one hand. In the other was something she couldn't make out. Not wanting him to see the box yet, she scooted through the kitchen, box in tow, and raced down the hallway and into David Payne's office. It was dark, so she put the box down on top of something and slipped out before Cooper could see her.

"Cooper! Stop a minute," Claire said, following Cooper, who had gotten something out of a kitchen drawer and was headed back toward the front door.

"Leave me alone, please." His voice oozed with conviction, and he moved like a boy on a mission—a young man on a mission.

"Stop a minute, Coop. What are you doing?!" Claire yelled ahead, trying to catch up with him. Story followed Claire. At least they hadn't turned on her yet.

As the three of them watched Cooper run out the front door, toward a sky still filled with a few twinkling stars, Hans touched Claire's arm. "Let him go, Claire," he said. "Give him a minute."

Story remembered what Cooper said to Sonny the bird. *If it doesn't happen, I'm gonna do it.*

Fearing he had a giant butcher knife to his throat, Story tried to get past Hans, who was holding the women back. "Let him get some air, ladies," Hans said.

Claire and Story sat down on the bottom step of the staircase, and neither could look at the other. Hans stared at them both, and smiled, until, suddenly, he turned his head and looked out the front door. "Um," he said, with growing nervousness, "he doesn't need any more air." And then Hans tore outside.

Claire and Story followed Hans, and the three of them stood on the sidewalk, watching Cooper's satisfied eyes widen as flames rose higher and higher. On the cement below was a book, aflame. Smoke billowed up from the ground, but in the patches of clear air, a few words on the cover were still visible: *Once*, *Moonflower*, and *Baxter* held strong for a few seconds, then disappeared with the smoke, drifting away into the black horizon.

No one knew what to say, so Hans whispered, "At least he didn't do it upstairs."

Story couldn't stand it any longer, so she walked closer to Cooper and his fire. "I'm so sorry, Cooper."

But he put out his hand, keeping her back. "Let it burn. It's a kids' book anyway."

Feeling like a fraction of a person, Story looked at Cooper, who looked older—like he'd skipped nine, and moved on to ten or eleven.

Satisfied that the book was thoroughly burned, Cooper said, "I need to talk to someone," and walked back in the house as the Phoenix sun began to wake up.

FORTY-ONE

T here are some journeys in life that seem longer than others, regardless of distance. For Story Easton, her longest journey began at a cracked piece of cement in front of Cooper Payne's house, and ended when she arrived in David Payne's office.

On his way to ask Sonny the bird why the world was a magic-less piece of shit, Cooper saw something that made him stop, and crouch down. Something that actually made him smile.

By the time Story, Hans, and Claire came through the doorway, Cooper already had his hands on it. And within seconds of touching it, the office light came on and the electrical hum of the house returned. With the renewed light, the three of them found themselves entranced by the wonder in progress. The treasure box looked even more ornate and beautiful than it had before, but when Story glanced at the wall behind the treasure box, she knew she was witnessing something beyond her control.

Claire's jaw dropped when she saw it. "Oh my God, Coop," she said in a soft, astonished voice, looking at what used to be a blank wall, but had been turned into a floor-to-ceiling, three-dimensional rainforest. "This must have taken . . ." But her voice trailed off in amazement as she took it all in.

While his mother had packed the night before, Cooper had built his very own rainforest out of paper. He'd rummaged through the closet in his dad's office, piling its contents in the center of the office floor. One of the boxes had contained art supplies, so Cooper pulled out a multi-colored package of construction paper and created a floor-to-ceiling snapshot of the rainforest, 3-D style, so if he closed his eyes, he could reach out and feel the trunk of a kapok tree, the current of a forest stream, the fur of a giant sloth—things he wanted Sonny to see.

And so the night before the big trip, Cooper set out to rebuild the empty space. He first looked down at the hardwood, wondering if he should begin there, where the forest floor would grow, but then he looked up toward the textured ceiling, where the canopy would try to break free. *Where do I begin?* he wanted to ask his dad, but with Sonny silent, he remembered what his dad would say—*begin at the beginning*—his way of reminding Cooper to trust his instinct. Cooper decided the rainforest had no real beginning or end, but was more of a circle, each layer regenerating and flowing into the next, just as Mrs. Stewart had explained at school.

Cooper began with the most important layer of the rainforest, the understory, where nearly all forest life existed. He cut out tree branches from brown paper, then several leaves from a big piece of green construction paper, placing small, rolled-up pieces of tape to the backs of all of them, and stuck them on the wall. He then drew and cut out several animals—a sloth, a snake, a capybara, a jaguar, and several rainbow-colored birds—and placed them in cozy homes all over the forest-covered wall. Some were close together, some farther apart, but he knew they all depended on each other.

When he realized what was missing, Cooper fashioned a giant kapok tree by rolling gray paper into a big tube, and once it was fixed to the wall, he added droopy fern-like branches that projected from the wall, ready to tap a passerby on the shoulder. Cooper looked down at the base of the kapok tree, imagining a magic treasure box obscured by buttress roots and leaves, but as he stared at the exposed hardwood floor, it was a glaring reminder of what he needed to find. And he knew he had only twenty-four hours. Taking in the rainforest view in front of him, he vowed not to turn nine without finding it. He vowed to do his very best. He vowed to be a rainforest superhero.

Suddenly, mid-masterpiece, the room turned black. Cooper sat for a moment to formulate a plan, but not once did it occur to him to leave his forest unfinished, so in the dark, he felt his away around his dad's desk until he found it—a long, heavy, and silver grown-up flashlight.

Finally, with his father's light propped up on a nearby chair, Cooper finished a meandering river and a forest floor tangled with vines, so he could move on to the canopy. He then created the heavenly emergents, the few trees tall and robust enough to break through the canopy's threshold and reach for the sun. Armed with his flashlight in one hand, he stepped onto the desk chair and reached for the ceiling. He wasn't tall enough to reach it, but he was old enough to know how it felt to try, and he used his last few minutes to cut a circle out of yellow paper. He placed it on the wall, as high as he could reach, using extra tape to ensure it would hold strong if it should try to shine.

And as his eyelids grew droopy, Cooper turned off the flashlight and real nighttime fell upon a paper forest and a talking bird.

Hans and Story stared at the wall in front of them, amazed at each paper layer of the Amazon, and they both were mesmerized by the sloth's paper tail, clinging to a branch, hanging on indefinitely. They both looked up to the tip-top of the giant kapok tree, and then moved their eyes downward, ending with Cooper and the treasure box sitting at the base of the tree.

And just as Martin had described in the book, the treasure box was nestled among roots—not exactly buttress roots, but another kind. Sitting snug in the cardboard box that had come from deep inside the closet, the treasure box sat among framed family trees with centuries of Payne lineage—roots David Payne had been compiling for Cooper. It had been a project that David loved, and was proud of, but when fate interrupted, it was ultimately a project that had been relocated to the bowels of the closet.

As Cooper's small hands slid back and forth, gliding over the treasure box, morning announced itself, sending one giant shaft of light through the wooden office blinds. With the sunlight hitting it just so, the treasure box attained an ethereal glow, and the kapok tree carved into its lid looked just like the giant construction paper kapok tree that towered above it.

In Cooper's interpretation of an Amazonian kapok tree, its many paper branches grew in horizontal tiers, in keeping with Mayan tradition—Mayans believed the souls of the dead climb up the stairway of branches, up into heaven.

Story walked closer to Cooper. When she leaned over the box and caressed the woody-vine lianas, which Hans had braided into an ornate handle, a shiver shot through her body, and she said a secret thank-you to whatever had helped recreate what they all so desperately needed. They were not in the rainforest. It didn't smell like the rainforest. It didn't sound like the rainforest. But the way the light came in the window, touching only things it wanted to be seen—the treasure box, the paper forest, Sonny's cage—cast an otherworldliness over the entire room. They stood now not on hardwood floors in an office, but on the forest floor with a canopy above, and possibility lurked in the shadows.

The beauty of the scene swept over Story. Cooper still believed, and Story alone knew what small miracle awaited them. For the first time in twenty-five years, Story Easton shed a tear—two, in fact. Without warning, she felt the drops escape from her eyes and trickle down both cheeks until they met on her chin and converged. As they combined, gaining momentum, the joined droplet fell, and she knew a piece of her would forever mark the sacred ground. She then said something like a prayer, in hopes that the treasure she'd put in it one day before would be enough.

Story crouched down next to Cooper, who said in his softest, most hopeful voice, "I knew he was right. I knew I would find it. Somehow." He inspected the box for authenticity. He let his small fingers glide over the carved lid, and then he gripped the handle with authority, and whispered, "The vines are braided . . . just like the book said." He turned around, and said to Claire, "There's only one, right, Mom?"

She nodded. "Only one." Claire took another breath, but not a deep one, because the magic trick was far from over. As Cooper lifted the lid in slow increments, Hans took Story's hand in his. They watched as the lid rose and, finally, rested on its hinge.

Cooper stared into the open treasure box. He cocked his head to the side, and tried to figure out what he was looking at. When he lifted it out of the box, everyone except Story was puzzled.

Cooper held in his hands a small, portable DVD player with a fold-out screen, and when he figured out what it was, he turned back to Claire with a restrained, but disappointed, look. Claire crossed her fingers behind her back, hoping the big, magical finale wasn't *The Jungle Book*.

Then Cooper looked to Sonny. They all waited for Cooper to say something, or Sonny to say something, but both boy and bird just stared at each other. The yellow and orange tuft of feathers on Sonny's head vibrated a bit, and soon Cooper began to smile, and he let out a laugh, as if the two of them had had some sort of discussion—not a mimicry session, but a real conversation where questions are asked and answered. And although it seemed weird to think a bird could look happy, he did look different, at least to Story, as if he'd been flying for thousands of miles and finally reached his destination.

It had been just last night when Story realized what she needed to put in the magic treasure box—not on her own, of course, but with the help of a simple word which had, until then, always failed her. "Abracadabra," she'd said with hope but not much confidence. She sat in her living room after she'd packed, looking for something, anything, that could pass as magic. And as her gaze darted around the room—book, *no*, candle, *no*, bottle of wine, *no, no, no*—she'd glanced on the shelf below the TV, fixating on the magic right in front of her.

"Maybe you should push play, Coop," Story said.

Cooper lifted the player out of the box, sat down cross-legged, and let his weight settle onto the floor. He took a deep breath, pushed the button, and waited. After a few seconds, an image appeared on the screen, and when it did, Claire brought her hands up to her mouth, and Cooper laid his gentle hand, spread wide over the familiar face, and said, "Dad."

FORTY-TWO

When Cooper removed his hand from the screen, there sat David "Sonny" Payne, smiling and relaxed, his olive skin tan on-screen. He sat at his office desk, in the very office they were all in now, taping a late-night message that neither Claire nor Cooper knew existed.

"I just came from upstairs, watching you sleep," said David, repeating the words Story had already heard. As Cooper watched, rapt, his dad smiled and said, "So I figure I'll give you my best advice about life, while it's still fresh in my brain."

Then he stared straight into the camera, lost his smile, and said in a deep, raspy voice, "Cooper, *I* am your Faaaather." And then he put his arm in the air, hiding his hand inside his sleeve like a Vader-inspired amputee.

Claire and Cooper smiled.

"Sorry. Seriously. You'll probably never see this, Coop, but your school project got me in a . . . chatty mood." He threw his hands up and said, "And I figured, what the hell, tell the kid what he needs to know, just in case. Let's start with some quotes near and dear to my heart. Here it goes. 'Outside of a dog, a book is a man's best friend. Inside of a dog, it's too dark to read.'"

Claire laughed, tears in her eyes.

"'Always forgive your enemies—nothing annoys them so much.'" He folded his hands and placed them on his desk. "Let's see, oh, yeah, 'You can observe a lot by watching.' That means, shut up every once in a while." Then he pointed his finger at the camera, and said, "Don't you dare turn this off yet," then added, 'Cheer up, the worst is yet to come.'" He raised his eyebrows and said, "Thank Mr. Twain for that one."

He looked up, and to the left, borrowing from his memories. "Okay, before

you're eighteen, see *This Is Spinal Tap*. Read *To Kill a Mockingbird* and pretend
your dear old dad is as cool as Atticus Finch. Own at least two Beatles albums and
know at least five Bob Dylan lyrics. By heart." He tapped his fingers on his desk.
"Oh," he said, putting his finger up again. "Three important things you should
learn how to say, and say a lot . . . to women. One, 'You're right.' Two, 'I'm sorry.'
Three, 'It'll never happen again.' Hmmm . . ." he said. "This is harder than I
thought. Um . . . if you start something, finish it. And . . . your word should be
gold, but where the other guy's concerned, get it in writing."

He then folded his arms and said, "Learn to set up a hammock, hammer a
nail, work the grill, and change a tire. Ask me—I'll teach you. Let's see, always,
always, keep your eye on the ball." He smiled. "Santa, the Easter Bunny, the
Tooth Fairy, they're real, and . . ."—he said this with passion—". . . they don't
stop coming, they're just in disguise. And magic does exist," he said, laughing.
"Just look at me . . . here . . . talkin' to you . . . there."

After a sigh, he said, "Don't ever get a tattoo. You don't need the story. *You*
are the story," he said, starting to get serious. "Ah, love. At the touch of love, everyone becomes a poet. And so will you," he said, blushing a little and laughing.
"God, the first time I laid eyes on your mother, I turned into T. S. fucking Eliot."
He grimaced. "Oh, and don't swear . . . It's not becoming. By the way, don't get
married because you want to get married. Get married because you want to marry
her. And don't worry about not knowing . . . When all you want is for her to be
happy, you'll know."

Claire looked into David's eyes. She almost felt as if he looked back.

Cooper stared at the screen, hanging on every word. "Look," said David, "I
know you think I'm a hero, but I have a secret for you. Heroes are only heroes
because someone makes them *feel* like one. And in case you ever want to know
what I love about you . . ." He paused, breathed in, then out, and blinked three
times. "I love the way you didn't give up when you were learning to ride without
your training wheels." He continued with a strong, proud smile. "I love the way
your hair looks all messy when you wake up. I love the way your chest moves up
and down when you sleep. I love how you gave your coat to that boy who needed
one at the park."

Unable to contain it, his smile grew wider with every word. "I love how you
want to wear your Halloween costume all year long. I love how you always kiss

Mommy back, even when you're embarrassed. I love that you want to know all the great things that have happened to me in my lifetime. But I'll save you some time, kiddo." And with this, he stared into the camera and pointed with such feeling, it looked as if his finger might come through the screen and touch Cooper in the flesh. "*You* are the greatest thing that ever happened to me."

And then he gave his head a slight shake and squinted a bit. "And just in case you ever wonder, I know you love me."

Cooper finally took a deep breath, and this time, when he let it out, it seemed to float out the window, away with the breeze. The wall-forest itself seemed to be listening to David now, all the paper animals quiet and attentive.

"Don't look back," David Payne said, "unless it makes you smile. No regrets. Only forward." He looked into the camera, through the camera, with a mysterious smile. "When you come to a fork in the road, take it."

Then the screen turned to static and David Payne disappeared. Again.

FORTY-THREE

The room was filled with broken stories, rewritten by fate, and a new sun shined over them all. Story took in the scene around her, and when she stopped for a moment to absorb the sight of the treasure box one last time, she noticed something lying on the ground near it. Sticking out from underneath one of the framed family trees that had toppled over the box's side in the excitement was a tiny green umbrella.

A much smaller version of Cooper's big umbrella, it, too, was green with a wood handle, but it wasn't made for rain. Designed for happier times, this little cocktail umbrella with its toothpick stem and paper-green top must have fallen out of the box, perhaps a remnant from a party, perhaps a souvenir from someone's past.

Perhaps, Story thought, but then she stopped thinking of the possibilities. They were endless. Besides, really, there was only one answer to the question of why, and Cooper had already answered it. *It was an unexpected gift.*

Story Easton closed her eyes for a moment, trying to imagine any award or trophy more satisfying than how she felt right then, but the sound of a doorbell interrupted her.

Claire asked Story to get the door while she sat with Cooper, digesting what had just happened. When Story opened the door, in front of her stood Martin Baxter, staring at his barely recognizable book, still smoldering on the sidewalk. "Who's the Nazi?"

"Cooper," Story said, smiling. "But he didn't really mean it—"

"No worries. Cooper and my editor would get along great."

Then Story said, "Shouldn't you be at the airport?"

"Change of plans," he said, smiling with a sense of peace Story had never seen in him. Though Martin had decided the night before that *he* didn't need to go the rainforest, that morning, upon waking, he knew he could not let Cooper or David Payne down, and had decided to be their guide as promised. "Called the airport to see if you'd checked in, and when you hadn't, I knew something was wrong."

"Change of plans here, too." And after a coy smirk, Story said, "Here to see me?"

Martin shook his head. "Just came to drop this off." In his left hand he held a wrapped present, thin and rectangular, and when he looked back at the still-smoking book on the sidewalk, he laughed. "I don't think he's going to like it."

Story shrugged and smiled. "Never know."

Martin smiled back. "Never know," he said, and then, not sure how to ask, he just said, "Where is everyone?"

She knew who he was asking about. "Come with me."

Story led Martin Baxter through the Paynes' home, back to where Claire and Cooper sat on the floor together. When Martin came through the door, Claire sprang to her feet.

"Martin." She walked toward him. "On your way to the airport?" They stared deep into each other, trying to get a glimpse of what to say next.

"Nah," he said. "I heard the Amazon is really rainy this time of year."

"Oh," she said, holding back a smile.

Cooper perked up, concerned. "What about—"

"She's—" And then Martin stopped. "Once I see the moonflower in bloom, I have to stop searching for it." Cooper wasn't sure he understood, so Martin said, in a gentle voice, "It'll always be there. I like knowing that." He paused. "Ya know?"

Cooper nodded.

Martin hadn't yet said it out loud, and of all people, Cooper deserved to hear it first. "Besides . . ." he said, but his voice cracked and he abandoned his words.

With complete confidence, Cooper calmly, and without emotion, said, "Well, she wants to live there, you know. It's her new home."

Martin changed gears and handed Cooper the present. "This is a collector's edition, but from what I saw, I'm pretty sure you'll hate it."

"Did you see the sidewalk?" Cooper asked.

"Don't worry about it. I burn books all the time."

"Really?" Cooper asked.

"No," Martin said, smiling.

Cooper started to laugh but hesitated.

But then Martin looked at Cooper, and his opened treasure box beneath the kapok tree, and said, "Well, isn't this a home run?"

"You watch baseball?" Cooper asked casually, getting to his feet.

Martin spoke carefully, saying, "Can you believe the Diamondbacks this season? Might be time for a new manager." He watched for Cooper's approval.

"Yeah," Cooper said in a soft voice, "might be."

Hans, Martin, Claire, and Story sang "Happy Birthday" to Cooper, who was finally able to turn nine. He extinguished the tiny blue candle jutting out of a stack of pancakes. Mid-bite, Story's phone rang, and she excused herself from the table.

"Story, dear? I just got your messages. Jail? Jesus, Darling. What happened? Do you need a lawyer?"

As Story tried to answer her mother's barrage of questions, Story heard someone in the background. "Who's that?" she said.

"I'm, um, having tea with someone," said Beverly. "For the second day in a row."

Story let out a suspicious laugh. "You hate tea."

"I know." She paused for a second, and then spoke in a slow, intentional tone. "He's a *gardener*," she said.

"Oh," Story said, caught in a pleasant surprise, "*that* kind of tea—good for you, Mom."

"It's really weird, actually. Something must have gone haywire on my gas gauge because I thought it said full . . . Anyway, I ran out of gas and I ended up walking up his lane, and one thing led to another, he invited me in, and here we are, on his terrace, looking at his garden." In a whisper, she said, "He says I make him feel . . . sure of himself. He likes my questions. And he called me a delicate rose. Can you believe it?"

Story heard hammering, and Beverly explained that the gardener was building some sort of shrine for a photo of a special flower. "Sent some guy all the way to
the Amazon to capture it on film," Beverly said with confidence, "but I told him
to lower his expectations . . . Things are usually best kept in the imagination."

How does she always manage to be right?

Beverly Easton returned to her comfort zone and asked a question. "The
moonflower. Ever heard of it?"

"Yeah, I've heard of it," Story said, happy to be interrogated. She almost told
her mother there would be no moonflower photo. And she almost got a little sick
thinking about how she'd have to explain how she didn't really work for *National
Geographic.* But then she realized everything else had worked out, and this would,
too.

Story then heard her mother laugh and talk with her mouth full. "I'm eating
Spam for breakfast!" Her voice quieted as she made a declaration. "Broke man
living in a mansion." Then, and in a sweet voice, as tender as a flower, she added,
"But he seems to be an extraordinary gardener."

Story thought of her father tending to heavenly daffodils, and then she embraced, for once, a book's last line. "So we beat on," she said, "boats against the
current, borne back ceaselessly into the past."

After breakfast, Story looked out the living room's back window at Claire,
Cooper, and Martin, who were in the backyard inspecting the two ailing saplings,
not yet ready to perish. And then she closed her eyes and saw the future. She saw
herself sleeping with Hans, and not wanting to be anywhere else. She saw herself
visiting Cooper on his tenth birthday, Claire and Martin looking on proudly,
while Story sought out new ways to invent magic for her own children. In the
middle of this warm blanket of a dream, Hans kissed her cheek.

"So, you're sure you want a third date?" she said in a whisper, leaning into
his shoulder. "You should know that I'm a pain in the ass." She paused so she
wouldn't leave anything out. "I have a crazy mother, I'm unemployed, and I'm
one catchphrase away from utter desperation. On a good day."

Hans put his arm around her. "Any *new* information?"

"Well, sounds like you're serious about me." She smiled. "So in that case, I should tell you I'm a millionaire. Probably a billionaire someday."

Though he looked skeptical at first, he had wondered how she'd come up with the money to send four people to the Amazon inside a week. After staring into Story's eyes, he focused his gaze toward the sky and performed an enchanting maneuver with his magic hands. "Abracadabra."

"That's *my* word."

"How about I sell it to you?" he said, kissing her on the forehead. "It's yours for . . . a million dollars."

It is a truth universally acknowledged, that a single woman in possession of a good fortune must be in want of a husband.

He took a moment to let the last two days sink in. "So, you've earned it now," he said. "Wanna know how it ends?"

"And so it goes," said Story.

He smiled. "Not that one."

"Enlighten me."

Looking into Story's eyes, Hans proudly recalled his favorite closing line from a book and recited it softly: "It is a far, far better thing that I do, than I have ever done; it is a far, far better rest that I go to than I have ever known."

Ah, real sleep, Story thought. *At home.*

When Story saw Cooper sit down next to Martin on the couch and open his new copy of *Once Upon A Moonflower*, she asked to hear the rest of the story. Martin asked Story where she'd left off, so she pointed to a picture of Hope standing before a vicious leopard, and said, "Right about here."

A story has no beginning or end; arbitrarily one chooses that moment of experience from which to look back or from which to look ahead.

After taking a deep, cleansing breath, Martin read the story he knew would eventually have to end.

As if he wanted to give me one last lecture before he ate me, the Fierce One purred a final bit of predator wisdom. "You know, everything in the rainforest happens in unexplained synchronicity," he said, sounding more like my dad than a preachy jaguar. "A bird's flutter shakes an ant off its leaf home, the ant falls and is gobbled by an anteater below, and when a droplet of water falls from another leaf on another tree, it launches another chain reaction, starting the whole cycle all over again and—"

"Yeah, yeah, we're all connected. I get it," I said. "And your teeth are gonna connect with me, so—"

"It all happens for a reason," he interrupted, his furry ears now twitching with excitement, "much like in your world."

My impending death having purpose confused me even more, so I looked down at the treasure box still in my arms. If everything happened for a reason, why was I holding this pseudo (fake) magic box? I figured I might as well die with treasure in my arms, so I said, "Here's to you, Pandora," remembering a story I'd read in Greek Myths for Dummies, and gently pushed the Fierce One's head aside in order to lift the lid.

"You've got to be kidding," was all I could say when I saw my so-called treasure. Lying at the bottom of the wooden box was an infinitesimal (diminutive) (small) lantern, so tiny it looked like it'd been plucked from a doll's dollhouse. Its shiny metal was painted lavender, the same color as my pajamas. When I picked it up and placed it in the palm of my hand, a tiny, midnight-blue light flickered inside, as if to beckon its secret small owner.

The Fierce One, now breathing in my face, let out a growl, and this time it was truly fierce. But just as he was about to lash out at me, something weird happened. Suddenly, the lantern got bigger. Lots bigger. Or was I smaller? Clearly, I was smaller, because the leaf I stood on now stretched before me like a picnic blanket. That's when I remembered I was dinner.

When his paw swiped at me from above, at first it looked like a giant furry cloud closing in on me, but when he swiped the ground near me, it felt like an earthquake's first rumble. There was no more small talk, only me running for my life in-between giant piles of dirt and mazes of tangled tree roots while he searched for my new small self.

His paws hit the ground with T-Rex-sized thumps. As I ran as fast as my small legs would go, lugging my lantern as I sprinted, I noticed my pajamas were gone, and I now wore a gauzy, lavender dress, adorned with some sort of glittery dust, and what felt like crazy big shoulder pads attached to the back of my shoulders. (So 1990s.) We continued our cat-and-whatever-I-was chase for quite a while, until I noticed a familiar face.

"Sloth?" I whispered from underneath a big bucket-like plant filled with water. "Where am I?" I asked softly, just like I'd asked him before. "The Fierce One is after me, my outfit is horrible, and I've turned into Barbie's dwarf cousin!"

"You're back to where you started," he said in his unhurried way. "You've come full circle. And you're a fairy, by the way. An eventide fairy, in charge of bringing light to those who fear the dark." He blinked slowly. "Didn't you notice the wings jutting out your back?"

"Fairy?!" I said, much too loud, and then adjusted my volume. "Fairy?! I can't be a fairy. I have a soccer game tomorrow. And I just got a great new pair of jeans. I need to change back—"

"No," he said. "You wanted to fly, to be three years older, and to not be afraid of the dark."

"Am I three years older?" I smiled, thinking about the cute earrings Dad said I could wear when I was eleven.

"Not yet, but climb up here before the Fierce One decides he has an appetite for fairies," he said, unfurling his tail so I could climb on. After he hoisted me up to his branch, I scurried off his tail onto the bark, careful not to fall. "Now jump," he said with resolve.

"Are you crazy?" I yelled back. "Splat!" I said, gesturing my interpretation of a fallen fairy hitting the forest floor. "I'll never get home with broken legs."

He hung on without even trying. "Trust me," he said. By now I had wrapped my arms and legs around the branch, hugging it tight. "Letting go is the hardest part," he said. "It's the part that requires faith. But if you ever want to find your home, you must."

If I ever want to find my home? I loosened my grip a little, but then tightened again as I thought about the fall. Just then, the branch began to move, and when I looked up, I saw why.

"You missed the third riddle," the Fierce One said, licking a paw as he lounged on a nearby branch, "so you know what that means." He lifted his head, stared through me, and began to move to where I clung.

"This would be a good time to let go," the sloth murmured.

I closed my eyes, thought of being in my soft bed, and did what seemed impossible. I let go.

But then, mid-freefall, something tugged at my back, and after being in the air no more than a split-second, I stopped falling, and began to . . . hover. In the corner of my eye, I saw why—iridescent wings fluttered in a slow, easy pattern, and as if I were moving invisible limbs, my brain sent messages to my new appendages to move. I was flying.

The Fierce One growled from the branch above and lashed out in rage, but I flew far from his reach, and soon I was flying in the dark night, carrying my light to illuminate the way. With help from the wind, I stumbled upon a white flower bud made from tightly woven, pearly-white petals. Wanting shelter, I crawled inside, gently lifting one soft petal at a time until I was deep inside, enveloped in a silky-smooth sheath.

Exhausted, I fell asleep.

When I awoke, I found myself in total darkness. My lantern had burnt out, and when I realized I was in the dark, alone, I panicked. Gasping for air, I looked for a way outside, where the bright moon awaited me. But the petals had closed tighter, and each time I tried to pry the petals away from me, they closed in.

By morning, when I could see a hint of sunlight through the opaque petals, I remembered what they'd said, and I knew where I was—first the box, then the moonflower. I was inside the mysterious, night-loving moonflower, and I would be there for a long time.

Day after day, I waited, thinking of the place I used to call home. I gave up fearing the dark, and eventually learned to find comfort in nighttime.

Three years went by as I became one with the darkness. And then, one night, a beam of moonlight snuck through a small opening between the petals. As the light seeped in, the flower opened wider and wider until, finally, I saw the starry sky above me.

And then I smelled the sweetest, most intoxicating (alluring) (pleasant) scent I'd ever laid nose upon. The flower had bloomed by the light of the moon, and I had been released. I looked for my dad, but even if he'd come to rescue me, he wouldn't recognize me. I was a new person—older, wiser, able to fly on my own.

As soon as I took flight, my lantern lit up, and that's when I knew I had an important role in my new home, and my new life. I was an eventide fairy. I would bring light to those who needed it. I decided to collect some unlikely souvenirs for my parents, for I would see them again. Sometime. I grabbed a moonflower petal for Mom, in hopes of convincing her I once lived inside a flower so beautiful it had its own soul.

And then I made a secret promise to my dad, that when I learned to fly high enough, I'd bring him a piece of my old, beloved friend, the golden star, and he would finally know, firsthand, the power of the sun. But until then, seeing the same sun as Dad saw hanging in the sky was enough.

And while I was in my new home, for however long, I decided to make every day an adventure. So I hung on to hopes of tomorrow, and let go of yesterday. I think that's what

we're supposed to do. *Life is just a series of knowing when to hang on and when to let go.*
Then I did what every parent wants his child to do.
I ate my broccoli. (*Kidding!*)

I lived happily ever after.

The End.

ABOUT THE AUTHOR

Elizabeth Leiknes grew up in rural Iowa and can make thirty-seven different dishes featuring corn. She attended The University of Iowa as an undergrad, and The University of Nevada, Reno for her Masters.

Her previous published novel is *The Sinful Life of Lucy Burns*. *Black-Eyed Susan*, *Future Perfect*, and *Let Them Eat Corn* are works in progress.

The inspiration for *The Understory* came one night while reading her sons a bedtime story about the rainforest.

Elizabeth has a love/hate relationship with great white sharks, and a slight penchant for speaking in hyperbole, which she says she never does.

She now lives near Lake Tahoe, Nevada, with her husband, and two sons, Hardy and Hatcher. She also teaches English there.